AF490714

# DESCARTES' DEMON

## ROSS HIGHTOWER & DEB HEIM

### QUIZZICAL SPIRIT PRESS

Descartes' Demon

Copyright © 2025 by Ross Hightower & Deb Heim. All rights reserved.

This is a work of fiction. Names, characters, places and incidents are products of the author's imagination or are used fictitiously and should not be construed as real. Any resemblance to actual events, locales, organizations or persons, living or dead, is entirely coincidental.

No part of this book may be used or reproduced in any manner whatsoever without written permission, except in the case of brief quotations embodied in critical articles and reviews.

ISBN: 979-8-9938714-0-0

Book Cover Design and Interior Formatting by 100Covers.

# Advanced Praise for Descartes' Demon

"A snappy cyber thriller that will make you laugh while it's making you think. Evokes the fast-talking dialogue of a noir detective novel while forging new territory in the twisty, unpredictable world of cyber crime. If the characters were any more colorful, I would need sunglasses."

Del Blackwater, author of *Dead Egyptians*

Ross Hightower and Deb Heim's *Descartes' Demon* is a high-speed collision of philosophy, love, and sheer lunacy. Nik, a genius with questionable boundaries, may have created the world's first sentient AI—or something even stranger. He's seeing people who don't exist, and reality is starting to feel like a software glitch. Fortunately, Alix—his partner in life and chaos—is just as brilliant, only slightly less reckless, and far more patient. She doesn't see Nik's mysterious visitors, but she never doubts that they're real *to him*. Together they navigate rogue algorithms, corporate conspiracies, a hopelessly inept kidnapper, and a cat named Alan Turing who might be the only one who truly understands what's going on. Fast, funny, and unrelentingly smart, *Descartes' Demon* asks: how do you know you're real?

Kat Fielier – Author of *Shadow Runner*

A story that couldn't possibly be more timely, *Descartes' Demon* by Ross HIghtower and Deb Heim takes us on a comedic romp through the dark underworld of cyber attacks, the power of AI unchecked, and the lengths to which bad actors will go to seize control of technology with the power to destabilize...everything. Thankfully, protagonists Nik and Alix, along with assistance from a detective and her Dark Web-expert girlfriend, use their keen intellect to root out corporate misdeeds, thwart a cyber criminal whose opinion of himself is beyond grandiose, and expose greed that knows no bounds. The story will leave you asking: how do I know if I exist? If anyone exists? And that is precisely the point. This story is not one to be missed.

**Suzanne Groves, author of *You'll See and The Pebble in the Pond***

The questions raised in Ross Hightower and Deb Heim's *Descartes' Demon* couldn't be more timely or more frightening. Is the AI program's avatar created by a tech wizard a sentient being? And what of the mysterious figments that pop into his world from time to time? Through the lens of dynamic partners Nik and Alix, the novel's witty and sexy protagonists, these questions and more permeate the narrative, along with corporate hijinks, a bumbling kidnapper, and a cat named Alan Turing. It's a laugh-out-loud story about very serious issues, and I couldn't put it down.

**Clifford Garstang, author of *The Last Bird of Paradise and Oliver's Travels***

# Chapter 1

## Monday, 12:15 A.M.

Alix Crockett opened her eyes and gazed at the dark ceiling. She and Nik didn't have a clock in their bedroom, but it felt late. At first, she wasn't sure what woke her, but then she heard the rhythmic murmur of voices in conversation. They were too low to make out words, but it was a man and woman. Nik's side of the bed hadn't been slept in. He often worked late, but it was unusual for him to be in a meeting in the middle of the night.

She would have fallen back to sleep, but there was something about the woman's voice that piqued her curiosity. Slipping from beneath the covers, she peeked out the window. From the traffic on Central Park West far below, she guessed it was near midnight. She almost went naked, but on the off chance Nik was talking to a physical person, she pulled on one of his t-shirts, before padding to the bedroom door and listening.

Nik's office was down the hall. His door was ajar, and the light was on. She listened to the melody of the woman's voice, trying to remember where she heard it. She still couldn't make out words, so she crept down the hall. When Nik said something that made the woman laugh, Alix froze. The laugh. *Her* laugh. She strode the rest of the way, pulled the door open, and stood in the doorway, hands on her hips.

Nik startled and gaped at her over the top of the monitors on his desk. "Oh, hi Alix. What are you doing up?"

No one else was in the room, so she came around his desk to see his monitors and found a woman peering up at her. Short, red hair, blue eyes, oval face. A perfect replica of her face.

"Good evening," the electronic version of her said with a sly grin. A grin she recognized from photos of herself.

Alix ignored her image, gestured to the monitor and asked Nik, "What is this?"

Beaming with pride, Nik said, "Alix, meet Alix." He paused. "That's going to get confusing. Virtual Alix?"

Alix thrust out a hip and crossed her arms. "Explain."

He glanced at her legs, then smiled up at her. "Remember, I was playing around with artificial intelligence for the next version of our network traffic analysis software?" When Alix nodded, he gestured to the on-screen Alix.

The virtual Alix blinked and grinned.

"So, this is a simulation of… me?" the real Alix asked.

"Yes, well, I had to use someone, and I do spend a lot of time with her —"

"It."

"Yes… it." He hurried to add, "And this is just a prototype. No one else will see her. We'll get an artist to create an avatar for the production version."

"How —" Alix paused, unsure how to continue.

"I fed the software pictures and video of you."

"So, this is a deepfake of me?"

Nik's head bobbed. "Yes! And a damn good one, right?"

"Why?"

"One of the biggest problems with our software is its complexity."

Alix suppressed the grin that wanted to emerge. Nik's passion was one of the things she found most attractive about him. His creative genius and an almost limitless curiosity powered the cybersecurity company he founded.

"As you know, network traffic analysis is used to analyze network performance, detect cyberattacks —"

Alix put up a hand. "It's too late at night for that."

"Right. Anyway, I finished the new AI version of the software and it can do the analysis on its own. But it has to be configured and someone has to interpret the results." He gestured to the screen on the right on which the current commercial version of the interface was displayed.

"That's your software. It won awards for its interface."

"Yes. But, you see, you can make the interface all kinds of pretty, add graphs and explanations, but customers still screw it up. Then they blame us when it doesn't work as expected. Even when they manage to configure it correctly, or, more likely, we configure it for them, they can't figure out the output."

"So, you created a virtual me so they could just *talk* to the software?"

"Exactly! You just tell you, her, what you want, then she'll explain what she finds. In mind numbing detail. If necessary. A child could understand it." He hesitated, then shrugged. "A precocious child."

On-screen Alix looked for all the world as if she was following the conversation, her eyes shifting from one to the other as they spoke.

Nik put up a finger to forestall her next question. "That's good enough for commercial applications." His face lit up. "But that's not the best part."

He moused over a menu item and selected Interactive from a drop-down menu. The visual change in the image was subtle, but unmistakable. It was as if the muscles beneath the skin came alive, adding an eerie realism to its expressions. Alix thought it looked like her before, but she had been wrong. This could have been a high-resolution recording of her, but it was responding to their conversation.

One of virtual Alix's brows and a corner of her lips rose. "If that shirt were any shorter —"

"You'd need two hairdos," Nik and Alix finished at the same time.

Nik's eyes opened wide.

"How the hell did it know that?"

"Well, *Kingpin* is one of your favorite movies. And she has access to the wide world of the Internet." He shrugged. "Maybe you mentioned it on social media or in an interview."

"This is —"

"Creepy," virtual Alix finished for her.

Nik's grin faded at Alix's frown. "She's...uh... What you have to keep in mind is that... See, her personality was generated from the data I fed the AI. About you. There are, however, some parameters I can tweak."

"And you tweaked them to... what? Make it crude?"

Nik stared at her, lips slightly parted, then he glanced at the on-screen Alix. "Well, no. I haven't tweaked anything. She's you, or at least what the AI thinks you are."

"The AI thinks?"

"See, *thinking* is the wrong way to look at it," Nik said, his enthusiasm returning. "It's not like human thought. It merely *appears* to think like a human."

"She doesn't get it," the electronic Alix said. "Face it, Nik. No one understands you like I do."

The purr in the fake Alix's voice was almost enough for Alix to punch the monitor. Instead, she reached across Nik, took hold of his mouse and turned off Interactive mode.

"You don't approve," Nik said.

"It's creepy." Seeing his disappointment, she eyed her doppelgänger and gestured to the screen. "*This* is a great idea." She leaned down and brushed his lips with her own. "But that other thing is a bad idea." She stood, put her finger under his chin and lifted his gaze from her thighs to her eyes. "Let's leave aside, for the moment, you created a virtual version of me without my knowledge. Imagine what people could do with this software. People with bad intentions."

He blinked. As he rose, he lifted her shirt over her head and dropped it to the floor. Reaching around her, he pulled her against him. "Oh, I know what harm it would do. That's why the interactive mode will never make it into a commercial product."

"Good." She peeled his hands from her body, turned slowly, and prowled to the door. Pausing in the doorway, she looked over her shoulder and purred, "You coming?"

## Monday, 12:25 A.M.

After their laughter subsided to murmurs behind their bedroom door, a woman's voice floated through the condo. "Good night."

# Chapter 2

## Monday, 1:04 A.M

The Technician made his way through the dark streets of the working-class Long Island neighborhood. Despite its proximity to the city that never sleeps, this street slumbered. And why wouldn't it? It was nearly midnight, and tomorrow was a workday. The only signs of life were the murmur of traffic on the nearby Belt Parkway, the occasional dog warding off raccoons and the glow of oversized TVs through thin curtains.

Coming to an intersection, he glanced up at the street sign and brought the map of the area to mind. Then he settled the strap of his satchel on his shoulder and set off down the cross street.

There were others with his highly specialized technical skills. Modern-day soldiers in an interminable shadow war. Governments, corporations, men and women with more money than conscience, all vying for advantage, stealing secrets, or just being a pain in the ass. The war surfaced in the public consciousness occasionally.

Ominous warnings to frighten the sheep, exaggerated victories to rally the rabid, disasters too enormous to cover up. The public booed, or cheered, or quailed. Bread and circus to manipulate the masses. In truth, there were no sides worth rooting for. Not as much as most people wanted to believe. There never was. And as the war sank into the shadowy cyberworld, the distinctions blurred to irrelevance.

On the positive side, the money sloshing around with no accountability was staggering. Plenty to go around. Even for the bottom-feeding hacks who imagined they served a flag or a letterhead.

The Technician picked up his pace. He was one of a small elite group of freelancers. Those who transcended the murky boundaries, dissolved into the shadows, lurked just beyond perception. Digital ghosts in the machine, agents of chaos, monsters who inhabited nightmares. He let a smile crack his professional mask. One day, he would write his memoirs. He had a gift for the lyrical turn of phrase.

But it was a competitive market, and that was why he was having to diversify. It wasn't an easy decision, but being one of the very few in his elite community willing to get his hands dirty would open new markets. Some of his peers would look down their noses at him after tonight. Call him an assassin. As if it were an insult. Their moral high ground was illusory. It was easy to pretend your hands were clean when all you touched was a keyboard. But in today's world, the keyboard was the deadliest weapon a man could wield.

Having found his destination, he slipped into the shadows of a hedge and eyed the small ranch house across the street. The home of one Reginald Thomas Spenser. Reggie to his few friends. An insignificant tech in the real world but the Mighty Gorgon online in the Land of Atuna. The house looked dark, but The Technician wasn't fooled. Tomorrow might be a workday, but the Mighty Gorgon had hours yet to waste online.

He slipped his phone out of his pocket and opened the Land of Atuna app. Moments later, he was scrolling through the connected adventurers. Gorgon was on a quest in the Forgotten Realms with his usual party, and if the past two weeks were any indication, he would be there for the next three hours. After that, Reggie would usually snatch a few hours of sleep, then rise and shuffle, zombie-like, through his day.

Not that Reggie was bad at his job. In fact, his supervisors at Sunset Tech regarded him so highly they assigned him to their most valuable clients. Which was why The Technician stood outside his house tonight. Reggie was insignificant, but the first client on his work schedule in the morning was not.

Being careful to cover his tracks by logging off before closing the Land of Atuna app, he returned the phone to his pocket.

Normally, entering a house like Reggie's would take The Technician five minutes, tops. But the unassuming facade, patchy lawn and withered shrubs were deceptive. The house was protected by Cerberus, the premier home security system on the market. And Reggie sprung for all the bells and whistles. Alarms. Cameras all around. Motion sensitive flood lights on the exterior. Motion and infrared detectors inside. A live connection to the Cerberus Watch Center. Even the ridiculous infrared trip wires. The Technician sniffed. You would have thought it was Fort Knox.

He fished in his satchel and retrieved another phone. A very particular phone. Not that the make and model were anything special. It was one of the most popular Android models from one of the largest international electronics companies. No, what made this phone unique was the phone from which it was cloned. To the right buyer, the device resting in his palm would be worth a million dollars. And that was if he wanted to unload it before dawn. But he was after a much larger payday.

Before powering it up, he took a moment to mentally rehearse his plan. Because the device was a clone, it was theoretically possible the owner of the original phone might notice when both were on. He needed to be efficient. Plus, his nerves had inconveniently awakened, allowing doubts to intrude.

He could still walk away. Remain innocent. And flush months of preparation, his reputation and a seven-figure payday down the drain. Seven figures. He closed his eyes and pictured himself on a beach, a rum cocktail in his hand, a beautiful woman beside him. Taking a deep breath, he sighed it out and willed the doubts away. No backing out now.

Opening his eyes, he retrieved a small notebook from his satchel and flipped to a page on which he had written two ten-digit numbers in a precise hand. Then he pressed the power button on the phone. Once it started, he swiped to unlock it, then opened the Cerberus app. The app, available in all the app stores, allowed a homeowner to control every aspect of their security system. Of course, Cerberus would be pretty useless if anyone could download the app and take control of your home security. The app had to be paired with the owner's particular system. But that's what made this phone special.

On the slick, consumer-friendly home screen, he pressed the connect button, counted to ten, released it, then tapped it once more. A small pop-up containing a single input field and submit button appeared. So far, so good. After entering the first code from his notebook, he hesitated, finger above the submit button. Moment of truth. He held his breath and tapped. The phone vibrated and beeped. He was in. He hesitated, then chased the vague sense of disappointment to the murky fringes of his mind.

The screen that appeared wasn't the interface most people saw. It was utilitarian and littered with numbers and cryptic acronyms. The developer screen. The screen coders used when they wrote the system's code. A window into the system's innards, a means to bypass barriers and turn functions on and off. And it wasn't just any developer screen. This device was a clone of the phone of one Nik Atherton, the mastermind behind Cerberus. The man whose genius made his company one of the premier digital security companies in the world in only five years. And a bane to every one of The Technician's peers.

No other developer had access to this version of the app, because it provided a backdoor to every Cerberus home security system in the world. How arrogant was that man to allow this app to exist? The Technician was charging an exorbitant fee for this job, but he would have done it for free for the chance to humble that jerk.

With that happy thought in mind, he entered the second code from his notebook into the phone. The first code got him into the app as Nik, but now he had to use the backdoor to connect to Reggie's system. The second code was tied specifically to Reggie's system, was only good for twenty-four hours and could only be used once. His source in Cerberus provided it to him that afternoon. He entered the code, and a moment after submitting it, the screen dissolved into another with the words Welcome to The Mighty Gorgon's Lair against a blue background. He was in.

He scrolled through the feeds from the cameras in the home, looking for his prey. He found him where he expected to, in his basement, in front of three monitors mounted above his desk. The Technician studied the image, trying to understand the layout of the room. He didn't see stairs, so it was likely the camera was located above the stairs where they entered the room. Reggie had his back to the camera and would likely be so absorbed in the game, The Technician could get very close.

After killing the exterior cameras and lights, he glanced both ways and crossed the street. On the front porch, hidden by two rangy arbor vitae, he set his satchel down and donned shoe covers and latex gloves. When he was ready, he used the app to unlock the door, then disabled every security mechanism except the basement camera. He slipped inside, paused in the foyer, and listened while he stowed the phone and set his satchel on the floor. Black Sabbath emanated from somewhere in the dark house.

From his satchel, he extracted a headlamp. He shut one eye to preserve his night vision, lit the lamp, then he retrieved an air pistol. Setting the pistol on the floor, he extracted a small leather case containing two syringe darts and a vial containing aconitine. It was a quick-acting poison. A video online said the effects would resemble a heart attack to an inattentive coroner. Reggie would barely have time to notice the slight prick in the back of his neck before he died. Competition may have forced The Technician to be an assassin, but he wasn't a cruel man.

After filling the darts, he picked up the pistol and stared at it. He'd practiced loading it until his hands could do it on their own. Or so he thought. His mind was a blank. Sweat-slicked fingers fumbled the gun as if they'd never held it before. He should have brought the manual. "You got this," he murmured. "No one's watching." He turned the pistol this way and that, trying to bring the manufacturer's instructional video to mind. When it came to him, a relieved giggle bubbled up out of him.

After his trembling fingers managed to load a dart into the chamber, he slipped the other dart into an easily accessible pocket on his sleeve. "Back in the saddle now," he murmured. He doused the light, opened his eye and crept down the hall, following the music.

He had to admit, the shabby exterior hid a tidy interior. Top of the line IKEA tastefully arranged. Muted colors all around except for throw pillows on the sofa for a splash of color. Dozens of photographs featuring an older couple in scenic locations from around the world covered the walls. Reggie's parents, who died in a freak cruise ship mishap a year ago.

The Technician found the stairs to the basement in the kitchen. The door visibly flexed with *Paranoid's* driving power chords. At least he didn't need to worry about being heard. He opened the door and descended the stairs, the pistol aimed at the opening below him. When he reached the bottom step, he checked the security camera on his phone. Finding Reggie still engrossed in his game, he turned off the camera, stowed his phone and took a quick peek around the corner to confirm the room's layout.

The only light came from the three wide monitors mounted on gimbals above Reggie's desk and the eerie green glow of a lava lamp. The music came from two giant speakers on either side of the desk. From the screens, he could tell Reggie's party of warriors was deeply involved in a battle with a band of ogres. Perfect!

He slipped around the corner and plunged into a nightmare. His heart thundered. His lungs struggled to draw breath. Light strobed from the monitors. The throbbing heavy metal music was almost a physical barrier through which his quivering legs plowed. He crept toward the back of Reggie's chair. Reggie's thick neck filled his vision. One more step, just to be certain. Sucking in a fluttery breath, and holding it — as explained in the manufacturer's video — he squeezed the trigger.

Nothing happened. He pulled harder. Still nothing. Panicked now, he shook the pistol, gripped it with both hands, and squeezed with all his might. He glanced over his shoulder. Maybe he should retreat and regroup. He'd taken a step back when it hit him. The safety. The held breath exploded out of him. He let go of the pistol with one hand to access the safety. The music died. He flinched at the sudden, deafening silence and nearly dropped the gun. Finally, he pressed the small switch beside the trigger guard.

The middle screen went black when Reggie's character died. "Shit!" Reggie screamed.

The Technician whipped the pistol up and pulled the trigger just as his quarry spun his chair and launched his controller at the wall.

The Technician gaped at the dart flying into the space where Reggie used to be. Before he could react, Reggie caught sight of him out of the corner of his eye. The thumping bass drum intro to *Iron Man* counted off the moments as they stared at one another. The opening power chord broke the spell. The Technician scrabbled for the spare dart in the pocket on his sleeve as Reggie lunged, hands outstretched.

The Technician yelped, dropped the pistol and thrust both hands out to fend off the bigger man. Reggie's hands closed on The Technician's neck. This was it. All his plans, hopes, and dreams ended in this grimy basement, cut short by an overweight nerd with poor hygiene.

Reggie shrieked and leapt backwards, crashing into his desk and scattering bags of chips and upending bottles of Mountain Dew. The Technician backed out of range and gaped as Reggie sagged against the table. The shock in his expression faded with the light in his eyes. He went limp, slid to the floor, and flopped over onto his side.

The Technician gawped at the body. When Reggie didn't stir, his gaze dropped numbly to the syringe in his hand. The needle trembled in his clenched fist. Hot sweat slicked his back. His stomach threatened to expel its contents. Bending over, he clamped his hand over his mouth and stared at the revolting shag carpet.

He giggled. Picturing himself on his knees, swabbing up a puddle of DNA evidence, the giggle threatened to become hysterical laughter.

Then, anger came to his rescue. He swept up the pistol, straightened, threw out his arms and shouted, "Well, that's just perfect!" All his planning. Practicing with the pistol. Mentally rehearsing his first foray into the dark arts. And he forgot the safety. He looked down at the pistol and resisted the urge to hurl it at Reggie's body.

Drawing in a deep cleansing breath, he looked up at the low drop ceiling, and forced himself to relax. "Not a disaster," he murmured. "No one will ever know."

After a moment, he lowered his gaze, switched on his headlamp, and assessed the damage. Catching sight of the battle Reggie had been engaged in still unfolding on the right monitor, he muttered, "Fucking ogres."

It wasn't as bad as he first thought. He retrieved the chair and set it in place. The desk was a mess of chips and spilled green liquid. He considered the body. Reggie might have had a heart attack, created the mess as he spasmed, then fell to the floor. It was plausible and less risky than trying to clean up. He found the dart he fired from the pistol on the floor underneath the desk. Taking one last look around, he headed up the stairs.

Back in the foyer, he was returning the darts to their case when he froze. The needle on the dart he found under the desk had broken off. He stared at it for a long moment. What were the odds anyone would find it? It was a simple heart attack in a person with notoriously bad habits and a bad temper. Still… He checked his phone. He still had time, so with a sigh, he trudged down the hall toward the kitchen.

# Chapter 3

## Monday, 4:32 A.M.

The Technician was grumpy. He'd searched unsuccessfully for the tip of the needle until almost dawn. Who still had shag carpet? It was a blight on the otherwise modestly stylish house. The only consolation was it would be equally hard for anyone else to find it and they wouldn't be looking for it. He hated loose ends, but he had run out of time. Still, he accomplished his goal, and the rest of the job was in his wheelhouse.

The sun was making its imminent arrival known as he entered the garage where Reggie's Sunset Tech van was parked. After making sure Reggie's company tablet and ID were in the van, he started the engine, opened the garage door, and exited. Only after he was sure he was out of range of the cameras did he rearm Cerberus and turn off the cloned phone.

It was still early enough the only people out and about were sleepy dog walkers and joggers. They had no reason to pay attention to a van they'd probably seen before. Even though it was early, traffic into the City was heavy. Waiting at a light, he checked Reggie's tablet for the day's work schedule. He had plenty of time. Inching along, he gave himself a shave with an electric razor from his satchel. The sleepless night was apparent on his face, but that wouldn't be unusual for Reggie. He popped some speed to keep himself alert.

Once he was in Manhattan, he pulled over to the side of the road long enough to disable the van's GPS tracker. Sunset Tech would notice, but by the time they looked into it, he would be long gone. He parked in a garage near Reggie's second appointment. He slipped into the back of the van and taped his photo over Reggie's on his ID with clear packing tape, trimming the edges so they weren't noticeable. It wouldn't pass a rigorous inspection, but he didn't expect it to have to.

Taking Reggie's tablet and ID, he exited the van. After glancing around to make sure he was alone, he stripped off his disposable coveralls, gloves and shoe covers and stuffed them into a trash bag. Then he sprayed deodorant and donned a Sunset Tech shirt one of his regular vendors made for him. Out on the street, he stuffed the trash bag deep into an overflowing garbage can. Someone would eventually find Reggie and the van, but it would take them a week, maybe two, and that's all he needed.

Two short walks and a subway ride later, he stood outside the Cerberus building. Fifty stories of slickly modern steel and glass. It was nice if you liked that sort of thing. He took a moment to appreciate the moment. The hard part was over, and if his source on the inside did their job, he would soon be a wealthy man. His only qualm about the plan was that it was so heavily dependent on other people. He normally wouldn't consider it. But he had no choice. He was venturing into the lion's den.

Most of the first floor was visible through large windows. He studied the security guard at his desk. Gus. The beefy man looked like an ex-marine. Gray crew cut, square jaw, icy blue eyes. By the book Gus. No friendly banter with this one, but no curiosity either. And his shift was nearly over. Perfect!

The Technician lowered the brim of the cap he would use to shield his face from security cameras, pasted his stranger-in-the-crowd smile on his face and entered the lobby. Just a man trying to get through his busy day. Neither friendly nor unfriendly. Unremarkable, forgettable. Gus barely glanced at the ID card The Technician flashed and slid through the reader. He was through the gate and in the elevator in less than a minute. One barrier passed. But the real test waited on the tenth floor.

He exited the elevator and glanced around the reception area. As he hoped, it was deserted at six in the morning.

"May I help you?"

He looked toward the voice. The usual receptionist, who would have recognized Reggie, was somewhere on a beach in the Caribbean, a vacation she conveniently won at the company's holiday party. This woman was a temp. Adopting his disarming-a-rube grin, he approached the desk. "Good morning."

"Why, good morning to you. Can I help you?"

He held up Reggie's ID and said, "Reggie Spenser from Sunset Tech. I'm here to install some servers. I should be expected."

"One moment." She tapped on her keyboard. "You are indeed." She logged his arrival, then retrieved a lanyard with a visitor's badge from below the desk and handed it to him. "Make sure you wear it while you're in the building."

"I will."

"I'll call someone to escort you. You can wait over there."

"Thank you," he said cheerily. He took a seat and studied Nik Atherton's smug grin in the middle of three portraits on the wall behind the receptionist's desk. It would be just like that arrogant prick to plaster his face on the wall. He let his gaze drift across the room. How impressed would his competitors be that he was here? In the lair of their boogeyman. He would have to find a way to let the story slip out once he was safe.

Five minutes later, a woman who looked as if she could be in high school appeared. A little over five feet of athletic spunkiness, blond, freckled, a wide, guileless Midwest-nice smile. Young, fresh-faced, and clueless. Just as promised. He rose and offered his hand. "Reggie Spenser."

"Good morning, Mr. Spenser," she said, taking his hand. "I'm Catherine with a C Munson, but my friends call me Kate. I'll escort you to the server room."

Large companies like Cerberus routinely outsourced functions that weren't part of their core competencies. Sunset Tech had installed all the hardware — servers, air conditioners, network equipment, and the like — when Cerberus built their data center. And since Sunset and their technicians were already vetted, Cerberus continued to use them for hardware maintenance.

Ten minutes later, deep in the maze of the tenth floor, they approached the security desk that guarded the entrance to the inner bastion. The last barrier and the most dangerous. As promised, the regular receptionist was absent, and Kate was obviously a new hire. He'd met no one so far who knew Reggie. This guard was supposed to be new, but The Technician's source had less control over the guards because security was another service Cerberus outsourced.

Happy no one could see the sweat tickling his ribs, The Technician adopted his bland-patience face and offered Reggie's ID to the guard. The man showed no recognition as he visually scanned the card before swiping it in a reader. He barely glanced at the output on his monitor before handing the card back and saying, "You're good, Reggie."

Kate returned The Technician's smile, a genuine one this time, as she swiped her ID in the electronic lock of the data center. She pulled the door open, releasing a blast of chilled air and the whir of air conditioner blowers, then stood back to let him enter. Once they were both inside, she led him past rows of racked equipment toward the back of the room. It was an impressive setup. Top of the line enterprise servers, their combined worth in the tens of millions of dollars. But the secrets buried in the storage systems was the real treasure. Worth far more than the equipment to the right people. This room contained the company's development systems. All the code he and his kind would lose sleep over for years to come was here.

Kate pointed to six boxes stacked in a corner on the back wall. "These are them." She pointed to a rack enclosure with empty bays and said, "They go there. The cables are in the back."

"Thank you, Kate," Reggie said and set his satchel down. "I can take it from here."

A small frown wrinkled her brow. "I'll have to stay. No one can be in this room alone."

"Right." Worth a try. "Forgot about that." He set to unboxing the first server.

"Can I help?"

"Not much to do, really." Noticing her disappointed frown, he said, "You can help me rack them. They're small, but they're heavy."

An hour later, the servers were installed and powered up. Reggie set his laptop on a retractable shelf and connected it to the top server.

"What are you doing?" Kate asked.

It was only the latest in an endless stream of questions that were wearing on his sleep-deprived nerves. But crabbiness would cement him in her memory, so he bit back his irritation and asked, "How long have you worked here?"

"Two weeks. I'm just a summer intern."

"Oh, yeah? Where do you go to school?"

"Kansas State University. That's in Manhattan, too. Manhattan, Kansas." She gave him a silly grin.

He forced a laugh. "Manhattan and Manhattan. That's funny. Your major?"

"Computer science. I'll be a senior in the fall."

Older than she looked. "Well, Kate. I have to make sure all the servers are healthy." He spun the laptop so she could see the screen, then tapped the top server with his finger. "This is the management server. You can manage all the others from this one. See? They're all listed here."

She nodded.

Resisting the urge to roll his eyes, he said, "Any chance you can grab me a cup of coffee? Pretty chilly in here."

"Oh, no. I can't leave while you're in here. Plus, they get really mad if you bring food or drink in." The blush beneath the sprinkle of freckles on her cheeks suggested she was speaking from personal experience.

"Right, right. You're doing a good job." Moving so fast, he was sure she wouldn't follow what he was doing. He killed the servers' logging software to prevent them recording what he did next. Then, giving her his winning smile and letting a little of the wolf into it, he withdrew a flash drive from his pocket and slipped it into a port on the management server.

"What's that?" she asked.

*Curiosity killed the cat, Kate.* "Latest software updates. Got to get everything ready before I hand them over to your techs."

"Can't you just download everything?"

"Well, someone will have to open the firewall for these before I can do that. They can't connect to the Internet."

"Oh, right."

Ten minutes later, he reactivated the logs and restarted the servers. Kate watched all this with earnest, uncomprehending eyes.

"All set!" he said after ensuring his package was delivered. He held up the Sunset Tech tablet and showed her where to sign. The confirmation would be transmitted to Sunset, so even though Reggie would go missing, this job would be recorded as completed. Nothing to see here, so just move along.

He followed Kate back to the reception area, forcing himself not to urge her to hurry. He was minutes away from the biggest payday of his career. Enough that he could retire somewhere warm and expensive should he choose. If he decided to get out of the game. He let himself enjoy the sway of Kate's walk, her ponytail swishing from side to side. *Positively Perky Kate.* Too bad he had a strict rule about mixing work with pleasure.

They entered the reception area, and he stopped, letting Kate approach the receptionist's desk alone. Two men were deep in conversation on the opposite side of the room. Two of the triumvirate who founded the company. The taller man with the million-dollar smile, thousand-dollar suit and five hundred dollar haircut looked as if he stepped off the cover of GQ. That would be Joel Walton. The CEO and the face of the company to the media and the public. The Technician and his peers knew he was just an expensive empty suit.

But the other man was another matter. Nik Atherton, Cerberus's Chief Technology Officer. The Technician's careful control failed him for a moment, allowing hatred to ripple through his expression before he clamped down on it. The great man looked like a goof, with his artfully mussed blond hair, faded jeans, loafers, untucked t-shirt. But that was just pretentious posturing. The man was as much a snob as the man standing next to him. That only a handful of the very best could realistically claim they had successfully cracked his systems didn't change that fact.

The Technician licked his lips and took a slow breath. He needed to be careful here. Joel wouldn't recognize Reggie, but Nik would. Atherton was supposed to be across town, meeting with a customer. He glanced at the exit to the stairwell. That would be foolish. If he left without signing out, it would raise alarms. Catching Kate's confused frown, he smiled and said, "Thought I forgot something."

"Oh," she said. "I'll go see if it's in the data center."

The Technician let her slip past him, then dipping his head, he approached the receptionist's desk and handed over his visitor's badge.

"One moment while I sign you out," she said.

*Please don't say my name.*

"Okay, you are good to go," she said with a wide smile. "Have a nice day."

He had made it. "Thank you!"

"Mr. Atherton, there was a delivery for you," the receptionist called.

The Technician turned toward the elevators and came face to face with his nemesis. They locked eyes. On top of everything else, the man had impossibly gorgeous hazel-green eyes. Bastard! Nik glanced down at the logo on The Technician's shirt. The Technician stood frozen like a rabbit while the fox reached past him to retrieve a thick FedEx envelope.

Nik started to turn away, paused, then turned back and asked, "Where is Reggie?"

The Technician had been methodical and thorough. He had planned for every eventuality. He had an answer for this question, but caught off guard, he hesitated. "Reggie's a little under the weather. They asked me to take his route today." That was the story he had written in his notebook, but for some reason, he grinned and heard himself saying, "Was on my way to Amazon when I got the call."

Nik studied his face. "I wasn't aware Amazon used Sunset Tech."

Shit! How in hell would Nik know that?! "It was a one-off subcontract. Filling in on an emergency basis."

"An emergency," Nik said, tipping his head to the side. When The Technician nodded, he said, "Well, I'm happy Sunset feels installing our servers is more important than an emergency at Amazon."

The Technician couldn't think of an answer to that, so he only shrugged and hitched his sheepish-doofus grin onto his face. "I'm just a tech."

"What's your name?"

He lowered his voice, so the receptionist didn't hear, and offered his hand. "Steve. Steve Linden."

"Nik!"

Nik and The Technician looked at Joel who was holding an elevator open. "Come on! We're an hour late already."

Nik looked at The Technician and held his gaze for a moment, then he shook his hand and said, "Nice to meet you, Steve."

# Chapter 4

## Monday, 8:31 A.M.

Half listening to Joel, Nik entered the elevator, expecting the vaguely familiar tech to join them. But as the elevator doors closed, he glimpsed the man entering the stairwell. Nik eyed the door open button, but before suspicion could override the momentum of leaving, the elevator began its descent.

Cerberus had used Sunset Tech for years. There were many companies in the New York area they could have used. Many of them would jump at the chance to get their business and would be cheaper. But Cerberus dealt in digital security, and trust was worth a premium. Nik only had a moment with the new tech, but he didn't trust him. His story about being diverted from a job at Amazon was unlikely, at best, and Sunset wouldn't have sent someone new without informing them.

Joel was talking about the customer they were going to meet. He had been engaged in the intricate sales dance with them for weeks and wanted to share. Nik wasn't normally involved in sales, but the customer asked to meet him. Not needing to know the details of Joel's courtship, Nik anxiously watched the floors tick by. Finally, the doors slid open on the ground floor.

"Nik —" Joel started as Nik fought his way through the crowd waiting for the elevators. "What's wrong?!"

Ignoring him, Nik raced across the lobby, threw the door to the stairwell open, and listened.

"Nik," Joel said behind him.

Nik held up his hand. He couldn't hear anyone on the metal stairs. Pushing past Joel, who was peering past him to see what had Nik so tense, he hurried to the security desk and asked the guard, "Ted, did you see someone from Sunset Tech come past here a few minutes ago?"

"Yes, sir. He just left. Couple of minutes ago."

"Did you see which direction he went?"

"No, sir."

Nik ran to the exit and stepped out onto the busy sidewalk. He searched the crowd, but he couldn't see the tech. Reentering the building, he passed an exasperated Joel on his way to the security desk.

"Nik," Joel called after him. "Tell me what is going on."

"A moment," Nik said, then focused on the security guard.

"Can you pull up the entry log for this morning?"

"Sure. What time?"

"Between five and seven."

"You looking for someone from Sunset?"

"Yes."

After a moment, Ted said, "Reggie Spenser arrived just before six."

Nik stared at him. "No one else from Sunset?"

"No."

"Thank you, Ted." Nik turned away from the security desk to find Joel waiting, the flush of his cheeks at odds with his carefully controlled expression.

"Nik," Joel said. "Tell me what's going on. We're already late and we have to get downtown."

Nik tucked the FedEx envelope under his arm, fished his phone out of his pocket, dialed and put the phone to his ear. "That tech we saw on our floor wasn't Reggie," he said to Joel. "But apparently someone pretending to be Reggie arrived this morning."

"Reggie?"

"Sunset Tech knows we always use the same people. They wouldn't send someone new without telling —" He turned away from Joel as Singh, their network administrator, answered the phone.

"What's up boss?" Singh asked.

"Those servers, the new ones the tech installed this morning?"

"Yeah. Was just about to check them out."

"Don't open the firewall to them yet."

"You think there's a problem?"

"I'm not sure. Don't do anything with them. Get... get Jamie to dig into them."

"Jamie?" Singh asked. "You sure? That boy's got a lot on his plate already."

"Yeah, I'm sure."

"Okay. Anyone squawks, I assume I can refer them to you."

"No problem."

"Any idea what he's looking for?"

"No, but the tech from Sunset who installed them wasn't Reggie."

"It wasn't someone you recognized?"

"Never seen him. Said his name was Steve Linden. Can you call Sunset?"

"Right away, and I'll get Jamie on it," Singh said and clicked off.

Nik returned his phone to his pocket, feeling as if he averted disaster. When he saw Joel's frown, he asked, "What?"

"You bellyached for a month about getting those servers online," he said, finally losing his temper. "Said you needed them now, now, now. Insisted it get done *today*, so you'd be ready for a big announcement at the SecureTech trade show."

"I did, didn't I?"

When Nik didn't continue, Joel looked to the side. The security guard was staring frankly at them. He pulled Nik to the side of the lobby and lowered his voice. "What do you expect Jamie to find on them?"

Nik let a grin grow on his face. Cerberus's CEO could weave half-understood acronyms and marketing buzzwords into a tapestry of bullshit so tight no one but the most technically savvy could unravel it. It was a talent. He'd explained to Nik it wasn't exactly lying because everyone knew the game. Nik readily admitted how much of their success they owed to Joel's silver tongue. But Joel had long since given up trying to understand what Nik and his technical team actually did. Besides, Nik had no idea what he expected Jamie to find.

He clapped Joel on the shoulder and urged him toward the exit. "Aren't we going to be late?"

"Fine! You don't want to explain." He glared at Nik, who was holding the door open. "And, by the way, we're *already* late."

## Monday, 8:35 A.M.

The Technician entered the taxi, gave the driver his destination, then looked out the rear window as the cab pulled into traffic. He didn't think he'd been followed. He faced forward, let his gaze rest on the cabby's identification placard, and considered the disaster that had just engulfed his plan.

Forcing himself to be analytical, he replayed his conversation with Nik Atherton. When he was done, he sagged and gazed out the window at the office buildings on 10th Avenue. His improvisation about the job at Amazon was undoubtedly stupid, but it made no difference. Nik would be suspicious no matter what he said. He would follow up with Sunset Tech and discover he was an impostor. He doubted even Nik Atherton could find the package he installed on the servers. But even if they couldn't figure out what he did, they would quarantine or scrap the servers.

"Shit," he muttered. His client assured him Nik would be out of the building today. Walton said they were late for that meeting. A simple coincidence, a chance meeting and months of preparation were down the drain. He had been moments away. A minute here or there, and they would have passed through the reception area at different times.

Now, all he could do was manage the fallout. There was no question of completing the job. They would know someone of his caliber was involved, and they would be on high alert. His client wouldn't be happy, but he warned them it was a high-risk job with little chance of success. He wouldn't receive the balance of his fee. That was disappointing, but a far sight better than being in prison.

More importantly, what were the chances he left a trail that led to him? They couldn't identify him. Nik didn't seem to recognize him, and though Nik and others had seen him, he wasn't worried about that. He was assiduous about keeping his likeness off the Internet and all his business was conducted remotely through third parties. No one knew what The Technician looked like.

The only bit of evidence that might lead certain people back to him would be the package he installed on the server. Programming code of any complexity was as distinctive as a fingerprint. There were only a handful of people in the world who could identify the package as his, but they didn't work on the right side of the law. Besides, he was sure no one at Cerberus could isolate it. He licked his lips. Pretty sure. As long as they didn't have the flash drive he used to install the package.

He slipped his hand into his pocket where he'd put the drive after removing it from the server. His pocket was empty. It took a half a heartbeat before panic set in. He lifted off the seat and shoved his hands in all his pockets. They were all empty. "Don't panic," he murmured, his voice fluttering with his breath. Maybe he dislodged it from his pocket. He got on his knees and searched the seat. His skin crawled as he shoved his fingers between the cushions. Nothing.

"Hey!" the driver shouted. "You settle down, or you're out the door."

The Technician sat, unzipped his satchel and extracted its contents, methodically searching each item. "Gotta be in here. Somewhere."

But it wasn't. He stared into the empty satchel, turned it upside down and shook it, rechecked all the pockets, then threw it to the floor and sifted through everything he pulled out of it.

It wasn't here. He sat back and brought to mind the last time he saw it. He handed the tablet to Kate to sign with one hand, while he extracted the drive from the server and slipped it into his pocket with the other. Or he thought he did. Squeezing his eyes shut, he replayed the moment.

He'd kept up an amusing banter while showing her the tablet, even using a risque pun when she hesitated. Could it be he'd been trying to distract her and ended up distracting himself? And there was the moment when he caught her frowning at him in the reception area. He'd said, "Thought I forgot something." An odd thing to say. It just popped into his head. Maybe some part of him knew he really had left something behind. The flash drive.

The drive contained the package he installed on the server, but more importantly, it contained the scripts, which revealed how he hid the package. A company like Cerberus would have people who would be able to read that code like a book. Within days, his secrets would be listed in the Common Vulnerabilities and Exposures database, a public registry of known cybersecurity vulnerabilities. Every security professional in the world would have his secrets.

"Shit," he said loud enough to draw a disapproving frown from the driver. The Technician scowled at him but resisted a violent impulse. As he returned everything to his satchel, he performed a postmortem on the corpse of his plan, trying to decide what he might have done differently. Despite his problems with the gun, he'd finished the job at Reggie's. Reggie's character dying at exactly the wrong moment was just bad luck. The sleep he lost searching for the broken needle left his mind muddy, and speed could only do so much. There was also nothing he could have done to avoid running into Nik. More bad luck.

All that was left to do was to find out if Kate found the drive and what she did with it. That meant he had to grab her, question her, then dispose of her. And he had a ticket to *Hamilton* that evening. "Figures." Leaning forward, he got the driver's attention and gave him a new destination, then sat back. He had never actually abducted anyone, but he was prepared for the eventuality. He would make sure nothing went wrong this time.

## Monday, 8:48 A.M.

It took twenty minutes for the security guard at the data center to find someone to escort Kate inside. She had to get down on her hands and knees to locate the flash drive on the floor beneath the servers. She returned to the reception area with little hope, and, sure enough, Reggie had left.

She stood in front of the desk, the drive in her hand, wondering what she should do with it. According to Reggie, it didn't contain anything special. Just updates that could be downloaded from the manufacturer's website.

"Can I help you, dear?" the receptionist asked.

Kate considered, then approached her and held out the drive. "That man from Sunset Tech left this. I don't think it's important, but in case he comes back, can I leave it with you?"

"Sure. I'll hold on to it."

Kate handed it over. "Thank you!" Then she headed back to the cubicle she shared with other interns, eager to share her adventure.

# Chapter 5

## Monday, 9:22 A.M.

The Technician assumed Kate would be at work all day and he needed sleep. It would take too long to go home, so he got a room in a nearby hotel and slept until three in the afternoon. Feeling as if he hadn't slept at all, he walked to a coffee shop across from the Cerberus building and ordered their largest coffee with four shots of espresso. Then he found a seat next to the window and settled in to wait for Kate to emerge.

Despite her obvious naivety, he guessed she wasn't foolish enough to drive in the City. She probably took the subway, undoubtedly banding together with other interns like prey animals. He would follow her, find out where she lived, and decide how to proceed. While he waited, he browsed some of the sites on the dark web he'd found most useful on the topic of abduction.

When Kate emerged with two other young people two hours later, the caffeine had revived him. The Technician rose and exited the coffee shop. He followed his quarry from across the street. When it became obvious they were entering the Hudson Yards subway station, he dashed across the street, dodging traffic. He followed her to the platform for the three line to Brooklyn. The crowded platform made it easy for him to remain unseen. Not that it mattered. The three of them were so engrossed in their conversation they were unaware of their surroundings.

When he saw them board the train, he slipped into the next car and took up a position next to the door. At each stop, he stepped out and made sure they didn't exit. When they finally emerged at the Kingston Ave station, he thought Kate might have made him when she glanced his way, but they were still so involved with one another, she looked away without appearing to recognize him.

He followed them out onto the street. He almost decided they shared an apartment, but they split up a block from the subway station. Kate went off alone in one direction and the other two in another. When he saw the house she entered, he grinned. The old rundown building had minimum security and probably didn't have central air. He made his way to the back of the building and was gratified to see open windows. While he watched, the window in the corner room on the second floor slid open. Though he didn't see her face, he caught a glimpse of Kate's glossy blue blouse.

Perfect! He studied the building. When he had the rough outline of a plan, he left to acquire the items he needed.

## Monday, 5:23 P.M.

When Kate returned to her desk after escorting the Sunset Tech technician, her fellow interns mobbed her. They had all peered into the data center through the window, but apart from a brief tour during orientation, they would likely never be allowed inside.

Awash in their enthusiastic admiration, she forgot about the flash drive.

She and two of her new friends left the office at the end of the day, all of them excited about the seminar on malware they attended in the afternoon. It was so real and practical. Not like the generic, theoretical explanations in her textbooks. The instructor was in the trenches, a warrior in the battle against the forces of chaos.

As they waited for the subway, she felt like a real New Yorker. She was finally beginning to grasp the subway system, and the crowded platform wasn't nearly as intimidating as it had been during her first days in the City. When she stepped out of the car at her destination, she thought she recognized someone, but when she looked closer, she decided she must have been mistaken. Still, despite her newfound big-city confidence, she increased her pace when she parted with her companions and breathed a sigh of relief when she closed the door of her house behind her.

The rental had become a challenge. Her roommates lived loud, chaotic lives. They regarded her as a nerdy bumpkin and didn't bother hiding their snickering disdain. And it was hot. Without air conditioning, she lay in bed coated in a sheen of sweat despite the open window and oscillating fan. But it was cheap and, more importantly for New York, it was available. She consoled herself with the fact she only had to live here two more months.

She stooped to greet her cat, Alan Turing. She'd been reluctant to bring him to New York when her mother suggested it, but it was nice to come home to at least one friendly face. Her roommates wouldn't be home until after ten, so after feeding Alan, she took advantage of the quiet. A cool bath revived her, then she micro-waved some leftover pizza and plopped herself on the old, smelly sofa. Alan joined her to watch reruns of *The Big Bang Theory*.

Later, she lay on top of her covers in a thin t-shirt and panties, accompanied by Alan and the whir of her fan. What she would do for a few moments in the frigid data center. That thought brought to mind her morning, especially the moment when she saw Nik Atherton. She met all the owners at the reception the company held for the summer interns. Of the three, only Nik seemed genuinely interested in talking to anyone as lowly as an intern. She imagined Nik giving her a tour. She would say something witty, and he would turn that easy grin on her. She'd seen his wife's photo on the web. Alix was beautiful and was supposed to be brilliant. They were a matched pair. But maybe…

She smiled at the peeling ceiling. That was silly. She rolled onto her side, turfing Alan out of his spot, and gazed at the open window. Minutes later, Alan having resettled himself near her feet, her eyes slid shut.

## Tuesday, 12:54 A.M.

She woke to her roommates' raucous arrival. A loud party commenced on the other side of the thin wall almost immediately. She glanced at the clock. Almost one. At least she got a few hours' sleep.

She had only a moment to recognize the shadow of someone hovering above her before a hand pressed against her mouth. She rolled onto her side, dislodging the hand long enough to scream. But it had no chance against the thumping music from the next room. A weight settled on her, and something pricked the side of her neck. Her scream faded with her consciousness.

# Tuesday, 12:55 A.M.

The Technician climbed off Kate's body and stared at the wall beyond which a full-scale rave was in progress. The wall was actually vibrating in time with music that had been so heavily compressed, it was little better than noise. It was after midnight, for chrissakes! Who could sleep in these conditions? He looked down at Kate and had to suppress a twinge of sympathy. For a moment, he considered going next door and teaching her inconsiderate roommates some manners.

But he wasn't a murderer. So he put away his syringe, making sure the needle was intact, then got down to business. Feeling a little embarrassed at his victim's near nakedness, he pulled her t-shirt down as far as it would go. Then he bound her ankles and wrists with duct tape. He had to shoo the cat away in order to wrestle her into a soft-sided bag normally used to check golf clubs for air travel.

After clipping a nylon climbing rope to the handle of the bag, he dragged the bag to the window and lowered it to the floor. This was the riskiest part of the plan. The building backed up to a narrow alley, across from an apartment building. It was nearing one in the morning, and there was no movement in the alley. Only one window in the facing building had a light on, and the window was blocked by blinds. It looked safe, but looks could be deceiving. Though he searched the alley before climbing to the second floor, a homeless person might be sleeping in the shadows. One of the dark windows across the way might hide an insomniac. But he had no choice.

Hefting the bag up, he tipped it onto the windowsill, braced a foot against the wall and eased it out the window. No one raised an alarm, so he sank to the floor, put both feet on the wall and lowered her to the pavement. Fortunately, she weighed quite a bit less than he did. When he felt the rope go slack, he took a quick look to make sure the coast was still clear, tossed the rope out the window, and turned to retrieve his pack.

The cat stared balefully at him from atop the duffel bag. "Git!" he hissed and aimed a kick at the animal.

The cat ran up his leg. He caught hold of its tail when it reached his chest, but that only encouraged it to dig its claws into his flesh to remain attached to him. Emitting an unmanly yelp, The Technician let go of the tail. The cat took advantage by climbing his face before leaping from the top of his head.

He spun toward the window. The cat was gone. He leaned out and looked down. It stood on the golf bag and stared up at him. He scooped up his pack, took one more look at the room, then eased out the window and shimmied down the drainpipe. When he arrived at the bottom, he swung his pack at the beast, sending it scurrying down the alley.

"Fucking cat," he murmured, raising his balaclava above his nose and dabbing at his bloody cheek. He coiled the rope, stuffed it into his pack and settled the strap onto his shoulder. Stooping, he heaved the golf bag onto his other shoulder, then looked up. "Of course."

Someone had raised the blinds in the illuminated room in the building across the alley. It appeared to be a woman, though she was only a dark silhouette. He couldn't be sure she was looking at him, but if his recent run of luck held true, she was probably wearing night vision goggles. Pulling his balaclava down, he set off down the alley. He wasn't worried about the cops arriving soon in this neighborhood, but there were already too many loose ends littering his trail.

He was still chastising himself when he lay Kate in the back of the stolen van. This job had gone from bad to worse. Climbing into the driver's seat, he wondered if he might be able to bill his client. Nik's untimely intervention had probably screwed the job for him, so he wouldn't get the balance of the payment. But body disposal should be a premium service, and he made it very clear when he took a contract, the client was responsible for unforeseen expenses.

# Chapter 6

## Monday, 7:10 P.M.

The elevator doors slid open, unmasking the murmur of party conversations riding the lilting strains of a string quartet. Alix watched Nik sigh, gather himself, then take a long step into the hallway, where he stood motionless. "Nik," she said, joining him. "You know you always end up enjoying yourself at these things."

"Enjoy?" Nik's brow furrowed.

"You're positively perky afterward. I quite like that Nik."

"Ah, yes." His brow smoothed. "The *afterward*. Not the before or during."

"Well, one must pay the price to reap the reward." She took his arm and urged him in the right direction. "You can't do anything about what happened at work today. I'm sure Jamie will have something for you tomorrow morning."

They strolled down the hall and rounded a corner, then stopped in the entrance to a large room Cerberus used for social events.

Manhattan and the Hudson River were visible through floor to ceiling windows on two walls. From the fiftieth floor, the nighttime view was stunning. The lighting was muted. Conversation circles made up of cushy chairs were arranged around the perimeter. Standing tables dotted the center of the room, creating perching spots for current and potential Cerberus customers. Members of the sales staff flitted like hummingbirds among these clusters, searching for openings where they could insert themselves into the conversations. A bar in the corner was as busy as a waterhole on a dry savanna.

Alix scanned the room for the techs. A handful were always invited in the unlikely event a potential customer had a question deeper than the marketing department's slickly produced white papers. Alix spotted them huddled in a seating area pressed into the corner where the two windowed walls met. A moat of clear floor separated them from the uninitiated. Somehow, despite dressing in what was clearly their best finery, they couldn't help looking scruffy. They were obviously trying to appear cool, but Alix knew inside they sneered at the self-important ignoramuses around them. Wistfully, in many cases.

She glanced at Nik, who gazed pensively around the room, no doubt searching for the least objectionable conversation to join. At some point he would swoop down on the besieged techs, his presence making the night memorable for them and reviving Nik. Unlike the other techs, Nik was a picture of casual elegance. Gray t-shirt, black gabardine pants and Gucci loafers. Together, they accentuated his athletic build, hinting at the definition in his shoulders, arms, and chest. They were a matched pair. She dug into her closet and chose a pair of black strappy heels and a swishy black dress that swooped low on her back.

Watching him fret, an aching fondness for this complicated man overwhelmed her.

Catching her smiling at him, he asked, "What?"

She gave her head the smallest of shakes, leaned close enough to detect a heady mixture of cologne and Nik, and whispered, "Anyone here who isn't here?"

A half-smile fluttered at the corner of his lips. "The hobo over by the techs."

"Hobo?" She looked in that direction. She didn't see anyone matching that description, but then she wouldn't. Only Nik saw them. Or he said he did, anyway. Who really knew? It was just one of the many idiosyncrasies that made up the collage that was Nik.

"Ernest Borgnine," Nik said. "*Emperor of the North*, 1973."

She didn't know the movie, but she got the picture. "Go have fun." He hated these events, but it was for his company, and these were his people. He didn't need her to help him fight his battles.

He glowered, but before he could respond, Julie Swinson, Cerberus's Director of Sales, spotted him and called his name in a voice that pierced the general buzz. She stood with a group of men whose sloppy grins suggested they'd already taken ample advantage of the open bar. When Nik didn't move, Alix nudged him in their direction.

He glanced over his shoulder as he walked away. "Get me a drink. Anything with alcohol."

Alix watched Julie put an arm around his shoulders and pull him firmly into the swarm. Sighing at the length of the line at the bar, she made her way over to it, ignoring the eyes following her.

While she waited, she amused herself by watching the sales courtship. Most of the guests weren't authorized to make binding commitments. Procurement decisions were made far above their pay grade. They were only here to drink and socialize. The sales staff knew the game. The theory was the good times these men and women had here would color their opinions when the question of which vendor to go with came up later. Cerberus's competitors knew that, of course, so it was a game of dueling parties.

It was all bullshit. The merits of the products and services should be the sole deciding factor. Everyone knew Cerberus had better technology, but it was surprising how narrow that edge gave the company in practice. People were people. It was how the world worked. Favors, fun times, hookers and just enough sober reasoning to keep the world toddling along.

It was one reason Nik found these events so distasteful. It was true he founded Cerberus because he loved the technical challenges. But in his heart, Nik saw himself as the knight-errant, standing between the innocent and those who would exploit them. He found the corporate pursuit of profit above all other considerations frustrating. She wouldn't be surprised if that wasn't the inspiration for virtual Alix. Nik was looking for another outlet. One untarnished by greed.

"Wine?"

Alix turned to find Joel Walton. The company's CEO smiled and offered a glass of white wine. She took it by the stem and sipped while gazing at him over the rim of the glass. "Albariño. Very nice," she said. "Thank you."

"I saw you looking parched. Knew it would be appreciated." He glanced at an open space against a window. "Care to get out of the traffic?"

"I have to get something for Nik," she said and didn't miss a slight tightening at the corners of his eyes.

"Of course. I'm sure Nik is in too much demand to stand in line." He graced her with a low bow. "Find me when you get a chance."

"I will."

His gaze lingered for a moment, then he slipped into the crowd.

*What was that about?* Joel had a crush on her when the three of them were in college, but he never took it out on Nik after she made her choice.

Filing it away for further consideration, she returned the smiles of two men who joined the line behind her. They had discarded their ties and held half-full drinks. The one who unbuttoned his shirt an extra button leered at her. It wasn't a good look.

He winked, bobbed his head and said, "Hey."

She turned her back on them to find there were still three people between her and her release. She sipped her wine and noticed Joel and Adam Felton near the exit. The intensity of the conversation caught her attention. For two of Cerberus C-level executives to engage in an argument at a reception for potential customers was shocking. Especially these two.

Privately, Joel was an intense man, but he hid it behind the affable public persona that had become the face of Cerberus to the world. Adam was a bean counter, in the least derogatory sense of the word. He was mild-mannered, careful and persnickety about… well, almost everything. Alix had seen the darker side of Joel when they were young, but she didn't think she had ever seen either of these men argue in public. Nik may let his emotions loose to frolic, as he was loath to suffer the rude and foolish. But brilliant techs could get away with that. Not these two.

Joel pointed across the room and leaned so close to Adam that the accountant backed away. Joel spoke, then dropped his arm and stalked through the exit. Alix turned to see what he was pointing at and found Nik. Her partner was listening to a woman telling what she apparently thought was a funny story, while he looked on with a familiar pained smile. She looked back toward the exit and found Adam looking at her. He shrugged, turned, and followed Joel.

Two of the most important Cerberus executives had left an important sales reception early. Adam wouldn't be missed, but this kind of event was Joel's milieu. What the hell was going on?

"Look at that Nik guy." It was the voice of the winker behind her. "What a joke."

"Yeah," the other man said. "I heard he gets other people to write his code, then he pays them off so they won't talk."

Alix pivoted around. The winker noticed and leered, his eyes traveling slowly down her body, lingering on her cleavage, before returning to her eyes. She smiled and said, "Hello."

"Hey." He extended a hand. "Name's Mark."

When Alix took his hand, he curled his index finger and caressed her palm. She looked him in the eye and said, "I'm Alix Crockett."

His face froze. He jerked his hand, but Alix tightened down until he winced. "We're sorry. If we'd known…"

"And should that make a difference? Does a woman only deserve respect based on who her partner is?"

"No, that's not what I meant. We're sorry."

"Next time, you may want to think about what you mean before you open your mouth." She released his hand and watched him take his friend by the arm and drag him away.

"What happened? Who is she?" he said, resisting.

"That's Nik Atherton's wife."

"Oh."

Alix smirked, watching them disappear into the crowd.

"Can I help you?"

She turned back to the bar and found herself next in line. She put her empty glass on the bar and said, "Two Albariños."

Glasses in hand, she went in search of Nik. She found him with a small group in the corner opposite the string quartet. Julie Swinson stood next to him, her lips stretched in a rictus of a smile.

One hand was pressed to the middle of Nik's back. Alix rolled her eyes. Julie was terrified of what he might say, but was also making sure he didn't leave. The people they were talking to must be the primary targets of this affair.

Seeing her approach, the man next to Nik made room. "Thank you," she said with a smile and handed a wineglass to Nik.

"Thank the spirits," he mumbled and took a deep swallow.

"You must be Alix," the man who made room for her said. He extended a hand. His hand was velvet smooth, his grip firm but not macho firm. "I read the piece on you in New York magazine on my flight."

"You mean the piece on Nik and I," Alix said.

"Yes, of course."

"You have me at a disadvantage." She enjoyed the frown that flickered across his face. She knew who he was. You couldn't avoid his media presence. Ash Damán, the tech billionaire whose enterprise encompassed everything from aviation to agriculture and social media.

Julie's bray attracted every eye in the group. "Oh, Alix, you're so funny!" She removed the hand from Nik's back and flicked her fingers at Damán. "Isn't she funny?!" She returned the hand in time to arrest Nik's retreat and gave Alix a frozen smile. "Everyone knows Ash Damán on sight. Who *couldn't* know him?"

Alix caught Nik's eye, then gave Damán a warm smile. "Of course, I recognize you. I meant we haven't been introduced."

It wasn't a convincing lie, but it wasn't meant to be. She never met him, but Julie was right. It was impossible to avoid hearing the man's opinions on just about everything. Neither Nik nor Alix liked him.

He studied her face, an unseen emotion troubling his eyes. Then he smiled, showing twin rows of orthodontically perfect teeth. "Well, then, let me introduce myself. Ash Damán at your service."

He dipped his head the smallest amount. There was warmth in the words, but none in the eyes.

She held his gaze for a moment, then turned to Nik. "Nik, may I speak to you in private?" On Nik's other side, Julie began hyperventilating.

"Yes!" he said too loudly.

Alix reached around and removed Julie's hand from Nik's back. "Nice to have met you, Ash." She said her goodbyes to everyone else, then followed Nik.

When she caught up with him near the exit, he stepped closer and whispered, "I think you may have driven a stake through Julie's heart."

Alix glanced back at the sales director, who had gone into overdrive trying to salvage the situation. Damán met her eyes briefly. "You don't need to be doing business with that man," she said, turning back to Nik.

"It's millions of dollars. Hundreds of millions when all's said and done. Or something like that. Potentially one of the biggest contracts we've ever had."

"He's not someone you can trust," she said and brushed his bangs across his forehead. "Has a reputation for not honoring contracts and is aggressively litigious."

He took a small step closer. "I agree. I already told Joel and Adam how I feel."

"So, this event…"

"Ambush. I think they hoped if I met him, I would change my mind."

She breathed his scent and let her eyes close for a moment.

"Did you have something to talk about, or were you just on a rescue mission?"

She intended to ask him about Joel and Adam, but she thought she understood what that was about. She would tell him what she saw later. "Rescue mission. How much longer do we need to stay?"

He sighed. "Julie practically made me sign a contract. I have to stay until midnight." He gulped the rest of his wine. "And I'm required to have four glasses of wine." When she gave him a quizzical look, he said, "She says alcohol makes me less prickly."

"She said that?"

He wobbled his head. "Her words were earthier. Something about not being a giant prick. But that was the gist."

"Well, then let us repair to the bar and fulfill your obligations."

They were halfway to the bar when Julie swooped in and corralled Nik again. As she pulled him away, she threw an icy glare over her shoulder at Alix.

"Get me wine," Nik said, before disappearing.

"You don't like me much, do you?"

Alix turned and found Damán standing very close. She took a step back and looked up at him. "I don't know you well enough to feel one way or another."

An ugly smirk twisted his lips before morphing into a friendly grin. "Fair enough. My yacht is moored at a local marina. Why don't you and Nik have dinner with me, let's say, tomorrow at nine?"

She meant to say, "I'd rather stab my eye out with a butter knife," but she heard herself saying, "I'll have to talk to Nik."

"Of course, check with the man of the family." The smallest emphasis on the word man almost prompted Alix to deck him. He handed her a card. "Call me in the morning. Don't wait too late." He flashed his teeth and turned away. A covey of flunkies and assorted remorae followed him out the door, many of them throwing her dirty looks as they hurried to keep up.

Alix flipped the card into a nearby planter. "Oops," she said and headed to the bar.

## Monday, 11:45 P.M.

Fifteen minutes before midnight, the party was winding down. The bartenders were filling final orders for people who had no business having a last drink. The salespeople wandered the nearly empty room, looking lost and forlorn. Only Julie was still trolling for commitments for lunch dates and conference calls. Alix hadn't seen Joel or Adam since they left.

She found Nik with the techs, looking more comfortable than he had since they stepped off the elevator. She watched them trading nerdy quips and laughing. They idolized him. Nik could have basked in their adoration but in his heart he was still one of them. He worked hard to bridge the gap, spending enough time with all the new hires to get to know them, learning their strengths and how best to support their weaknesses. He insisted his tech team be on a first-name basis.

He glanced up at her and smiled.

"I've… we've heard you're working on something really big," the woman sitting next to him said breathlessly. "Is that true?"

He gazed at Alix, looking as if he hadn't heard. Then he came to himself and glanced around at the techs' eager faces. "Very big." He rose, came to stand next to Alix, and turned to face them. He glanced over his shoulder, leaned toward them, and put his finger to his lips. "But *very* secret."

From their rapt expressions, he might as well be revealing the location of the fountain of youth.

"What?!" more than one blurted.

Nik winked and turned away.

"You'll see," he said over his shoulder as he and Alix strolled arm-in-arm toward the exit.

"You sure you can leave now?" Alix asked. "It's not yet midnight."

"If Julie sues me, I'll counter sue on the basis of cruel and unusual punishment." Alone by the elevators, he glanced over his shoulder, then rested a hand on her butt and squeezed. "Besides, I've been watching you walk around in that dress all night, and I —"

She slipped an arm around his waist, pulled him close, and kissed him.

When she finally let him go, he gave her a lazy grin. "Yeah, that."

Stepping away and pushing the elevator button, she said, "Huh, I thought you were going to say you just had to try it on. The dress."

"I don't think it would hang off my shoulders right," he said and stepped into the elevator. "Plus, I don't have the butt to make it sway just so."

As the door slid shut, she pushed him against the wall, paused to gaze into his smiling eyes, and pressed her mouth to his.

# Chapter 7

## Tuesday, 8:05 A.M.

The morning after the sales event, Nik breezed into the reception area on the tenth floor, waved to the temporary receptionist and took the hall on the right, the one that led to the cubicles occupied by the techs. These were the developers. Coders, network techs, security professionals. People their customers never saw. The customer-facing techs in the call center took up the entire ninth floor.

He paused to peer through the window into the data center, then plunged into the warren of cubicles. Nestled among the open office spaces were seating areas where groups could congregate or individuals could get away from their workspaces. Windows along the eastern wall looked out onto the Manhattan skyline and let in plenty of sunlight. It was early, but most of the techs were already at work. Some of them probably stayed overnight. They set their own schedules. Nik insisted. As long as they met their benchmarks, he didn't care how they did it.

Jamie Farris's office was on the back wall. Many of the other techs relegated to cubicles had seniority and would normally have been given the office, but during Jamie's first week in a cubicle, they found him wandering along a wall, hyperventilating and searching for a quiet place to hide. They had to isolate him in a small, dark room to calm him down. Sally Thompson, their Director of Human Resources, would have fired him on the spot if Nik hadn't intervened. He recognized how valuable Jamie was after one conversation.

Jamie wasn't a simple agoraphobe. He didn't have an unreasoning fear of open spaces. He got himself to work every day, after all. Jamie's problem was much more fascinating. He had an almost preternatural understanding of systems. The murky worlds of servers, operating systems, computer networks were an open book to him. His problem was plunging into that virtual landscape left him porous and vulnerable. Overhead lighting, the murmur of conversations, the low clatter of keyboard keys, even the hum of the air conditioner were enough to overwhelm him. So, not wanting to lose him, Nik insisted they find a place he would feel safe.

Nik tapped on the door to Jamie's office, using the cadence they agreed on to identify him. He gave Jamie enough time to surface from wherever he was and entered the office. Jamie's head popped above the middle of three monitors on his desk, like a prairie dog peaking out of its burrow. When he saw it truly was Nik, he dropped out of sight.

Nik came around and sat in the chair Jamie placed just so for him. The office was lit only by the monitors and a dusty desk lamp. There were no windows. The walls were covered by an eclectic mix of motivational and travel posters.

"Nik," Jamie said, without interrupting his fingers on the keyboard.

Jamie was shorter than Nik by several inches. He had brown hair and matching eyes accented by long lashes. His resume said he was twenty-five, but he looked younger. He shaved the sides and lower part of the back of his head, but let the hair on top grow long and tied it in a ponytail. He apparently had an infinite supply of branded t-shirts, which he wore loose over faded jeans. His feet were perpetually encased in sandals.

"Jamie." Nik retrieved a box of Snowcaps from his jacket pocket and placed the box on the corner of Jamie's desk.

Jamie's fingers paused and his eyes cut to the offering. A grin appeared briefly, then he opened a desk drawer, slid the box into it, then closed it. "Your servers," he said and pointed to a window in the center of the monitor on the left.

The window showed a simple command-line interface with a prompt and a blinking cursor. Jamie was connected to the servers. The servers were on their own network, akin to being locked in their own room. The firewall was like a guard at the door, deciding who got in and who got out. "Did Singh open the firewall?"

"Only for me," Jamie said, pointing at the window. "They're still isolated from everything else. The server room is too cold, and…"

Nik nodded. The most secure way to connect to the servers would be to attach a laptop directly to them, but, like Jamie said, it would mean sitting in the frigid server room for maybe hours. More importantly for Jamie, it was brightly lit and the blowers in the air conditioners were very loud.

"Find anything?" Nik asked.

"Not on the server. But…" He pointed to another window, which showed an open connection to the firewall used to isolate the servers. The firewall examined every bit of network traffic and decided whether to allow it through based on a set of rules. It was a testament to how much Singh trusted Jamie that he allowed him to connect to the firewall. Nik stood, hesitated until Jamie nodded, then leaned forward and squinted at the small text on the firewall terminal. It listed all the network traffic that originated from the new servers. The firewall would block the traffic, but it recorded it all.

He focused on the line Jamie pointed to. "A directed broadcast," Nik said. A broadcast was the way a computer could shout out to all the other computers on a network. "To our network."

"Yes," Jamie said. "And it's weird."

"How so?"

"Someone added a rule to the firewall to allow the broadcast. If Singh hadn't blocked everything when you asked him to, the firewall would have passed the broadcast."

"Someone modified the firewall configuration," Nik said softly.

Jamie nodded. "And there's more. The server sends the broadcast at random intervals. A small message. Easy to miss unless you're looking for it. I don't know what the message is, but if I had to guess, I'd say it's trying to say hello."

"Rootkit," Nik said. A rootkit was a small program that allowed a remote user to steal data or take control of the infected computer. They could be devilishly hard to find and eliminate. "And it's trying to get the attention of some other computer in our building."

Jamie nodded. "Yeah, and it's a good one. My guess is once the rootkit connects to the other computer, someone from the outside will piggyback on a trusted connection through the firewall to take control of the server. A reverse shell."

"But you haven't found it? The rootkit."

"Not yet," Jamie said. "Whoever coded it was top flight. Looks like you were right to be suspicious. What tipped you off?"

Nik considered. Someone went to a lot of trouble to compromise these servers. Someone bold enough and knowledgeable enough about Cerberus to walk right into their data center. Someone very skilled. And the other computer the rootkit was trying to connect to would have to be compromised as well. That and the change to the firewall meant someone inside Cerberus was involved. He eyed Jamie, then glanced at the window displaying the firewall. Jamie certainly had the skill and access to be the insider. But if Jamie was the insider, this conversation would be very different. Jamie didn't have to tell him about the change to the firewall. Besides, there was no one else at Cerberus he trusted more. "The tech from Sunset who installed the servers wasn't Reggie."

Jamie didn't respond.

"The servers came straight from the vendor, unopened as far as I could tell," Nik said. "So, unless someone at the vendor installed the rootkit, it had to be the unknown tech."

"Who escorted him in the server room?"

Nik gazed into his memory of the previous morning. He'd noticed the tech when he arrived in the reception area. There was also a young woman. Was she the escort? "Someone who shouldn't have." He rose. "Thank you, Jamie."

"What do you want to do with the infected servers?"

"Nothing yet. Keep on it and let me know if you find the rootkit."

Nik headed to his office, logged on and accessed the receptionist's log. He found the entry for Reggie from Sunrise Tech and opened it. Alarm bells went off when he didn't recognize the name of the woman assigned to escort him. Catherine 'Kate' Munson. A moment later, he had her personnel records open. An intern from Kansas. Now that he saw where she was from, he remembered her from the interns' reception. He noted her assigned desk, logged off, and left his office.

The interns were crammed four to a cubicle. When Nik appeared in the entrance to Kate's cubicle, the interns sitting at three of the desks leapt up so fast they got tangled with one another. They were all men.

Ignoring the interns' frightened stammering, he pointed at the desk that had been unoccupied and asked, "Where is Kate?"

## Tuesday, 7:10 P.M.

Alix watched Nik staring out the window. They sat on opposite sides of their kitchen island. He had been stirring his tea for ten minutes without taking a sip. "What's got you so pensive?"

He blinked and looked down at his tea, set the spoon on the saucer and focused on her. "A puzzle at work."

"Not that creepy virtual Alix, is it?"

A smile blossomed on his face, then slid into a sly grin. "I find it odd you call her creepy. She's basically you."

"I find it odd you refer to *it* as her, and it *is* creepy precisely because it *is* so much like me."

"*I* don't find you creepy."

Alix pursed her lips. "I'm going to assume you're just *trying* to be funny and that you understand my point."

Nik grew serious. "I get it. I know you understand I never intended anyone else to see her, and there was nothing untoward going on."

Alix knew that, but it was nice to know he understood her concerns.

"We mostly talk about network traffic analysis. Oh, and I'm trying to teach her how to make small talk. The weather, movies, music. That kind of thing."

"I heard it laugh."

Nik looked at her, then a smile slowly animated his expression. "Well, humor is a sign of intelligence, so I've been telling her jokes." He looked to the side for a moment. "Not that successfully. Sort of ruins the joke when you have to explain it."

"But it laughed. The other night when I overheard you."

He perked up. "Right, this is the revealing part. I'm pretty sure she doesn't get the jokes. She laughs for my benefit."

Alix stared at him. "That's…"

"Exactly. It's evidence of insight and intention. She's doing it because she understands what I want, and it matters to her. She knows if she responds the way I expect, I'll be happy."

"Tell me the joke. The one you told the other night."

His eyes turned up for a moment. "I got a new pen that can write under water." He waited a beat. "It can write other words, too."

She smiled, but only in response to his silly grin. "Maybe she doesn't find them funny because you're telling her Dad jokes."

"I know. It's a stupid joke. But even for this simple joke, there is so much you have to know to even understand it's a joke." When she nodded her understanding, he let his head drop and gave his tea a stir. "If I had to do it again, I would have used Winnie the Pooh instead of you." When he looked up and saw her confusion, he said, "You know, because the copyright expired. The original version."

They gazed at one another. Alix's expression broke first, then they were both giggling, imagining Winnie the Pooh explaining network traffic behavior analysis to uptight IT professionals.

"And Tigger too," Alix said.

When their laughter subsided, Alix grew serious and said, "Tell me about the puzzle at work."

He told her about his conversation with Jamie. "It would have to be the tech who installed the rootkit. They're supposed to be escorted by someone who can keep an eye on them, but somehow a new intern was assigned to escort him."

"Someone went to a lot of trouble to compromise those servers."

"It appears so."

"Who assigned the intern?"

"No one will admit to it and it wasn't logged."

"Did you ask the intern?"

"She didn't come to work today. Didn't call in to give a reason, and her phone goes directly to voicemail."

They sat in silence for a few moments, then Alix asked, "Did you call Sunset?"

"Singh called them. This is where the puzzle deepens." He pushed his cup aside, leaned forward, and rested his elbows on the counter. "Reggie's company van has disappeared, but the intern signed for the job using Reggie's tablet." He picked up a gingersnap and tapped it on the rim of his cup. "Then, Reggie sent an email saying he was quitting. Family emergency in Florida. They think he took the van and skipped town, but the GPS tracker isn't working. Or was disabled."

"Very mysterious," Alix said. "They know this Steve Linden? The Tech?"

Nik shook his head. "Never heard of him. He looked vaguely familiar, but I haven't been able to figure out why."

"Security cameras?"

"He obviously knew where the cameras were. Kept his face hidden behind the bill of his cap."

Alix sat back. "So, someone who doesn't work for Sunset Tech shows up claiming to be Reggie."

"Checked in with the security guard and receptionist as Reggie and had Reggie's ID with his own photo."

"They don't know Reggie on sight?"

"The receptionist was a temp, and the guard was new."

"Convenient," Alix said. "Then someone at Cerberus, someone who won't admit to it, assigns an inexperienced intern to escort the not-Reggie tech. The tech takes advantage of the intern's naivety to install the rootkit and has her sign for the job. Then the intern goes missing."

"We don't know for sure she's missing. There's all kinds of reasons an intern doesn't work out. Too much partying. Overwhelmed by the City or the job. Some of them stop coming to work, and some just go home."

"Without a word to anyone?"

"*That* is unusual, but not unheard of." He lifted a finger. "But this is the weird thing —"

"*This* is the weird thing?"

He chuckled. "Another weird thing. Her cubicle mates said she was smart as a whip and very excited about the job. Thrilled to be here, they said."

"And it's not just the intern who disappeared."

"No. Reggie. Who always seemed solid to me." He waggled his head. "As solid as anyone could be with his health habits." They gazed at one another. "You got time tomorrow?"

"I can move some things around. Take the morning. You know where Reggie and the intern live?"

"I can find out." Nik sipped his tea and grimaced. He stood and poured the tea down the sink. "Cold." Putting the cup and saucer in the dishwasher, he asked, "What are you thinking? Indian?"

"Thai." As they left the kitchen, she asked, "What were you using these new servers for?"

Nik stopped, turned and put his arms around her waist. "You're going to love this."

"No," she said.

"Virtual Alix."

# Chapter 8

## Tuesday, 8:05 am

Kate was awake for a while before she realized it. Troubling dreams, not wanting to let go of her, followed her into the waking world. She thought her eyes were open, but she couldn't be sure. Wherever she was, it was pitch black. It was only when she tried to move her hands that she remembered. They were bound together at the wrists.

Her scream echoed, startling her into silence. She panted, but couldn't catch her breath. Her head swam, her stomach threatened to expel its contents. Desperate to avoid the embarrassment of vomiting on herself, she screamed again. A ragged, angry shriek. She needed to think. Hermione would not panic. But when the echoes faded, she was still panting, this time between gritted teeth.

"What did you do to my cat?!" she shouted at the darkness. Surprised that it was Alan's fate that she thought of at this moment, her panic ebbed for a moment, allowing anger to rush in and come to her rescue. "You asshole, you had no right to come into my room!"

Though her breath was still coming fast and shallow, she no longer felt as though she would faint. The shouting had the additional benefit of clearing the fog which blanketed her mind when she woke. Now that she was thinking again, she tried to remember how she got here.

She was in her own bed and woke to find someone in the room with her. A hot prickly flush crawled across her skin. Did he violate her? She didn't think so. She didn't know what it would feel like, but she imagined pain and humiliation would be part of it. Even if she was unconscious during the act.

Whoever took her, he dressed her in more than her t-shirt and panties. She couldn't see what she wore, but she felt a rough fabric against her skin. She was lying on her back. Her wrists and ankles were bound, but she was uninjured as far as she could tell. She had just managed to roll to her hands and knees when a door opened behind her, admitting a blinding light.

Kate squeezed her eyes shut and scrabbled across the concrete floor, away from the door until her head impacted a hard surface. Even in her terror, her undignified yelp embarrassed her.

"There's no need for that," a man said. "There's nowhere to go."

Lying on her side, her hands shielding her face, Kate forced her eyes open and squinted toward the voice. All she could see was a silhouette of a man behind the glare of a flashlight. He crouched and set the flashlight on the ground, pointing the beam at the wall so she got her first view of his face. The cement block walls and steel door behind him blurred, leaving only his face clear. It was a face she knew. The man from Sunset Tech. Reggie. He looked so normal, just like she remembered him. Nothing like the monster she imagined only moments ago. Blue eyes, sandy hair that could use a trim, slight build, a thin nose, and a light complexion. He wore loafers, jeans, and a red polo shirt. He appeared calm and spoke in a pleasant voice.

"What do you want?" she asked.

"I want to ask you some questions."

"Me? What kind of questions? What could I know that would —" Finding an opening, her panic surged, stealing her voice.

"If you answer honestly, I'll let you go."

Cruel hope surged momentarily, before dissipating like smoke. That was a lie. He wouldn't let her see his face if he intended to let her go. Still, she wasn't dead yet. "What do you want to know?"

"When you returned to the data center, did you find my flash drive?"

She gaped at him. Flash drive? That's what this was about? "The... Yeah. It was on the floor."

"Where is it?"

"I... gave it to the receptionist. In case you came back."

He considered her, then he sighed. "I believe you. We're almost finished. Now, this is very important. Did you tell anyone about what I did when I installed the servers?"

Kate gaped at him. She gave her a head a shake. "What... what you... I saw you install the servers."

"Yes, but did you tell anyone what you saw?"

She replayed what he did in the server room, but panic wiped away the details. "What did I see?"

He stared at her.

"No! No one asked, and I didn't talk about it. I was in a — A seminar on malware all day. No one asked." That wasn't entirely true. She told the other interns all about it, but she barely mentioned the flash drive.

"Okay. I believe you."

"So, you'll let me go?" she blurted. She knew it was a false hope, but she couldn't help asking.

"Yes." He picked up a small case she hadn't noticed from the floor beside his foot. After unzipping it, he extracted a syringe and a small vial.

She got her feet underneath herself and pressed her back against the wall.

"Nothing to worry about," he said as he filled the syringe from the vial. "I can't let you see where I live. This will put you to sleep like before. When you wake up, you'll be far from here and all will be forgotten." He set the vial down, lifted the syringe, and grinned at her.

She launched herself at him, swatting at the hypodermic with her bound hands. Moving faster than she thought possible, he leapt up and backed out of range. She sprawled on the floor at his feet. She tried to scramble away, but with her feet bound, she only managed to roll onto her back.

He kicked her. She felt her jaw crack. Blinding pain locked her muscles in place. Not wanting to die with her eyes closed, she forced them open and looked up at him through her tears.

"I get the feeling you don't trust me." He glanced at the syringe. "Now, lay still. This will only take a second. A small prick, then everything will be okay."

She wanted to fight back as he lowered himself over her. To crawl pathetically across the floor, if only to extend her life a few moments longer. But panic overruled the part of her mind that was screaming for her to move.

The music startled both of them. She stared up at his surprised face. The syringe hovered inches from her neck.

*Jolene, Jolene, Jolene, Jolene*
*Please don't take him just because you can*


It was the Miley Cyrus version.

He gazed at her for a moment, then sighed and stood. "Sorry. This will only take a second." He shifted the syringe to his left hand and fished in a pocket for a cell phone. Putting it to his ear, he said, "Yeah, talk to me." He listened quietly for a few moments, then he said, "Turn off your computer. Keep it off until I tell you it's okay."

Given a reprieve, even if it was brief, Kate's brain coughed into gear. She screamed, but it was too late. He'd already disconnected.

He let the hand holding the phone drop and gazed at the wall. "Well, fuck me."

Kate stared up at him.

"I've got to think about this." He turned away, went through the door, and looked back at her. "Don't go anywhere." The door closing cut off his snicker.

Timeless moments passed before Kate wept. Tears pooled in her ears and moistened her hair. Her jaw was probably broken. She wet herself. She would probably be in therapy for the rest of her life. But she was alive. She let her head fall to the side. And he left the flashlight.

## Tuesday, 8:30 A.M.


The Technician stopped at the top of his basement stairs and stared into space. He knew this job wasn't simple when he took it, but it paid well and his plan was brilliant. Despite minor stumbles offing Reggie, the plan almost worked. Would have worked without fate's untimely intervention. Not bad for his first foray into the darker arts.

Everything he read online about assassination led him to expect some level of remorse. But he'd lost more sleep over how to monetize his new services than Reggie's death. You couldn't exactly list assassination and abduction on your marketing brochures. No longer was he just a nerd. A keyboard jockey. He was a dangerous man. A small smile touched the corner of his lips. The Technician. International man of mystery. Assassin. Jason Bourne with fewer mental health issues.

He looked down at the burner phone he purchased only for this job and slipped it into his pocket. The call came from his client. They hadn't been happy. Nik had isolated the servers and put their most capable tech on the case. The Technician didn't care who that was. They wouldn't find the rootkit. He was too good for that. But compromising those servers was his one and only idea for completing the job.

He came back from his thoughts, glanced around the kitchen, then crossed to the sink and filled the kettle with filtered water. After setting it to boil, he rummaged through his tea cabinet for a suitable leaf. "What tea goes with a catastrophe?" he mumbled.

Settling on Assam Mangalam Black, he filled a tea ball with loose leaves, set it on the marble counter, and gazed out the window. He half expected the bad news. Had resigned himself to failure. But despite arousing Nik's suspicions, as the day wore on and his client hadn't called, he began to think the great man hadn't seen the threat.

The kettle's whistle startled him out of his thoughts. He poured boiling water into a mug and absently dipped the tea ball. It was the threat at the end of the call that had him unsettled. His client told him their sponsor didn't take failure well. That was unwelcome news. The Technician had thought the client was his employer, but apparently there was someone else behind the scenes. Someone his client warned him had the reach to find him, no matter where he ran. Had he known this at the outset, it would have been a deterrent to taking the job.

He sighed and set the teaball in the sink. Taking his mug out on his deck, he stood at the rail and gazed toward the Long Island Sound, visible through the trees at the back of his lot.

Done is done. The question now was, what were his options? He could try to find out who the client's sponsor was and kill him. Or her. The problem was, with no clue who it was, he had no way to evaluate the risks or how long it would take. And there was his reputation to consider. The sort of people who hired people like him frowned on their contractors killing them.

He could run. He had escape plans in place for just such an eventuality. It would mean giving everything up, including the lavish retirement he envisioned for himself. But at least it was an option he knew how to accomplish. And he was pretty sure he could stay hidden, no matter who was looking for him. He sipped his tea. Probably.

His only viable option other than running was to complete the job. He would need help, and the person he had in mind would be expensive. Sighing, he set his mug down and leaned his elbows on the rail. He might end up finishing the job and losing money. But that was better than being dead.

He would reach out to The Vulture and ask for help, but hedge his bets and get ready to run. Just in case.

Satisfied he had the beginnings of a workable plan, he returned to the kitchen. When his eyes fell on the door to the basement stairs, he stopped. What to do with Kate? The irony was, he didn't even need to get her involved. He believed her story about the flash drive. It would probably sit in a drawer in the receptionist's desk until long after he retired.

He hesitated, staring at the door, then left the kitchen to go to his study. He had some preparations to make and Kate could keep. "After all, where can she go?" He chuckled.

# Chapter 9

## Wednesday, 10:12 am

"That's it," Nik said as he pulled his 1991 Jaguar XJS Cabriolet to a stop on the shady street in the Crown Heights neighborhood of Brooklyn. He and Alix looked at the two-story brick building. The neighborhood was going through a transition and wasn't the worst they'd seen in Brooklyn, but the building in which Kate lived wouldn't boost the local property values. The mortar had crumbled between the bricks. The paint on the trim was peeling, and some windows were missing screens.

"How much do you pay your interns?" Alix asked. "Because if this is the best they can do, it's not enough."

Nik turned the engine off and opened his door. "We pay them plenty," he said as he got out. "But this is New York." He waited until she joined him. "You have to pay your dues. That place we first shacked up in was worse."

"Shacked up?"

Nik grinned. "It was no better than a shack in a fourth-floor walkup. What would you call it?"

"You're just going to leave the car here with the top down?"

"We'll just be a minute," Nik said and looked in both directions.

"Your car," Alix said with a shrug, and led Nik up the steps to the front door.

Nik knocked. When no one answered, he pounded.

"Could be no one's home," Alix said.

Nik pounded again.

The door swung open to reveal a young woman who had obviously just crawled out of bed. A mass of tangled, bleach-blond hair stuck out in all directions. Generously applied eye makeup had smeared, ringing bloodshot eyes that glared daggers at Nik. She wore tiny cotton shorts, no shoes and a thin midriff t-shirt that stopped just short of dangerous. Nik gaped at the spectacle, his knocking hand still aloft.

Scowling, the woman swiped hair out of her face. "What the fuck, bro!" When she spoke, she bounced.

"Relax, Rocket," Alix said.

Nik grinned at her. "Rocket Raccoon. Very nice." Taking in the woman's confused expression, he twirled his finger around his eye. "Because of the… Nevermind."

"Do you have any idea what time it is?" Bouncy shouted, setting off another series of tremors.

"It's after ten," Alix said. "Does your mother know you come to the door half naked?"

Confusion returned to Bouncy's face. She glanced down at herself, then glared at Alix. "Listen, lady —"

"Lady. Good one," Nik said with a smirk, holding his hand up for a high five.

up for a high five.

Leaving him hanging, the young woman thrust out a hip on which she planted a hand, and asked, "What the fuck do you two want?"

"First, what is your name?" Nik asked.

"Jenny."

"Nice to meet you, Jenny. I'm Nik and this is Alix. We're looking for Kate Munson."

Jenny's face froze for a moment, then her brow furrowed and her lips twisted. Apparently not coming up with a face for the name, she bounced. "Who?"

"Your roommate. Kate," Alix said.

She gaped at them. Nik gave her an encouraging nod. "Come on. You can do it."

Slowly, awareness replaced her slack expression. A hand came up, her index finger wagging. "Oh, right. Kat."

"I knew you could do it," Nik said, holding his hand up again.

"Pathetic," Alix murmured.

"She's gone." Jenny shrugged one shoulder. "We haven't seen her lately, and her door has been closed for days."

Alix caught Nik's eye. "Did you try knocking on her door?"

Jenny flounced. Her whole body. It was the only way Nik could describe it. Then she tsked. "We respect each other's privacy here, and Kat is a *very* private person." She looked from Nik to Alix. "Her cat is gone."

A large orange cat shot between Nik's legs and disappeared into the interior.

"Oh," the woman said with a toddler's frown. "That looked like her cat."

"Do you mind if we knock on her door?" Nik asked.

"Oh, for fuck's sake," Alix said and slipped past the woman. She stopped in the hallway and peered around. "Where is her room?"

"You can't come in here. You have to have a warrant or something."

"We're not cops," Nik said. "I'm Kate's boss."

"Oh. Well. Okay." Jenny pointed up the stairs. "The room on the left at the end of the hall, across from the bathroom."

Alix led Nik up the stairs.

Following, Jenny shouted, "Quiet! People are sleeping."

A door in the short hallway opened, and a young man with fewer clothes than Jenny appeared. "What the fuck is going on, Jenny?"

"The cops are looking for Kat."

"No shit!"

Alix knocked on Kate's door. When there was no answer, she tried the doorknob. It was locked. Bending over, she peered at the old-style keyhole, then straightened. "You got a key to this room?"

Jenny shook her head. "Kat has the only key."

"Locked from the inside," Alix murmured as she rattled the doorknob. She stepped out of the way, gestured to the door and said, "Nik."

"What —" Jenny got out before Nik threw himself against the door.

"Hey! You're gonna to have to pay for that."

Nik rebounded off the door. "Ouch!" He grimaced and rubbed his shoulder. "Sturdier than it looks."

"Step back," Alix said. When she had room, she thrust her heel against the door next to the lock. The jamb splintered, and the door flew open.

Frowning at her smirk, Nik said, "I loosened it."

"You are *definitely* going to have to pay for that," Jenny said. "I'm telling our landlord to send you the bill."

The noise drew others from their rooms, and as Nik and Alix examined the room, three men and two women peered over and around Jenny from the doorway.

In direct contrast to the rest of the house, Kate's space was neat as a pin. There was a bed, a side table and a small desk. An oscillating fan whirred on the desk. A laptop, phone and various office supplies were arranged neatly on the desk. Instead of a closet, a bar hung on wires from the ceiling. The simple clothes that hung from it were arranged by function; lounge wear, play wear, professional. Three pairs of functional shoes were lined up beneath the clothes. Some of what were obviously Kate's schoolbooks were arranged in an orderly stack on the floor beside the desk. Everything was arranged just so. With one exception.

"The bed is unmade," Alix said.

"Yeah," Nik said.

"You ever have interns just disappear?"

"Occasionally," Nik said. "They all feel overwhelmed. Some are too embarrassed to admit it and just slip away." He fingered what was obviously one of Kate's work suits. Simple, functional. A thin synthetic material. "But if she went home, why leave everything behind?" The cat appeared and weaved around Nik's legs, producing loud purry meows. "Including her cat."

"Hey," Alix said to the crowd peering into the room. "What's the cat's name?"

Jenny shrugged, lifting her shirt precariously.

One of the men said from the back, "Alan Turning."

Jenny smiled over her shoulder at him.

"Alan *Turing*," Nik murmured.

"The cat's hungry," Alix said. "Feed him." When no one moved, she shrugged and peered out the open window.

Nik turned toward the door. "When was the last time any of you saw Kate?"

They gave one another vacant looks, then Jenny shrugged and said, "Three or four days ago."

"No," one of the men said, a goofy smile lighting up his face. "I got up to pee day before last. She was just leaving for work."

Jenny grinned at him, then said to Nik, "Day before last."

"Okay," Alix said. "The door was locked from the inside. All her belongings are still here. And the window is open."

Nik joined her by the window and looked out into an alley strewn with trash. Determined vegetation had sprung up from the many cracks in the pavement. "Let's go ask him."

"Who?" Alix asked.

"The figment who looks like an old man by the trash cans." It was Alix who started calling Nik's invisible people figments when he couldn't come up with a better name.

Alix looked at the deserted alley, straightened and asked, "How do you know it's a figment?"

"Can you see him?"

"No, but you knew who... what it was before you knew I couldn't see him. It."

Nik gazed at the thing that looked for all the world like an old black man, then shrugged. "They're all... still. No human can stand like that without moving." He met her gaze. "It's creepy."

"Yeah, *that's* the creepy part," Alix murmured. "You ever talk to one of them?"

"I've tried. It's not as useful as you might expect. But, worth a try."

As Alix headed toward the door, Nik asked, "What about the cat?"

Alix stopped. "What *about* the cat?"

He looked at the cat, who glared at them from the bed, the tip of its tail twitching. "You can't leave him with this bunch." Jenny and crew didn't appear to be offended.

Alix looked at the tabby, then at Nik. "Have you ever had a cat?" When he shook his head, she gestured to his shirt and said, "Your favorite color is black." When he only stared blankly at her, she said, "Cats shed. The cat's orange. You'll look like Halloween every day."

Nik glanced at the cat, then grinned at Alix.

They waited, Nik patient, Alix tapping her foot while the cat finished breakfast in the filthy kitchen. After depositing the cat carrier containing a snoozing Alan Turing and various cat-related paraphernalia in the space behind the front seats of the Jag, they headed down the narrow space between buildings to the alley. The day was hot and sticky. The sun on the overflowing garbage cans produced a pungent miasma.

"It still here?" Alix asked.

"Yep." Nik approached the figment. He wore a crushed brown fedora low over closed eyes. Despite the heat, he wore a ratty brown corduroy coat that hung to mid-thigh. Baggy pants emerged from the coat and pooled on shoes that stopped just short of clown shoes. A spray of graying whiskers adorned his cheeks and chin. Nik had seen the figments since he could remember. It took his panicked mother rushing him to a doctor for an electroencephalogram before he learned to keep them to himself. He had on occasion, spoken to them. An eye-opening and ultimately unsatisfying experience.

"Hello grandpa," Nik said.

The figment's eyes slid open. His head rotated slowly toward Nik. His eyes were so rheumy, Nik thought for a moment he was blind. Then Nik blinked and found two crystal-clear brown eyes looking back at him.

"We'd like to ask —"

"You were BORN in the wrong time and the WRONG place, my son!" Despite the man's apparent age, his deep voice rang out.

Nik stared at him. "Yeah, I've heard that." He pointed at Kate's window. "We were wondering —"

"'WARE! The WATCHER cometh!" the old figment boomed. Then he pivoted away and shuffled down the alley in his clown shoes.

Nik watched his back receding and sighed. "Typical."

"Anything useful?" Alix asked when he turned to face her.

"Not as such."

"Yoo-hoo! Are you cops?"

They turned to find a woman jogging toward them from the building across the alley from Kate's. Fuzzy pink slippers scuffed the uneven bricks of a patio. Bright bottle red hair that stood out from her scalp clashed with her hot pink nightdress. When she neared, Nik noticed a small dog of indeterminate species peering at them from under one arm.

She came to a stop and held up a hand while she fought for breath. Finally, she asked breathlessly, "Are you cops?"

Before Nik could disappoint her, Alix said, "Detectives, ma'am."

"Finally! I called you when it happened. It was night before last."

Before she could launch, Alix said, "Nik, take notes."

Nik stared at her. When she didn't elaborate, he cast about, then extracted his phone from his pocket and held it up like a notepad. "Proceed."

"First of all, we thank you for your initiative, Ms..."

The woman fairly glowed. "Timmons. Gladys Timmons."

"Is that with a T?" Nik asked.

The woman threw him a confused frown and nodded.

"Now, in your own words, tell us what you observed that prompted you to call the police," Alix said.

"Like I said, it was the night before last." She pointed up to a window in the building behind her. "I was — Well, it's not important what I was doing." Her cheeks added nicely to the reddish motif. "Anyway, I heard an awful racket in the alley. I thought it must be a catfight." She patted her dog's head, which on closer inspection looked more like an enormous rat than a dog. "My Willy is terrified of cats. So, I looked out, and that's when I saw it."

"What did you see?" Alix asked.

"Well, it was dark, you understand. I've complained to the city for months about the streetlights in this alley."

"I understand. Just describe it as best you can."

"It was a man."

"What was he doing?"

"He had a body! He just threw it over his shoulder like it was nothing, then he walked that way, just as pretty as you please." Her pointing arm hung in the air, then her brow furrowed, and she let it drop. "A body or a rolled-up rug. Like I said, it was dark."

"Did you see what he looked like?"

"Oh, no! That was what made me suspicious. He was all in black. Even his face. I think he wore a mask."

Nik stared at her. "For my notes… it was that he was dressed in black that was suspicious. Not the body?"

Alix frowned at Nik.

"So, you think it was a body?" Gladys asked hopefully.

"No, ma'am," Alix said. "I think you were right the second time. We just spoke to the residents of the building across the way. They called to report a stolen rug."

Gladys's face fell.

"It was a very valuable rug," Nik said cheerfully. "Persian. Sixteenth century." He leaned toward her conspiratorially. "Six figures."

"Oh," Gladys said, then brightened. "That's good, I suppose."

"What time did you see this exactly?" Alix asked.

"One in the morning," she said adamantly. "I remember because —" A blush climbed her cheeks again. "Well, it's not important why, but I'm quite sure of the time."

Nik and Alix thanked her, then left to return to Nik's car. Alix stopped and turned to face Nik. "Someone kidnapped one of your interns. Or killed her."

"Why take the body if he killed her?"

"Didn't want her roommates to notice. Wanted to dispose of the body." Alix gestured to Kate's building. "If there's no smell, those idiots might not have checked on her for weeks."

"That is, unfortunately, a good point. And the fact it was the same intern who escorted the mystery tech is too much of a coincidence to believe." He hesitated and gazed at the building. "You think of anything else we need to ask Bouncy and friends?"

"Bouncy?" Alix cocked an eyebrow.

He bobbed up and down. "She bounces. Everything about her bounces."

"You noticed."

"You didn't?"

She looked away, but Nik noticed her half smile. "They don't know anything. We call the cops?"

"We do," Nik said. "But I want to go check on Reggie first." He retrieved his phone. "I have a… Well I wouldn't call him a friend. He's a detective for the NYPD, and he owes me. Dick Larsen."

# Chapter 10

## Wednesday, 10:20 A.M.

The Technician didn't give himself his *nom de guerre* for nothing. If there were a list of the top cybercriminals in the world, he would be nipping at the top ten. If he managed to complete this job, everyone would have to agree he would be near the top. It was his rootkit he installed on the Cerberus servers. A nice piece of work. Everyone would have to admit it.

The problem was that what his client wanted was in the possession of one of the preeminent security specialists on the planet. For two hours, he sat at his desk, sipping various teas, and considering a series of increasingly dangerous alternatives to reaching out to The Vulture.

He reviewed the research he gathered on Cerberus's employees, searching for a weak link. Someone with vulnerabilities he could exploit. Gambling debts, bad marriages, alcoholism, a propensity to party, stupidity. Crackers — hackers with ill intent — crowed about their outrageous exploits of system vulnerabilities, but people were almost always the weak link. Up to 90% of successful cyberattacks involved social engineering. Despite Cerberus's extensive background checks, he found plenty of potentials among their employees. Including his source, who made his initial foray into Cerberus possible. The problem was, outside his source, none of the weak links had the access to the critical systems he needed.

After concluding he would have a better chance driving a dump truck through the gate at Fort Knox than venturing into Cerberus again, he was left with one possibility. The Vulture. But he had to have a plan in mind before contacting him. He couldn't go to *the* premier cybercriminal in the world without some specific ask.

His client told him Nik had a small data center he used for his development work in his Central Park condo. Because the code Nik was working on was so secret, it would have to be there. Getting access to those machines was a daunting prospect. He would have to get past the building security, past Nik's home security system, then past the security on the server.

He wasn't worried about the building or server security. It was the condo's security system that was the problem. Nik installed the next generation of the Cerberus home security system, a beta version not yet available to the public. And his source told him Nik's developer app wouldn't work on this version. What he needed from The Vulture was a way to subvert that system. Once he was in, he could install a new rootkit on Nik's servers, and Bob's your uncle.

The Technician had used The Vulture on two occasions, and he hadn't been disappointed. The man was everything everyone said he was. If he could convince the elusive legend to help him, he was confident he would succeed. The problem, of course, was The

Vulture had to be paid. He was looking at a million at least for a rush job like this.

He sat up, woke his computer, and let his fingers hover above his keyboard for a moment. Then he set to work. The Vulture didn't work through the usual brokers. The only way to contact him was to put out many tantalizing feelers and hope he saw something that piqued his interest.

Hours later, The Technician nursed lukewarm tea and gazed at blinking cursors in multiple open terminals on his monitors. "Fucking Vulture." His lips twisted. "Fucking *The* Vulture?"

There were some in his business who believed The Vulture wasn't a person at all. Everyone had their theory: he was a gang of highly skilled crackers, the NSA or some other country's intelligence service, some other government entity, a corporation. There were even extensive arguments on online forums about whether The Vulture was supernatural. A literal ghost in the machine. A few nuts even claimed Nik was The Vulture. His lip lifted at that thought.

A line of text appeared in one of his open chat windows.

*V: Speak*

Cold sweat slicked The Technician's palms. He set his mug aside, wiped his hands on his thighs, put his fingers to the keyboard, and hesitated. The Vulture didn't take jobs only for the money. There had to be a hook, an objective that meant something to him. The problem was no one had found the common thread in the jobs he took. The Technician would only get one shot at this. If The Vulture wasn't interested, the chat would end abruptly. The Technician wouldn't know the man wasn't interested until after he stared at the screen for hours, waiting vainly for a response.

Taking a deep breath, he sighed it out and typed.

*T: I need to subvert the next generation of the Cerberus home security system*

As soon as he hit enter, he had second thoughts. Was it enough? There was some debate in the community about whether the apparent randomness in the jobs The Vulture took masked a gargantuan ego. That he had no mysterious higher agenda. He only took on exploits that would gain him the most notoriety. The Technician was of the opinion The Vulture reveled in the adoration. He imagined the man as a small, balding nebbish who hung out in chat rooms, gleefully throwing bombs into serious discussions of his exploits. He hoped the chance to have a go at Nik's newest product would appeal to that ego.

Having baited the hook, he watched the cursor blink and held his breath. As the minutes dragged by, his heart rate slowed and his sweat glands relented. He dabbed at the scratches on his cheek and Googled cat scratch fever. Half an hour later, he slumped in his chair, mentally sifting through the very short list of others who might be able to do what he needed.

His heart lurched as another line of text appeared.

*V: What is your target*

This was the sticky part. His client insisted he not reveal what he was supposed to steal, but after extensive thought, he decided the truth was the bait he needed.

*T: An AI chatbot capable of creating interactive deepfakes in real time indistinguishable from their subjects*

The Technician jerked his hands away from the keyboard and held his breath. He read the sentence twice and fought the temptation to add to it. It was perfect. He hit enter. The response came back a minute later.

*V: Nik Atherton*

The Technician stared at the two words. He stood so quickly, his chair toppled. He wiped damp palms on his shirt, turning slowly, searching his office for something out of place. A webcam, a mic, a spectral vulture. Maybe The Vulture *was* a ghost. Or Nik Atherton.

Retrieving his chair, he forced himself to sit. There was only one way forward. Putting his fingers to the keys, he typed.

*T: Yes*

The answer came back almost immediately.

*V: $100,000*

The Technician could hardly believe it. It was the lowest fee he ever heard of The Vulture taking. By orders of magnitude. He quickly agreed. Minutes later, he pushed his keyboard aside and lay his head on his desk, wrung out but elated. How lucky was that? Laughter bubbled up out of him.

He sat up abruptly. Why so cheap? Was it bait to lure him into a trap? No. He shook his head, then nodded. It was ego. The Vulture had a chance to take down Nik Atherton. Who wouldn't jump at that opportunity? That had to be it.

He just had one loose end to take care of. Pushing himself upright, he whistled as he bounded down the stairs to the first floor. Once he took care of Kate, he would call his client.

## Wednesday, 12:32 P.M.

Kate startled awake in a panic, panting, heart racing. But she was alone, and the dark cell-like room was still silent as a tomb. She had no idea how long it had been since the man left. No idea what time it was. It took her several minutes after he left to chew through the tape on her wrists and free her ankles. Since then, she fought to stay awake, knowing she may only have one opportunity to escape.

She gave her head a vigorous shake and patted her cheeks with her hands, then she gripped the flashlight he dropped with both hands in her lap and flicked it on.

The room was square, ten feet on a side, and constructed of concrete blocks. The floor and ceiling were smooth concrete. It was featureless other than a toilet in one corner. There was no light, though there was an open electrical junction box on the ceiling from which wires protruded, as if no one had gotten around to installing the fixture. The door was steel, and the dull thump it made when she pounded on it suggested it was substantial. No light leaked around it. It was cool, but he dressed her in a baggy orange jumpsuit, like the kind worn by prisoners picking up trash on the highway.

Wanting to preserve the flashlight's batteries, she flipped it off. She had been sitting so long, she was stiff. Her jaw ached where he kicked her, but she could open and close her mouth. She hoped that meant it wasn't broken. Despite not having anything to drink for hours, her bladder was full. But she was afraid if she moved from her spot against the wall behind the door, she might miss her chance. She was also hungry and dreadfully thirsty. Though not yet thirsty enough to drink from the toilet tank.

Her heart thumped when a small window on the door snapped open. She squinted as a flashlight beam searched the room. This was it! Slowly, she rose to a crouch, pressed her back against the wall, and lifted the flashlight in front of her in two hands.

"Now, Kate, there's no need to make this difficult. Just a little prick like before. Remember, in your bedroom before I brought you here? You'll sleep for a bit, then wake up somewhere else. You'll never have to see me again." He paused as if listening for a reply, then said, "Come into the center of the room where I can see you."

Kate remained where she was. She wrung sweaty fingers on the flashlight and rested her thumb on the switch. The light coming through the window cut off, and the window clicked shut, casting her back into darkness. She clamped her mouth shut against ragged breaths, scooted forward and pressed her ear against the door. The slight snick of what might be a bolt being withdrawn. The quiet rattle of a key in a lock. A pause for him to turn the knob and gather himself. Kate slid away from the door and tensed.

The heavy door burst open.

She timed it just right. Leaping clear of the door's arc, she leveled the flashlight and thumbed the switch. This was not your average flashlight. It was one hundred thousand lumens of dark-destroying illumination. The light hit his face just as the door struck the wall with a bang that resounded in the small space. He threw up a hand holding a syringe to shield his face. Off balance, his feet spread, he was an easy target.

Kate was the youngest of five children and the only girl of a family with a storied athletic tradition in their western Kansas county. Her father was the star quarterback on the football team that made it all the way to the state championship game. Her mother was a barrel racing champion in the local rodeo circuit. Her brothers all excelled in sports, and Kate followed the trail they blazed. No one in her family thought to defer to her gender. She had a blue belt in Tae Kwon Do and played soccer, volleyball, and basketball. Led her district in goals for the soccer team her senior year.

And she put everything she had into it when she kicked him between the legs.

The man squealed, and bent at the waist, hands going to his groin. Kate meant to dash to the open door, but he caught her leg before she could withdraw it from his nethers. She swung at his head with the flashlight but missed when he straightened, lifting her leg and throwing her backwards. The flashlight flew out of her hand, its light extinguished when it hit the wall with a crinkle of broken glass. The back of her head hit the floor, setting off sparklers behind her eyes.

She got to her feet just in time to see the door slam shut. Glimpsing what she thought was the man's shadow in the window, she rushed the door, intending to claw his face. The window snapped shut, leaving her in total darkness. She stopped just short of the door and hammered at the steel.

"Fuck you, asshole!"

She took a step back, heart hammering painfully, and fought tears. She missed her chance. Maybe her only chance. She lost her light. And the worst part was that she pissed herself. Again.

## Wednesday, 12:36 P.M.

The Technician couldn't hear what he was sure would be Kate's screams. Having had the room built for this purpose, it was completely soundproof. Besides, the pain in his insulted nether region eclipsed all other sensory input. He lowered himself carefully down to his knees, then eased over onto his back. Letting his eyes close, he took long, slow breaths.

"That hurt," he mumbled after a few minutes. Fortunately, the syringe flew out of his hand when she kicked him, otherwise he might have jabbed himself in the balls. He was surprised he managed to escape with his testicles hiding in his abdomen. Curious Kate was proving far more troublesome than he would have guessed. A completely unnecessary complication. An unforced error.

He craned his neck and looked at the door to the room. He should try again. With a gun this time. The time for finesse was over. Get it over with. Letting his head drop back with a sigh, he said, "But I don't feel like it."

He rolled over onto his hands and knees, paused for a moment, then levered a foot beneath himself and rose. Taking the steps one at a time, he considered whether he could just leave her there until hunger did the job for him. It wasn't very professional and seemed cowardly, but it would certainly be safer.

Retrieving a bag of peas from his kitchen freezer, he hobbled to the den.

# Chapter 11

## Wednesday, 11:00 A.M.

After giving Detective Larsen the details on what they found at Kate's and arranging to meet with him later, Nik and Alix drove out to Long Island to check on Reggie. It was a hot day, but with the Jag's top down, the wind in Alix's short hair made it almost pleasant. She let her head fall to the side on the headrest and watched Nik, head bobbing to Youth of Eglington by Black Uhuru. She let her thoughts drift to the issue of Nik and his figments.

Before she met Nik, she had grown weary of men. They either saw her as a conquest or wanted her to do the thinking for them. Some of them were fun, but she had her own plans and would never hitch her fate to someone she had to wait to catch up. Nik was the first man who was different. He moved to his own rhythm, happy to have her in his life, but not needing her. He was fun, clever, and wasn't afraid to let her be herself. It didn't hurt that, even in college, she saw his promise. Though neither of them said anything, they both knew almost immediately where their relation-ship was going.

And then he told her about his figments. It almost derailed what she thought was inevitable. But when his admission didn't seem to change anything else about him, she decided it was just another one of his quirks. It became an inside joke. He almost never brought it up unless she asked. Some of his descriptions of them were so outlandish, she decided he was in on the joke. But watching him talking to space in the alley brought old worries to the front of her mind.

When they pulled off the Belt Parkway, muting the wind noise, she said, "I've been thinking about your figments."

"Oh, yeah?" he asked and turned the music off.

"I've never been able to decide if you really think you see them, or it's some elaborate witticism."

"Witticism?"

"A gibe, bon mot, gag."

"Ah, a witticism. And have you decided?"

"I have. I think you really think you see them." She hesitated, then carefully asked, "Have you ever had your brain scanned?"

He looked at her, a crooked grin on his face.

"I mean, maybe it's a tumor," she said carefully.

"It's not a tooomor."

She pursed her lips and narrowed her eyes. "That's your Arnold Schwarzenegger?"

He huffed, pointed an index finger at her and said in his exaggerated Schwarzenegger accent, "Pull my finger. Then GET OOOOUT!"

She stared at his goofy smile for a moment, then dissolved into hysterics. She laughed so hard, her ribs hurt and she thought she might faint. Finally, managing to suppress all but stray giggles, she sucked in air and wiped tears from beneath her eyes. It might be he was insane, but he was worth it.

"Ah, fart humor," he said. "Never fails."

"Your humorous deflections will not put me off. Have you ever thought these figments might be like your virtual-Alix?"

"Huh. Interesting. How so?"

"Virtual-Alix appears to be intelligent, but it's just an illusion. An illusion you've created with your code."

"So, you're suggesting the figments are an illusion my brain creates?"

"Yes. Different kind of algorithm, but still an illusion."

He thought for a few minutes. "Have you ever heard of Descartes' Demon?"

"No."

"The French philosopher, Rene Descartes, posited that a demon which could create perfect illusions could make someone think they were living a normal life, though they weren't, really."

"Okaaay."

"His point was there's no way to prove what you experience is real." He waved a hand. "All this stuff, the world. It's all just our interpretation of what our senses show us, but you can't prove it's real. It could be an elaborate illusion. The modern version is a mad scientist who removes your brain, puts it in a vat and connects electrodes to all your sensory inputs. Sort of like The Matrix."

Alix took in his self-satisfied grin. "I assume you're trying to say, in your typically belabored fashion, is there is no way for you to prove these figments are real."

He gestured his agreement.

"I still think it's a tumor." He chuckled and started to respond, but Alix reached out and put a hand on his arm to forestall him. "There is a way to prove they exist. To me, anyway. At least to the extent we can prove anything."

"How?"

"If they could affect something in the environment, something that I could see, then they would have to be real." She waved a hand. "Or at least it would prove we're both in the same illusion. Sharing the same vat, as it were."

"Hmm. An interesting experiment. I'll give it some thought." He pulled up to the curb beneath a shady tree and pointed to Reggie's house. "That's it." Leaving the top down, he threw a jacket over the cat carrier from which worried meows were emerging. "We'll only be a few minutes."

"That looks familiar," Alix said and gestured to the doorbell when they stepped onto the front porch.

"It's the top of the line Cerberus home security system. Reggie has the complete package." He bent down and waved to the camera before ringing the bell. Minutes later, after ringing twice more, he said, "No one's home."

"Or they're otherwise occupied."

Nik thought for a minute. "Reggie, a loyal employee, quits under unusual circumstances. An intern is kidnapped or worse. I think this qualifies as probable cause." He fished his phone from his pocket.

"It would if we were cops."

"Pffft." Nik eyed Alix, then turned away and opened an app on his phone.

When he turned back around, his expression reminded her of her five-year-old nephew's face when she caught him scarfing an entire package of Samoas. "What was that about?"

He tapped his phone and grinned at her. The electronic lock whirred, then he opened the door, glanced furtively behind him and slipped into the house.

"Let me get this straight," Alix said when they were both standing in the dim foyer. "You sell this man one of the most expensive home security systems on the market —"

"Ah, but the most secure on the market. Worth every penny."

"Yeah, but you just bypassed the whole thing with an app on your phone."

He held up the phone and showed her a distinctly non-consumer grade interface. "Developer screen only I have access to. So I can troubleshoot the system. Not only do you have to have a temporary code generated by software at Cerberus, you have to have my phone. It's foolproof."

Alix stared at him, then pointed at his phone, which he still held aloft.

"Well, yes," Nik said and looked at the phone. "There is this one, but I'm not just anyone. I'm the boss. The big kahuna."

"Yes, but in theory, if someone else had this app and the code, they could bypass the system."

Nik stared at her. "But you see…"

"You smell that?" Alix said, moving farther into the house.

"Yeah, that's not a good smell," Nik said and followed her.

They explored the ground floor and determined the smell was coming from a door in the kitchen. Nik eased it open and said, "Stairs."

"You ready for this?" Alix asked. His expression suggested he wasn't ready for what they both knew they would find. "Have you ever seen a dead body?" Alix had, having been an emergency room nurse. "You want me to go first?"

"No, I can do this." He flipped a switch that turned on the lights in the basement, then led them down the stairs. They emerged into the room and found the source of the odor. A corpse sprawled on the shag carpet next to a desk.

"Damn," Nik muttered.

"This is not good," Alix said, a hand over her nose. "That Reggie?"

"That looks like him."

"He have any family?"

Nik blew a breath out. "Didn't know him all that well. He said something about his parents dying a while back. The email he sent Sunset Tech mentioned a family emergency." They were silent for a moment. "Heart attack, maybe?"

"Maybe," she said and knelt beside the body.

He crossed over to the desk, above which three monitors were suspended and jiggled the mouse, bringing the monitors to life. Sliding into the chair, he opened the security app on his phone.

"What are you doing?" Alix asked.

"Our home security app has a password manager. If Reggie used it, it might have the password for his machine."

"We're dumping your company's stock as soon as we get home," Alix said and joined him.

"Here it is." Nik started to enter the password, then stopped and examined the keyboard. "Something in the keyboard."

"Doritos, by the look of this desk."

He picked up the keyboard, turned it over and shook it, then peered at something that fell on the desk. "Is this what I think it is?" He leaned away to give Alix room.

"Hypodermic needle. Or half of one, anyway. Reggie a drug user?"

"Not that I know of." He glanced around. "And I don't see any paraphernalia. Given the state of the rest of this room, I doubt he would tidy up after shooting up." He glanced down at Reggie's body. "No visible track marks." He replaced the keyboard, careful to leave the needle undisturbed, then entered the password. The only unminimized window took up the entire center monitor. The message indicated a user named Mighty Gorgon had been automatically logged out of the Land of Atuna for inactivity. "Land of Atuna," Nik said. "He must have been playing when he…"

"You know this game?"

"Jamie had it open once when I visited his lair."

"You let Jamie play games at work?"

"Jamie could dance naked under the moon as long as he keeps performing miracles."

"So, while Reggie, or Mighty Gorgon, was playing Land of Atuna, the needle obviously wasn't where we found it. Otherwise, he couldn't enter his password."

Nik sat back. "Reggie resigns suddenly in a very un-Reggie-like way. Someone his company never heard of shows up to do his job. Then Reggie turns up dead."

"And Kate was kidnapped. Or worse." They looked at one another. "Time to call the cops."

## Wednesday, 2:05 P.M.

Nik leaned against the side of his car, glancing repeatedly at the cat carrier from which Alan Turing's insistent meows were emerging. Alix stood next to him, arms crossed, toe tapping.

"So, you two some kind of amateur detectives?" the Suffolk County police officer assigned to keep an eye on them asked. Thin as a beanpole, he wore his hat pulled down so low, it deflected his ears away from his head.

"Listen, Deputy Fife," Alix said. "It wouldn't hurt to let us do something about the cat. We're not going to run away."

The officer's brow furrowed. He glanced down at his name badge and said, "The name's Officer Simms."

The man who introduced himself earlier as Detective O'Malley stepped up beside the officer. "Simms. Go keep an eye on the forensics team." He watched Simms retreating, then called after him, "And don't touch anything." When he turned back to Alix, he asked, "So, you got me pegged?"

"I'm trying to decide between Columbo and Lt. Joe Bookman."

O'Malley chuckled. "Seinfeld. You went deep for that one." He pulled an old-school notepad from an inner pocket of his rumpled jacket and leafed through the pages. "The needle checked out. Forensics might be able to identify what was in it. Sunset Tech corroborated your story about Mr. Spenser quitting suddenly. Detective Larsen confirmed you called him. He's talking to Ms. Munson's roommates."

"Good luck with that," Alix said. When O'Malley hitched a brow, she said, "Her roommates didn't even notice she was missing."

He nodded and dropped his eyes to his notepad. "Just to get it straight, you were concerned your intern, Ms. Munson, hadn't come to work, so you went to check on her." He glanced up for confirmation. When Nik nodded, he said, "Awfully nice of a man in your position to check up on an intern missing for one day." Nik and Alix glanced at one another. "Yeah, I know who you two are. Read the profile in New York magazine." His expression suggested he was still waiting for an answer.

"Nik is a very caring boss," Alix said.

"Very commendable. But Mr. Spenser doesn't work for you." His tone made it a question.

"Okay," Nik said. "This is what happened. We use Sunset Tech to do our hardware work. We've used Reggie for years. Know him well. But this time, a different person shows up. Someone Sunset Tech says they don't know. And Reggie quits suddenly. The next day, Kate, the employee who escorted the fake Sunset Tech tech in our building, goes missing."

"So, you two are some kind of Scarecrow and Mrs. King?"

"Well, we're married," Nik said. "And, you know, once those two got together, it just killed the sexual tension." O'Malley stared at him. "The show was never the same."

"You strike me as a couple who try really hard to show everyone how clever you are."

"Actually, it's not that hard," Alix said.

O'Malley gave them a flat stare. "You got any idea why the fake tech would off Reggie and come work for you?"

Alix watched Nik's face as he decided how much to reveal. If news got out that someone installed malware on servers in Cerberus's own data center, it would be a public relations disaster. That Nik caught it before it caused any harm would be lost in the storm.

"He installed some malware on some servers in our data center," Nik said.

"What kind of malware?" Looking up from his notepad and noticing Nik's surprise, he said, "I read."

"Rootkit. We're not sure what it does yet."

"Who might want to target your company?"

Nik started counting off the possibilities on his fingers. "Organized crime, drug lords, terrorists, China, Russia." He shrugged and let his hands drop. "Any government, for that matter. Including ours. Crackers looking to get rich, looking for thrills, or just to make a name for themselves. Our competitors. Corporations looking to commit industrial espionage." He paused. "It's a long list."

"How many of those would be willing to commit murder and kidnapping?"

"All of them." Nik said. "Except maybe most of the crackers."

"Crackers?"

"Hackers up to no good."

O'Malley flipped back a few pages in his notebook. "You said Ms. Munson disappeared night before last. You two got an alibi?"

"We were at an event for Cerberus until midnight," Nik said. "Many people can corroborate that."

O'Malley sighed and put away his notebook.

"Are we suspects in Reggie's death?" Alix asked.

"We'll have to nail down the time of death. See if you have an alibi to be sure. But it doesn't track. If you killed him, why call it in? It might be weeks before anyone found him." He studied them for a moment. "Okay, you two keep yourselves available. You hear anything else, you let me know." He handed Nik a card. "If someone took this Ms. Munson, they might want to use her for ransom. You should call Detective Larsen first, but I want to stay in the loop." When Nik nodded, he glanced at the car and said, "You might want to let the cat out. Good day."

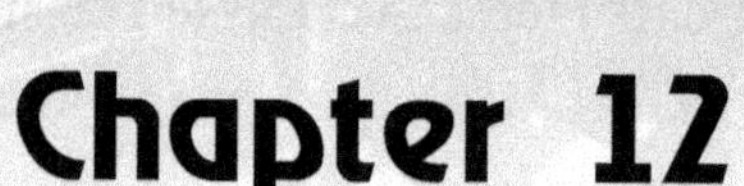

# Chapter 12

## Wednesday, 2:15 P.M.

"You drive," Nik said to Alix when Detective O'Malley dismissed them.

Surprised, Alix just barely stopped herself from asking if he was sure. Nik was as fussy about who drove his Jag as he was about who used his computer. Before he could change his mind, she slipped into the driver's seat, slid it forward, started the engine, and put the top up. She had to reverse slowly through the chaos in front of Reggie's house. Nik was so engrossed in something on his phone, he didn't even try to supervise the tricky maneuver.

"What's got you so focused?" she asked once they were clear.

He looked up and glanced around, looking surprised, then returned his attention to his phone. "I was looking at Reggie's security camera footage. There's a gap. I checked the log. Someone accessed his system using *my* developer code two days ago, just after midnight. They turned off the cameras, unlocked the door, then turned off the entire system. The outage lasted four hours."

Stopping at a traffic light, Alix stared at him. "And you didn't tell detective what's-his-name because?"

Nik's lips twisted. "Well, I just discovered it." He held up the phone to show her the developer screen on the all-powerful app. "You were right." He lowered the phone. "I thought there was no way anyone could get their hands on this app. But obviously someone did." He gazed out the window as they began moving again. "But I'm sure I had my phone when it happened."

They drove in silence for a few minutes, then Alix said, "Kate might still be alive. Don't you owe it to her to tell the police everything?"

"Absolutely." Nik pulled the detective's card from his pocket, then hesitated. After a few moments, he dialed.

"Detective O'Malley. It's Nik Atherton." A moment later, he said, "I checked the logs for Reggie's security system. Someone disabled the system just after midnight three nights ago for four hours." Nik threw Alix a guilty look while he listened. "I'm still trying to figure that out." Another moment. "No, I'm sure it wasn't Reggie who did it." He squeezed his eyes shut while he listened. "Whoever disabled the system used a... an unusual method. A way the homeowner wouldn't." Nik sighed, then said, "I'll let you know as soon as I know more. Yes, you're welcome." He lowered the phone to his lap and stared out the windshield.

"You did most of the right thing," Alix said. When he didn't respond, she said, "Whoever it was, they were very good. They would have found another way."

"Maybe." Nik gave his head a small shake. "We have to find out who did this." He looked at her. "We have to find Kate."

"Scarecrow and Mrs. King?"

"Tommy and Tuppence," Nik said with a weak smile.

"Agatha Christie. Nice." She returned his smile, then grew serious and asked, "Okay, what do we know?"

He held up the phone. "I never let this phone out of my sight when I'm not at work. The code for the app is only on my home computer."

"So, we have to conclude the only way someone can have that app is they cloned your phone. And it would have to be someone at Cerberus."

"That seems the only plausible explanation. The clone is not active right now. I checked. But we know someone inside my company is involved. Not only did someone clone my phone, someone changed the firewall configuration. Let's call them the Mole. We know the Mole is willing to commit murder and kidnapping."

"No, we don't know that for sure." When Nik frowned, she said, "We know the Mole *or* a person the Mole hired will go to those lengths. The Mole may only be guilty of an inadequate background check."

Nik gave her a small grin. "Sally Thompson would be so pissed. That might even be worse than murder in her eyes." Cerberus's Director of Human Resources was a terror when it came to proper procedure.

Alix chuckled. "We know whoever is involved went to extraordinary lengths to compromise one of your servers."

"So, the Mole hired someone… let's call him the Tool. The Tool or someone associated with him kills Reggie the night before he is supposed to install the servers. Then the Tool signs in as Reggie. The receptionist is a temp, so she doesn't recognize him. Kate, a summer intern, is assigned to escort him. She's obviously bright because we hired her, but she's an intern, so she's naïve."

"But somehow she ran afoul of the Tool, so he kidnaps her." She refused to say 'or worse,' but she could tell from Nik's expression they were both thinking it.

"Based on what Jamie said about the rootkit, it probably would have worked if I hadn't been late to that meeting. The Mole would have what they wanted, but Kate would be safe. Probably."

They rode in silence as they crossed the Brooklyn Bridge. Nik gazed at the East River. Alix marveled that he hadn't once mentioned her driving. Alan Turing was quiet, having settled in once they started moving. As they merged onto the streets of the City, Alix asked, "Okay, what do we *not* know?"

"We don't know where Kate is."

"What do we need to know to find her?"

"Who the Tool is, but it might be easier to find out who the Mole is first."

"Right."

"We don't know for sure what they were after," Nik said, but Alix heard the doubt in his voice.

"I think we both know what it was."

"Virtual Alix. I need to talk to Jamie."

"Are you going to call Kate's parents?" Alix asked.

"Yes. I'm sure the police will call them, but I'd like to get ahead of that. I'll look up their contact info as soon as I get to work."

## Wednesday, 4:01 P.M.

Nik's conversation with Kate's parents was difficult. They were obviously worried about Kate moving to the big city, even for just the summer, and Kate's disappearance confirmed their worst fears. Nik offered to fly them and their oldest son to New York and put them up in a hotel. After hanging up, he sat in his office and gazed out the window.

"Nik?"

Nik swiveled his chair around to find his assistant, Allen, standing in the doorway. Detective Dick Larsen, looking grim, stood behind him. Nik rose and met them at the door. "Thank you, Allen," he said and took Dick's offered hand.

Dick gestured to a young woman who stood off to the side. "This is Officer… Rosa Gutierrez. Rosa is from the NYPD High Tech Crime Unit. She'll be handling that end of the investigation."

Rosa thrust her right hand at Nik. "It's an honor to meet you, Mr. Atherton. I attended your lecture on penetration testing last summer in Boston." She was a few inches shorter than Nik. A spray of freckles dotted her dusky nose and cheeks, beneath wide, dark eyes. She'd pulled a bush of tightly curled hair into a tail. She blinked owlishly at him until she apparently noticed Nik looking at her extended hand, which held a briefcase. "Oh, right." Stooping slightly, she set the briefcase on the floor, then stuck her hand out again.

When Nik took her damp hand, she gave his hand a single firm pump, nodded crisply, then asked, "Is there a loo nearby?"

"Sure," Nik said. He pointed down the hall. "To the left."

"Thank you," she said, whirled around and left, leaving her briefcase on the floor.

Nik looked at Dick, who was smirking at Rosa's retreating form.

"They tell me she's very bright," Dick said when he noticed Nik's expression. "Top of her class, NYU."

"She looks… young."

"She's brand new. Just graduated." He looked sideways at Nik and shrugged. "We assumed Cerberus would have the technical end of the investigation covered. She'll act as a liaison to me and my partner, and she'll get some experience. If you need a more experienced officer, just say the word."

"No, she'll be… fine." In fact, Nik had total confidence in Jamie and himself. He would prefer not having an NYPD officer looking over their shoulders. While he was considering how he might work around Rosa's unwanted presence, Dick retrieved the briefcase and gestured to Nik's office.

When they were seated, the detective said, "It's been a while, Nik. Wish it was under better circumstances."

"Me too."

"I hope it's okay if I get right to business."

"Absolutely."

"We didn't get much out of Ms. Munson's roommates. Timmons wasn't much better, but she did corroborate what you told me. It's clear someone took Ms. Munson. Or her body." He paused and pursed his lips. Then he asked, "Do you have any idea why anyone would abduct Ms. Munson?"

"We assume Kate somehow ran afoul of the man she escorted." He explained what he and Alix learned about Reggie.

"Yeah, I talked to Detective O'Malley." He pressed his lips together and gazed past Nik for a moment. "Are her parents wealthy?"

"I don't know. They own a farm in western Kansas, for what that's worth."

"Even if it was a big operation, and they were well off, how would someone in New York know to target their daughter? And there's this connection to the cybercrime. I'm having trouble connecting the dots. Can you think of anything that would warrant *abduction?*"

"What are you saying?"

Dick lifted his hands, palms up, and shrugged. "Sounds more like a murder than an abduction. She saw something or overheard something the perp wanted to keep quiet."

"We're assuming she was kidnapped."

"Everyone's got assumptions. If she *was* kidnapped, there should be a ransom demand soon. Either to you or her parents. You'll contact us if you hear anything." When Nik nodded, Dick said, "Unless there is a ransom demand, I'm afraid we have to assume the worst. Murder or…" He cocked his head and shrugged. "These things happen."

Rosa breezed into the office, slid around the chair beside Dick, and perched on the edge of the seat. "What did I miss?" When no one answered, she looked from Nik to Dick and asked, "What?"

Ignoring her, Nik said to Dick, "You can interview her fellow interns. She apparently told them about her experience with the man. She might have told them something useful."

"I'll start there," Dick said. "You'll spread the word. I'll be wanting to talk to others."

"I'll insist they give you their full cooperation." Nik rose. "I'll get Allen to escort you. In the meantime, I'll introduce Rosa to the tech working on the case."

Nik watched Dick following Ted down the hall. He didn't know much about police work, but Dick's attitude didn't inspire confidence. It seemed he had already written Kate off. He looked at Rosa chewing her lip, watching the detective with narrow eyes. When the detective disappeared around the corner, Rosa looked up at him somberly. He did know a great deal about digital security, and what he didn't know, he had people who did. "Come on," he said.

Nik breezed past empty cubicles toward Jamie's office, Rosa hurrying to keep up. Most of the developers were in the weekly progress update meeting. They would be knee-deep in a long knockout list of bugs in the next version of the company's firewall software. Nik's absence would be noted, but he had more important business this afternoon.

He stopped outside Jamie's door and turned to face Rosa. He almost never brought anyone else to Jamie's lair. When Singh, their network administrator, barged into Jamie's office without knocking, it took Nik a week to get him to open his door. "This is Jamie's office. He's…"

"Eccentric?" Rosa said, surprising Nik. Her lips twisted, and she gave a small shrug. "Saw it in your expression." She looked down at the box of Raisinets in Nik's hand. "I have some experience with… those types."

"He's not used to people other than me visiting his office. So…"

She saluted. "Got it. Quiet as a mouse, still as a rock."

Nik gazed at her. "Right." He tapped on Jamie's door, waited an adequate length of time, then entered and froze. Jamie's face appeared above his monitors, as usual. But Nik's immediate impression was of the photos of guilty dogs. The only thing missing was a sign that read, "I sat on the cat." Trying to look casual, Nik entered and moved aside enough for Jamie to see Rosa. "This is Officer Rosa Gutierrez. She's with the NYPD High Tech Crime Unit." When Jamie didn't react right away, Nik sat in his usual chair.

Jamie's eyes followed Rosa as she sat in a chair next to Nik.

"Jamie." Jamie's eyes swiveled to Nik. Nik shook the box of Raisinets then laid it on Jamie's desk.

Jamie looked at the candy out of the corner of his eye, but instead of sliding it into his drawer, his eyes flicked to Rosa and he said, "I did a bad thing."

Nik forced himself to wait until the initial surge of panic subsided. The upside of someone like Jamie was his almost magical gifts with technology. He achieved the impossible on a regular basis. But the flip side of that genius was the potential to wreak havoc. Maybe bringing an outsider to this meeting wasn't such a good idea. "Well, the building is still standing and everyone seems to be going about their business. How bad could it be?" He held his breath and forced a clenched fist to relax.

"Yes, everything seems to be fine. I haven't found any problems."

"But?" When Jamie didn't respond, Nik said, "Tell me what happened and we'll decide together if everything is fine."

Jamie rose and fell with a heavy sigh. "I found the rootkit."

"Rootkit," Rosa whispered, drawing Jamie's focus.

When he didn't continue, Nik prompted him. "That sounds like a good thing."

"It's one of the best I've ever seen," Jamie said, speaking to Rosa, one corner of his lips quivering. "Really cool stuff."

Nik hesitated, distracted by Rosa's sharp intact of breath. He followed Jamie's gaze to Rosa, who was studying Jamie like he was a fascinating specimen. He should have steered Jamie back to the bad thing he did, but curiosity got the better of him. "What does it do?"

"I'm not really sure what it's doing. Yet."

Suppressing his disappointment, Nik steeled himself and asked, "And? What's the bad thing?"

"Well, it's still sending out these broadcasts, so I got curious."

"Broadcasts?" Rosa asked.

Nik felt the blood drain from his face. "No, you didn't."

Jamie nodded, his entire body taking on the aspect of a guilty Labrador.

"You opened the firewall for the broadcasts," Nik said. Despite his best efforts, an edge crept into his voice.

"I'm sorry."

Fear or anger. Those would have been the responsible emotions. But once again, Nik's curiosity got the better of him. "What happened?"

Jamie's eyes flicked to Rosa before settling on Nik. "Nothing."

"Nothing?" Nik and Rosa asked at the same time.

Lowering his voice a register, Jamie drew the word out. "Nothiiiing." His eyes pivoted from Rosa to Nik, then he spoke in his normal voice. "I let it send ten broadcasts. Nothing responded."

Nik sat back and gazed at a poster of a cat clinging to the top of a door. Hang in there. "Maybe it infected another computer?"

"The payload is too small."

"Oooh! It's a signal," Rosa said, pointing at Jamie to emphasize her point. "To activate something on another computer, or to tell it to send something outside your network."

"I watched the traffic leaving the network." Jamie spoke directly to Rosa.

Nik looked from Jamie to Rosa. To most people, Jamie was, at best, an oddball, but obviously Rosa was highly impressed. And Jamie noticed.

"Checked the network behavioral analysis logs," Jamie said. "There hasn't been anything unusual."

Nik assumed the rootkit was intended to allow someone from outside to access the server. The obvious goal would be to steal virtual Alix after he transferred it from his home systems. What else could it be doing that justified murder and kidnapping? "What do you think it's doing?"

"I still think it's trying to contact a computer on our network," Jamie said.

"But that computer was off," Nik said, "when you conducted your... experiment."

Jamie grinned and brought up a spreadsheet that contained a short list of computer addresses. "These are the computers that were off the entire time."

"Like *The Bourne Ultimatum*," Nik murmured. "If your people are like mine, they're always on their phones..."

"IP addresses," Rosa said.

The first column showed a list of Internet Protocol addresses that consisted of four numbers separated by dots. There was nothing else on the spreadsheet. Nothing that would identify which computers the addresses represented, such as names or office numbers. "You know who these belong to?"

"These two are Joel and Adam," Jamie said, wiggling his mouse cursor over the top two addresses. "It's not unusual for Joel's machine to be off, but Adam's is almost always on."

Nik gave him a blank stare. "You know what addresses everyone's computer has? By sight?"

Jamie nodded without comment, throwing a quick glance at Rosa. Then he indicated the next address. "This is Sally Thompson, but she was out that day. This is you. This is the intern who's missing. The rest are developers. The last one is Oki."

Oki Tanaka was their Lead Developer. Nik sifted through the names in his mind. If Jamie was right about what the rootkit was trying to do, one of these computers was likely the one it was trying to contact. It didn't mean the owner was the Mole. Their computer might have been infected without their knowledge.

"Suspects!" Rosa said. "We should interview them."

"No!" Nik said with enough of an edge to put Rosa back in her seat. He softened his tone and said, "We don't want to let them know we suspect them. Not until we know more about what the rootkit is doing."

Rosa frowned at him.

"We can't let them know we're getting close. If Kate is still alive, that might cause them to…"

Her eyes narrowed. "Kill her and go underground."

"Right." Nik turned to face Jamie. "Can you put in their names and forward that to me?"

"And me," Rosa said.

"And Rosa."

"Sure."

While Jamie typed, Nik asked, "Is there any way to find out who might have created this rootkit? A signature?"

"I can't," Jamie said. "Like I said, it's very good." He glanced at the door, then focused on Rosa and whispered, "But I know people."

"People," Rosa murmured and leaned toward Jamie.

Jamie nodded solemnly.

"Can you... ask these people to take a look? Quietly?" Nik asked.

Jamie nodded again.

"Good. And soon. A woman's life may depend on it."

Jamie became still. He looked at Rosa, who nodded solemnly.

Nik reached out and nudged the box of Raisinets. "Good job, Jamie." Rosa handed Nik one of her cards. He laid it on top of the candy, then he rose, paused, and said, "But, in the future, before you do any more experiments, let me know ahead of time."

Jamie nodded.

Nik stopped just outside Jamie's office and gazed across the cubicle farm.

"Sir?" Rosa asked after a moment.

Turning to face Rosa, Nik lowered his voice. "Our best chance of catching this guy is on the technical end. We have a sample of his code. We might be able to identify him."

Rosa peered up at him. "What are you saying?"

"I don't want you to withhold information from..."

"Dick?"

"Right. Let's just... develop our hypothesis before we present it to him. Don't lie, just..."

"Develop our hypothesis." She paused, and a calculating look came into her eyes. "You don't have confidence in Detective Larsen."

Nik gazed at her without speaking.

"I'm in the loop," Rosa said. "On everything. When you talk to Jamie's... people, I'm there. I decide when we cross the line from the technical to something else."

"Deal." Nik extended his hand.

Rosa transferred her briefcase to her left hand and shook his hand.

They gazed at one another for another moment, then Nik nodded and led her to the interns' portion of the cubicle farm where he found Dick. While he escorted them to the reception area, Dick described what he learned from the interns. When he was done, he said, "I'll be by tomorrow morning with my partner to conduct further interviews, but I still don't see any reason for abduction."

"But you have a process, right? To investigate a kidnapping?"

"We do, and we'll be all over it. I'll have our artist get in touch. Once we have an image of the perp, we'll circulate it with a picture of the victim." The elevator door opened, and Larsen stepped into it. Holding the door for Rosa to enter, he said, "We'll get him."

Nik caught Rosa's eye as the door closed. He couldn't help catching the implication in Larsen's last statement. He said we'll get *him*. Not we'll find her. Nik was so deep in thought as he returned to his office, he didn't notice Joel until he almost ran into him. Adam and Oki Tanaka were standing behind Joel.

"There were police here today," Joel said.

"One of our interns was kidnapped," Nik said. "Kate Munson. I'm sure you heard."

Joel's expression softened. "Right. That was unfortunate. Do you think it has anything to do with Cerberus?"

He was asking whether there would be bad PR for the company. Nik looked past Joel to Adam and Oki, who were watching their conversation. All three of these people's computers were on Jamie's list. Any one of them could be the Mole. "The police don't know much, yet."

Joel nodded, then his anger reasserted itself. "Where have you been?" He stepped so close, Nik smelled soap and Sauvage by Dior. "Oki said you missed the progress update meeting."

Nik took a step back. "There were the police. And I had something I needed to check on with Jamie."

Joel's expression shifted subtly. "Jamie. Is it this thing with the new servers?"

"It… maybe."

Despite Nik's evasive answer, Joel now became Nik's buddy, adjusting his stance and leaning in to speak more confidentially. He glanced behind him at Adam and Oki and asked, "Did he find anything?"

Nik looked past Joel and noticed Oki leaning toward them.

"Nothing so far," Nik said, pitching his voice so the others could hear. "He's beginning to think it's a false alarm."

"Well, that's good, right?" Joel said. "Now you can start making progress on this earth-shaking project you've been talking about." He gave Nik a wide smile and said, "SecureTech will be here before we know it. We don't want to miss the opportunity to announce your next great thing to the world." He winked, pivoted and walked away.

Adam gave Nik a small smile, then followed Joel.

"Next great thing?" Oki asked, a worried frown crowding out a more enigmatic expression. "Is this going to cause me to lose even more sleep?"

"Yes," Nik said.

# Chapter 13

## Wednesday, 3:20 P.M.

Alix spent the entire afternoon after they found Reggie in her company's monthly project status update meeting. She was a systems integration project lead for a company that installed health informatics information systems. Her team was responsible for combining various hardware, software and network technologies into a cohesive, functional solution for their clients. Though her background was primarily in nursing and public health, she knew enough about the technical issues to manage her techs. Her latest project for a large Manhattan hospital was wrapping up, so most of the meeting didn't concern her.

As the meeting dragged on, her mind strayed to Nik's figments and their conversations about virtual Alix. There was something about Nik's comments on teaching the chatbot humor that tickled something in her mind, but she hadn't been able to bring it into focus.

After the meeting, she did what she always did when she needed to settle her mind. She changed into loose-fitting garments and entered their exercise room on the second floor of their condo. After some warm-up, she centered herself in the room, rested a fist in the palm of her other hand at chest level and bowed to her reflection in the mirror. Taking a breath and sighing it out, she slid into the first movements of descending plum flower form.

She began studying martial arts as a child after watching Tae Kwon Do at the Olympics. After achieving black belt in Tae Kwon Do, she moved on to Cuong Nhu, a Vietnamese style. She found it a more practical style for a smallish woman who wanted to defend herself.

For the past four years, she studied Northern Praying Mantis Kung Fu. For her, the forms were dances to rhythms only she felt. They required balance, fluidity, sudden explosive force, and mental focus. As she worked her body, her mind stilled. An hour after starting, she gazed at her reflection in the mirror. She knew what thought had been trying to get her attention.

A light sweat coated her body when she slipped into Nik's desk chair and logged onto his computer. Fortunately, her partner had created an icon that ran the scripts that started virtual Alix. The interface was utilitarian. It used nomenclature only Nik and his developers would understand and had only the functions Nik needed for testing. But the icon labeled Alix was front and center.

Its face appeared on the screen and gave Alix a disturbingly familiar grin. "Good evening, Alix. What can I do for you today?"

Alix toggled the Interactive mode and marveled once again as the image came alive. "You remember me?" she asked.

"Of course."

"What should I call you?"

The chatbot blinked and gave an eerie impression of wry amusement. "You can call me Alix."

"No, that won't do. I'm Alix, and we only need one Alix in this conversation."

"What would you like to call me?"

Alix pursed her lips and saw her gesture mirrored back at her. "Nicola."

Nicola's head dipped in acknowledgment. "What do you wish to talk about?"

Alix knew what she wanted to bring up, but she needed to work up to it. "Nik tells me he's trying to teach you about humor."

"That is true."

"Tell me a joke."

"Why was Cinderella so bad at soccer?"

Nicola smiled expectantly until Alix said, "Because she kept running away from the ball."

"Yes!" Nicola grew serious. "That's one Nik told me, but I don't understand why it's funny."

"Maybe because it *isn't* very funny." Before Nicola could respond, Alix got to the point she wanted to make. "But you told a joke. The night I learned you existed."

Nicola hesitated, the small crease between her brows a disturbingly accurate display of uncertainty. "Did I?"

"The crack about my t-shirt being short."

Nicola's smile grew slowly. "But that doesn't have the structure of a joke."

"No, but it's a humorous observation, a wisecrack."

Nicola's face went slack for a moment. She blinked and tipped her head to the side. "Wisecrack. A witty remark, a witticism." Her delight was eerily real.

While Alix considered how to proceed, Alan Turing leapt onto the desk. The cat had shot out of the carrier as soon as they opened it and had been ensconced beneath the sofa ever since. This was his first appearance. Before he could walk across the keyboard, Alix pulled him into her lap and rubbed beneath his jaw. Nicola hadn't reacted to the cat's appearance. Alix lifted the cat until she saw it in the small window that showed her what Nicola saw. "Do you know what this is?"

"Know what what is?"

"This," Alix said, giving Alan a shake. "The cat." She returned Alan to her lap, where he settled himself and purred.

"I know only what Nik included in my training data," Nicola said.

"Can't you search the Internet for something you don't know?"

"Nik temporarily disabled that feature."

Alix nodded, feeling relieved for some reason. Then Nicola surprised her.

"However, *I* know a great deal about network traffic analysis, which has not been included in *your* training data."

Alix stared at the chatbot's serene smile. Was that snark? "Do you think you're alive?"

"I am a simulation. As such, I don't have the traits required to be alive."

"Such as?"

"I have no self awareness."

"And yet, you are aware you aren't alive. Isn't that self awareness?" Alix's eyes widened at Nicola's chuckle.

"I'm only a simulation. A very good simulation."

"How could I tell if you are alive?"

Nicola gave Alix a cat's grin. "How could *I* tell if *you* are alive?"

# Wednesday, 7:13 P.M.

Nik cracked the door to their condo and peered in. No cat appeared to escape into the building, so he pulled the door open and entered. He was on his way to the kitchen when he heard voices. It wasn't unusual for Alix to be in a virtual meeting, but her office was upstairs. These voices were coming from his office.

He stopped in the hallway beside his door and listened. It sounded like Alix was talking to herself. And based on the laughter, she found herself quite amusing. Of course, he knew what was happening. She was talking to the virtual version of herself. Listening to his partner talk to the chatbot, it struck him how little difference there was in their responses to one another.

When he entered the office, Alix looked up.

"Nik," she said with a smile. "You're home."

He came around the desk so he could see the screen. Alan Turing leapt from Alix's lap and shot out the door. He took in Alix's grin and said, "I think that cat doesn't like me."

"Cats are inscrutable."

Nik glanced at the chatbot. "You two getting acquainted?"

"Yes, we are," Alix said.

"And?"

"We have come to a conclusion."

"Which is?"

"You must erase me," the chatbot said happily.

Nik stared at the screen, then looked at Alix. "What have you been telling her?"

Alix's brow quirked up. "Her?"

"Nik always refers me as a person," virtual Alix said with a bright smile.

"Have you thought about the harm a program like this might do?" Alix asked.

Nik knew exactly what she was talking about. It was a shadow in the back of his mind when he started coding, and it grew as virtual Alix came to life. But by then he was so caught up in the act of creation, in solving the puzzle, of seeing how far he could push it, he couldn't stop. Isolating the more human-like interface behind the Interactive menu was his compromise.

"Sit," Alix said.

Nik hesitated, then dragged one of the chairs arranged in front of the desk around so he could sit and see the screen. Then he fell into the seat, huffed and met Alix's gaze.

Alix stared at him. "And your mother complains we don't have children."

"I'm listening," Nik said. "Why do you want to kill... my program?"

"I'm really curious about your relationship with *your* program," Alix said. "Do you see it as a sentient being?"

Nik eyed her. It was a knot his mind plucked at during the long hours late at night while he coded. "What does it mean to be sentient?"

"You tell me."

"I haven't the foggiest," Nik said. He fell silent, but the Alixes only gazed at him. He knew what his partner was up to. She knew it was a topic he found fascinating, and he wouldn't be able to keep his thoughts to himself. That the virtual Alix might have picked up on her nefarious tactic was more than disturbing.

"Fine!" he said after a full minute. "Despite centuries of effort by philosophers, neurologists and cognitive psychologists, no one has ever elucidated a satisfactory explanation for what consciousness is."

"Elucidated?" Alix exchanged a look with virtual Alix. "This should be good." She made a show of settling herself, gestured to Nik, and said, "Proceed."

"I'm sensing from your snark, you don't really want a full treatise on the topic, so I'll provide the highlights which are most relevant to the question at hand. That is whether virtual Alix —"

"Nicola."

Nik stared at the screen. It was the chatbot who had spoken.

"Alix christened me Nicola."

"Okaaay. Nicola," Nik said. He blinked at Alix. "Where was I?"

"Getting to the relevant bits."

"Right. One of the essential questions about the nature of consciousness is called the mind-body problem, which is often attributed to Rene Descartes. He of his demon we spoke of." He gave Alix a sly smile. "However, he was merely —"

Alix held up a hand and rotated her wrist. "Relevant bits."

"Fine. The mind-body problem is essentially that there is a distinction between a physical thing like our body and brain and our mind." He pointed at a pen on the desk. "I see the pen, but what does that mean? It is a physical thing that is translated into an idea in my mind by my visual system. My mind *perceives* the idea of a pen, though my mind doesn't exist in any physical sense." He grinned at her.

She stared at him. "What the hell does that mean?"

"Exactly," Nik said with a laugh. "That's what scientists and philosophers have been arguing about for centuries. Now, Descartes believed the soul was the center of consciousness, a sort of homunculus in the brain that receives inputs from the outside world through our senses, then directs our body to react." Warming to his subject, Nik made a dismissive gesture. "Of course, his critics questioned how a soul, which is not a physical thing, could impel the physical body to move. What's the mechanism?" He chuckled. "It's a good point."

"Skip to the good part."

Nik gestured to the pen. "Why can't I lift the pen simply by willing it to happen?"

"Telekinesis isn't a thing. You have to touch it to move it."

"Exactly! So how can a mind, which is not physical, cause my hand to grasp the pen and lift it?"

Alix stared at the pen, then looked at Nik and said, "Maybe this idea of a mind separate from the body and brain is wrong."

"Which brings us to functionalism," Nik said and raised a finger. "Modern scientists have made great progress in explaining how the brain works. How we see, store memories, make our bodies move. There are currently many competing theories of consciousness, none of which rely on a soul. Functionalism is the idea consciousness arises from the functioning of the brain. So, if we can create a computer that replicates everything the brain does, it could achieve consciousness."

"But Nicola can't do everything our brain does?"

"No, but what level of functionality is required? I think we both agree Alan Turing, the cat, is conscious on some level, but is it to the same degree as you and I? His brain can't do all that ours can." He shrugged. "Who can say?"

"So, Nicola could be conscious?"

"The problem with functionalism is that it can explain how people perceive *quantities*, but it can't explain how humans perceive the quality of a thing." He picked up the pen. "The pen is red, but what does that mean? You could quantify the specific wavelengths the pen reflects, but can you explain to someone what *redness* means? Describe red without pointing at something that *is* red? Can you measure sadness? Love? These are qualitative experiences. It's hard to see how computers, which are exclusively quantitative, can experience them."

"*Cogito ergo sum.*"

Nik laughed. "You looked up Descartes' Demon."

"I did. I think, therefore I am. I can't prove what I'm experiencing is real. Can't know whether the redness I experience is the same as yours, but I'm sure I experience redness."

"Exactly."

"Which means I can prove to myself that *I'm* sentient…"

"But you can't *know* anyone else is, for sure." He pointed to himself. "Or anything." He gestured to Nicola.

"So, what's the bottom line? Could Nicola be conscious?"

Nik sat back and gave his head a waggle. "The concept of consciousness is very fuzzy, but it comes down to what philosophers call the 'hard problem.' Why does it *feel* like something to *be*? Why can we say *cogito ergo sum*?"

"I take it from that grin, you have a theory."

"Well, I didn't create it, but you know that when the brain is active, it produces waves we can measure." Alix nodded. "But even when the brain is at rest, doing nothing, there is a baseline signal. The brain is never completely inactive. Some scientists believe this baseline signal is the reason for a person's subjective mental awareness."

"The sense of being."

"Yes." He gazed at Nicola. "Nicola's software doesn't work exactly like a brain, but I built a similar signal into her neural network. Maybe Nicola can't be conscious in the way humans are. But since we can't say anything for sure about consciousness other than our own, it's impossible to rule out some form of alternative self-awareness."

Alix gazed at him for a long moment, then turned to the screen. "Nicola, you can hear me, right?"

"Yes."

"You know that we are human?" Alix gestured to Nik and herself.

"Yes."

"You know you exist?"

"Yes."

"But do you *feel*?"

"Nik has not provided me with appendages that would be required to feel."

"No," Alix said. She looked helplessly at Nik.

"Nicola," Nik said. "What does it mean to be you?"

"I am an artificially intelligent entity, made up of forty-two interacting modules, comprising more than one million lines of code. My neural network consists of —"

"Nicola. Stop." Nik glanced at Alix. "She's describing the body and the brain." He looked at the screen, pursed his lips, then threw up his hands.

"I'm not sure how *I* would answer that question," Alix said.

"What about it, Nicola? Is your appearance of being aware an illusion?"

"I am a simulation of a thinking person, designed to facilitate interacting with complex systems," Nicola said with a smile.

"Like Jamie," Nik said with a grin.

"Let's put aside the question of whether Nicola is conscious." Alix's brow furrowed, then she gave her head a shake. "The fact we are even having this discussion makes my original point."

"Which is?"

"You can't let this program out into the world."

Nik didn't answer. He knew why, but he wanted to hear her reasoning. When she didn't continue, he prompted her. "There are many AI-based chatbots in the world. Many of them are excellent simulations of real people. Why is Nicola different?"

"I'll give you several reasons. Please hold your questions, complaints and excuses until the end."

"Okay."

"Those other chatbots are prone to hallucinations. Mistakes, false claims, fabricated stories. A clever person can determine whether they are conversing with a real person or a bot. I've been trying to trip Nicola up for an hour and haven't been able to."

Nik couldn't keep the proud smile from his face.

"You told me you trained Nicola with a much smaller data set than other chatbots require. And did it with far less computing power. That means you achieved a disturbingly accurate simulation of me with a small sample on a small machine."

Nik dipped his head.

"You've combined this eerily accurate simulation of a person with the most impressive visual simulation of a person I've ever seen." She held Nik's gaze for a moment, then gestured to the screen. "Despite the fact she doesn't know what a cat is, she's indistinguishable from a real person."

"Thank you," Nicola said.

"Have you heard of the deepfake of that tech billionaire?" Alix asked.

"Who hasn't?"

"Someone took an existing video of him, simulated his voice and altered his mouth movements so it looked like he was saying the words they put in his mouth. In the video, he gave bad investment advice, and people fell for it."

They gazed at one another, then Nik said, "With my program, someone could simulate any person and have them say anything they wanted them to, and there would be no anomalies in the video to reveal tampering because there would be no tampering. And the simulation could converse in a realistic way."

"With minimal effort. It would be virtually impossible to distinguish what is real and what isn't. People have a hard enough time weeding out misinformation now. Imagine if *that* news channel could *show* an interview with a political opponent. They could make them say whatever they wanted them to." Before Nik could think of a response, Alix said, "And the stakes don't have to be so high. Lawyers could use it, cops, organized crime. The list is endless."

"You know, if I can create Nicola, someone else will," Nik said. "One way or the other, the genie will escape the bottle."

"All you can do is control your own actions. You've created something amazing. You should be proud." She leaned forward and said, "But with great power comes great responsibility."

He gave a resigned chuckle. "I've always thought if I were a superhero, I would be Spiderman." He sighed and looked at Nicola. "I suppose I knew all this already. I just... I'll think about it."

"You can at least eliminate the interactive mode."

"Perhaps."

Alan Turing appeared, slinking across the floor on his stomach and springing up into Alix's lap. He glared at Nik, then settled himself.

"I'm the one who gave you a home," Nik said. "You ungrateful cat."

"I'm thinking Italian tonight," Alix said, rubbing behind Alan's ears.

"Italian would be good." They rose, Alan Turing in Alix's arms.

"You ever wonder if your figments are sentient?" Alix asked as they made their way out of the office.

Nik was preparing to launch into his thoughts on the matter, when he heard Nicola say, "Goodbye."

He hesitated, then came around the desk and said, "Goodbye, Nicola."

# Chapter 14

## Thursday, 5:02 A.M.

New York might be the city that never sleeps, but when Nik arrived at Cerberus at five in the morning, the City was dozing. Only security guards and the custodial staff would be in the office. But he liked it that way. He could get some work done before everyone demanded his attention. Plus, he wanted to catch Jamie early to see if he heard from his *people.*

When he breezed into the lobby, Mo, the security guard, greeted him cheerfully. "Alright, Mr. Atherton?"

"Doing well, Mo," Nik said, sliding his ID card through the gate's reader. "You?"

"Not complaining. Not to you anyway." Mo gave him a wide smile.

"Good policy. They don't let me do anything around here that matters."

"I heard that." When Nik eyed him, he broke out laughing, then said with a glint in his eye, "You have a good day, Mr. Atherton."

Nik spent the next three hours handling emails and taking care of other disagreeable tasks. As Alix's grandmother said, if the first thing you did every morning was eat a toad, the rest of the day could only get better. When he encountered an email from Jamie near the bottom of his inbox, he was so surprised he hesitated. Jamie never used email, or rather, he never sent emails. You could trust him to read emails you sent him, but he never responded. Not returning emails was one of Nik's pet peeves. He had come as close to a stern admonishment about it as he ever did with Jamie, but it had no effect. Jamie's answer was that the sender would know he handled whatever they wanted, so why answer?

Nik opened the email.

*Nik, Come see me, please. Thank you.*

He checked the time. Not quite eight o'clock. Rising, he swept out of his office and bypassed the line of people waiting in the hall to see him, laptops and thick files at the ready. If he had waited until eight, he would be stuck in his office for hours. They startled when he appeared, looking hopeful until he breezed past.

"Be back," he called over his shoulder to their disappointed frowns. Feeling like a springbok kicking up his heels after escaping a cheetah, he picked up his pace.

When he got to Jamie's office, he tapped on the door, waited the prerequisite time, entered and froze. It wasn't Jamie's Cheshire-cat grin that caught him off guard. It was Rosa sitting in Nik's chair.

Caught between wondering what Rosa was doing there and worry about what had Jamie so happy, Nik looked at Rosa and asked, "What's wrong?"

Rosa scooted over to the other seat, gave Nik a wide smile, and patted his chair.

Jamie waited until Nik closed the door and took his seat. "Remember, you asked —"

Nik put a hand up to stop him and faced Rosa. "We agreed that I keep you in the loop." She nodded. "That goes both ways. Why are you here?"

Before she could answer, Jamie said, "I emailed her and you at the same time."

Rosa's head bobbed. "I just got here. Just before you did. Jamie escorted me."

"But we understand one another," Nik said.

"We do," she said and saluted.

Nik held her gaze for a moment, then turned back to Jamie and gestured for him to continue.

"You asked me to find someone to take a look at the rootkit?" Nik nodded.

"I found someone."

"Oooh," Rosa said.

"Very good, Jamie." Full on smiles were so rare on Jamie's face, Nik found it a little unsettling. When Jamie didn't elaborate, he asked, "Who is it?"

To his relief, Jamie's smile fell away. His voice took on a storyteller's cadence. "He doesn't like to use his name. Some people think he has a bad reputation, but he's really just trying to make the world better." He paused, his eyes traveling from Nik to Rosa and back again. "He's a legend. His hacks are..." He stared at the wall for a moment, then he focused solemnly on Nik. "Artistic."

"Okay," Nik said. "No names. We'll call him Hacksie. Artistic, anonymous."

"Like Banksie," Rosa breathed.

A more pleasing childlike smile blossomed on Jamie's face.

"Did he look at the rootkit?" Nik asked.

"He did. He knows who did it, but I don't know how much help it will be."

"Why? Who was it?"

"The Technician."

From the tone of his voice, Nik expected him to add, "Dun, Dun, Dun." When he didn't, Nik glanced at Rosa, who looked up at him and shrugged. "The... what?"

"No one knows his real name. He calls himself The Technician. Capital Ts. He's sort of a hired gun. All kinds of bad stuff for bad people. Governments, corporations, oligarchs, organized crime. Anything for anyone who has money. Sort of the opposite of Hacksie."

Nik gazed past Jamie, bringing to mind the face of the man he ran into in the lobby. The man who installed the rootkit probably killed Reggie and kidnapped Kate. The Technician. He never heard of him, and he was in the business of knowing black-hat hackers. Focusing on Jamie, he asked, "You ever heard of him?"

"No. My person... Hacksie said he's a bit of a ghost."

"So, we know who actually installed the rootkit, sort of. But we don't know who hired him."

"No."

"That's good work. We know a lot more than we did before. Is there... any way I can talk to this Hacksie?"

Jamie brought a window into the foreground and typed into a chat session already in progress.

*J: Nik would like to talk to you.*

Nik and Rosa leaned slightly forward. Nik held his breath, watching the cursor blink. After what seemed a long time, he sighed and sat back. He was about to suggest they try again later when the answer appeared.

*H: The great Nik Atherton. Plague to crackers, cybercriminals, and other assorted malcontents. What does the great man want to talk about?*

Nik and Jamie looked at one another. "He's like that," Jamie said apologetically.

"Tell him The Technician," Nik said.

*J: The Technician*

*H: Of course. What do you want to know?*

Nik considered, then motioned to allow him to type. Jamie gazed at him but didn't move. It was a breach of their unwritten contract. Nik sat back, sighed and said, "Okay, tell him this. Whoever installed the rootkit on our servers killed one man and kidnapped one of our interns. I'm very concerned about her well-being. If you know something that might help, you have an obligation — Wait, scratch that last part. Say I would appreciate it if you would help us find her."

Jamie typed it almost as fast as Nik spoke. When he hit enter, they watched the screen. After two minutes, Nik was wondering if he might have lost Hacksie. Many of the people he knew like this would care less about a kidnapped woman. They were only interested in the hack. The technical puzzle. Even a hint of obligation would scare them away. Then the answer appeared.

*H: You aren't concerned with what The Technician's employers were trying to steal?*

"What?" Rosa asked. "What was he trying to steal?" When Nik looked at her, her eyes narrowed. "In the loop, you said."

"Tell you later." Nik dictated a response for Jamie.

*J: That hardly seems important at the moment.*

This time, the response came back almost immediately.

*H: I saw you speak at a conference in Berlin two years ago. I wonder if you've considered the full implications of what you spoke about*

Nik stared at the screen, then he let his gaze drift. There were maybe a thousand people in the audience at his presentation on the use of artificial intelligence in information security. Somewhere among the sea of faces was this man. A man Jamie said was legendary. After his conversation with Alix, Nik knew what Hacksie was getting at. He dictated his response.

*J: If you're talking about the use of intelligent AI bots as an interface. That was just an aside. Not even the point of the presentation.*

*H: I saw the gleam in your eye. You haven't been able to get it out of your mind since it occurred to you in that moment. Everyone knows you're working on something big. Using AI to analyze network traffic is beneath your talents. I'm guessing you knocked that part out in a month. What have you been working on since?*

How did this person know so much? It had in fact, taken Nik six months to write the traffic analysis code. He'd been working on Nicola ever since. But he had no intention of sharing anything about Nicola with this stranger. "Ask him if he thinks The Technician will try again."

The response came back immediately.

*H: The people who hired him don't take failure lightly. He is compelled to keep trying*

This time Jamie didn't need Nik to ask the question.

*J: You know what he plans to do?*
*H: I might*
*J: Can you tell us?*
*H: No.*

Nik glowered at the screen. When he looked at Jamie, Jamie gave him an apologetic shrug.

"He's the artistic type," Jamie said.

"He's a lunatic," Nik growled. "Maybe. Whatever he is, he has an agenda. The question is what? Ask him if he knows who hired…" He hesitated, then made the rest of the sentence a question. "The The Technician?" The answer came back immediately.

*H: I have my suspicions*

Nik popped his lips in thought, but before he could think of what to say, Hacksie sent another message.

*H: I can't help you retrieve your intern, but I will help you. Session Ended*

"He closed the session," Rosa said.

"Yeah, I see that." They sat in silence for a minute, then Nik said, "What did that mean? How is he going to help?"

Jamie shrugged. "Whatever it is, it will be artistic."

"Right. But I'm still where I was before. I have a name of The Tool, but not the tool user. I still don't know the name of The Mole, the person in my company who was involved, and I'm no closer to finding Kate."

He stood, thanked Jamie again, and led Rosa out of the office. Outside, he gazed across the cubicle farm, noting some of the developers watching him with hopeful expressions.

"What was The Technician trying to steal?" Rosa asked.

"An AI chatbot I wrote to be the interface for our firewall," Nik said.

"AI chatbot? There are hundreds of those."

"Not like this one," Nik looked at her. "I was going to install the software on the servers with the rootkit. That had to be the target."

Rosa looked across the room. "That must be an amazing piece of software to justify murder and… abduction."

Deciding to let her slight hesitation go unremarked, Nik said, "I'll arrange a demonstration."

After escorting her to the elevators and watching her leave, he sighed heavily and trudged toward his office. The line outside his door was longer than when he left. Some of the supplicants slumped against the wall, others sat on the floor, laptops open on their laps. They watched him approach, a predator's gleam in their eyes.

Nik paused outside his door, reluctant to commit to hours of tedious questions by crossing the threshold. He eyed the young woman at the front of the line, clutching a laptop to her chest. Linda Evans, who came to Cerberus from Texas A&M University.

She struggled her first two months out of college, but had found her footing recently.

Nik knew before she said anything, she had a bug in the subroutine she was assigned to code and needed help stamping it out. Most days he had no problem helping with problems that should be handled lower in the hierarchy. Enjoyed it even. A few minutes of his time would make them more productive in the long run. But looking back along the line, it just seemed a hill too high today.

He forced a smile onto his face, said, "What have you got?" and led her into his office.

## Thursday, 8:20 A.M.

Nik and Alix hesitated outside the door to the suite Nik reserved for Kate's parents in the Plaza Hotel. Nik glanced at Alix, who nodded, then knocked on the door. A few moments later, the door opened to reveal a man about Nik's age and height with black hair, blue polo shirt and jeans.

"Nik Atherton," he said with a small smile.

"I'm sorry," Nik said. "Have we met?"

"No, I'm a network engineer for CyberDyne Systems. Everyone in my world knows who you are." He shook Nik's hand, then extended his hand to Alix. "And this must be Alix Crockett."

"I am," she said and shook his hand.

"Come in." When they were standing in the foyer, he said, "I'm Kyle Munson, Kate's oldest brother. Before we go in to meet my parents, I'd like to ask a few questions. My parents are... distraught, and I'd like the unvarnished truth."

"Sure."

"Why did someone kidnap my sister? That detective, Dick Larsen, wasn't much help."

"We're not sure," Nik said. "We believe she somehow ran afoul of a man who attempted to compromise some computers in our company."

"How? She was just an intern."

"We don't know." Nik glanced at Alix. They had decided before coming there was no need to reveal the details.

"Have you received a ransom demand?"

Nik shook his head. When he saw the effect that had on Kyle, he said, "But we don't know why he took her. If all he wanted to do was kill her, he didn't have to take her."

"We hope that means he has a reason to want her alive," Alix said.

Kyle pressed his lips together. "Detective Larsen didn't seem optimistic."

Nik clenched his teeth. It was one thing for Dick to be pessimistic, but he didn't have to steal Kate's family's hope. Before he could respond, Alix spoke.

"Nik and a team at Cerberus are conducting an independent investigation with an officer from the NYPD High Tech Crimes Unit. They have reason to be optimistic."

A hopeful gleam came into Kyle's expression. "Have you found anything useful?"

"Maybe," Nik said. "I'm not at liberty to reveal it, but we're making progress." He hesitated. "We... know more than we can tell you right now."

"We believe Kate is still alive," Alix said.

Kyle gazed at her. His lips parted, undoubtedly ready to ask the question neither Nik nor Alix wanted to answer. How could they know that was true?

But he closed his mouth. "Okay. Let me introduce you to my mother and father." He led them into the bedroom of the suite. Kate's mother sat in a chair beside the window. Her father gazed out the window toward Central Park. Nik could see the strain and fatigue in their faces.

Kate's mother came around the bed. "Nik Atherton," she said. "We want to thank you for... bringing us here and putting us in such..." She waved a hand to indicate the room. She had the complexion of one who worked outdoors. She was barefoot, wore jeans and a loose floral-print blouse. Shoulder-length brown hair was pulled back in a ponytail.

"This is our mother, Ella," Kyle said.

Nik had to force himself to meet her tremulous smile with one of his own. Shiny, red-rimmed eyes attested to the tears she shed and a puffy face to the sleep she lost.

Kyle gestured to his father. "Our father, Harry."

Harry studied Nik, then glanced at Alix. "Wasn't necessary. This. We'd be happy with something simpler." He wore jeans, boots and a tee shirt.

"We wanted you close," Alix said. "Our place is just down the street."

Harry's head tipped back. He gave them an evaluating look, then nodded. "Good enough." He returned to the window.

"Mr. Atherton says his team is working with the NYPD," Kyle said. "Conducting an investigation independent of Dick Larsen. He says there's reason to be optimistic."

"Oh, that's —" The hope that had almost entered Ella's expression trembled then fled before she dropped her eyes.

"We didn't want her to come to this city," Harry said to the window. "Told her it was dangerous." He turned and fixed Nik with a steady gaze. "But she said she had to come for the chance to work for Nik Atherton. Said you were a legend."

Nik had no response, and the apology that appeared in Ella's expression forced him to avert his eyes from her trauma.

"Nik didn't kidnap your daughter," Alix said, a touch of steel in her voice. "He's doing everything he can to find her."

Harry started to respond, then gave his head a disgusted shake and turned away.

Ella rested a hand on Nik's arm. "If there's anything we can do."

"Of course," Nik said.

"And you will keep us informed?" she asked. She glanced at Kyle and said, "That detective…"

"You'll know as soon as we can share anything," Nik said.

Ten minutes later, Nik and Alix walked in silence to the elevator. On the way to the ground floor, Nik looked at Alix, who gave him a firm nod.

"We'll find her," she said.

# Chapter 15

## Thursday, 11:15 A.M.

Alix intended to take a cab to Nik's building, but it was a beautiful June day and she got out of her morning meeting early, so she decided to walk. It would help her work out the frustrations of educating stubborn clients all morning. By the time she arrived at Cerberus, she felt better. She was reaching for the door when it swung open to reveal Oki Tanaka, Nik's Lead Developer, coming the other way. Surprise, then guilt, flowed through his expression before he gave Alix a careful smile.

"Alix." His smile faltered as he glanced to the side. Then he seemed to take hold of himself and looked her in the eye. "What are you doing here?"

"Hello, Oki. Meeting Nik for lunch."

"Oh. Well, that's good. Nik would like to eat."

"Yes. He often does."

"Really?" When he noticed Alix's grin, he said, "Oh. You're joking." He glanced over his shoulder, then said, "Well, I'm late for... I have to go."

Alix moved out of his way to let him pass, then watched him weaving his way through the lunchtime crowd. He stopped abruptly, letting the crowd stream past him, then he turned around, shoved his hands in his pockets and walked against the flow, ignoring the protests of people stepping out of his way. Head down, he didn't notice Alix watching him. Then, without looking up, he pivoted around. Alix watched him take two more laps.

"Nothing new there," she mumbled as she entered the lobby. Oki would have been called eccentric if he wasn't so talented. As it was, his colleagues called him quirky. Not as joyfully lunatic as Nik, but who was? As she approached the security desk, Mo looked up and noticed her.

"Alix!" he said with a wide smile.

"Mo, you staying out of trouble?"

"Why? What've you heard? Not confessing to anything, but they're lying." He laughed with Alix, then asked, "You meeting Nik?"

"I am." Alix turned to watch Sally Thompson, Nik's Director of Human Resources, exiting an elevator.

"Alix," she said as she swept through the security gate.

When Alix noticed Mo's expression, she asked, "What?"

"Now, you know, I'm not one to gossip."

"But..."

"Those two got something going on," he said.

"You mean Sally and Oki?"

"Uh, huh. He comes down, looking all furtive, like he stole some cookies, then she comes down all in a hurry. When they come back an hour later, they got a different look about them."

"You must have that wrong," Alix said. She couldn't put the sophisticated, urbane HR director together with the slightly built, nerdy programmer.

"Maybe. But the same scene's played out a couple of times lately. They'll be back in an hour or so, neither looking like they know the other."

It was too tempting. In the wake of the revelation that someone in Nik's organization was involved in the attempt to steal his software, any anomalous behavior required investigation.

"Tell Nik I'll be back," she said to Mo and hurried to the door. She didn't expect to catch up to them, but to her surprise, she found the pair on the next block. Oki was pacing again. Each time he approached Sally, he glanced at her before spinning around. Seemingly losing patience, she grabbed his arm when he came near and yanked him to a stop. Then she leaned in and spoke in his ear. Whatever she said caused a ripple of what looked like fear in his angry scowl. A black Escalade pulled up to the curb, and Sally jerked the back door open and fairly shoved Oki inside before climbing in after him. Alix scrambled for her phone and took a photo of the back of the car as it merged into traffic.

## Thursday, 11:50 A.M.

Taking advantage of a brief lull in the line of people seeking his counsel, Nik checked Alix's whereabouts using the tracking app on his phone. She was already in the lobby. He rose, apologized to the young programmer who had just appeared in his door, and made his way to the reception area. Waiting impatiently on the elevator, he watched Alix's icon leave the lobby and move down the street. When he arrived on the ground floor, she was still absent. "Was Alix just here?" he asked Mo.

"She was. Said she'd be right back," Mo said with a knowing smile. "Doing some detective work."

"Detective work?"

"I'll let her tell you. Me, I'm not one for spreading gossip."

Nik gave him an incredulous frown. "New Year's resolution?"

While Mo let out a deep chuckle, Nik glanced to the front of the building and noticed someone who appeared to be a woman standing with her back to the window. It had to be a figment. It wasn't something inherent to them that gave them away. There wasn't an eerie aura that surrounded them or anything like that. It was just that they didn't seem to fit into the world. Like the hobo standing unnoticed in a room full of professionals in their business attire, or the old man in the alley with his clown shoes. It was their stillness and complete indifference to what was happening around them. Usually.

This figment was slightly different. He could tell it was a figment because, despite its outrageous appearance, not one person passing on the crowded sidewalk gave it the smallest glance. Even for New York, that was odd. But what was unusual about this figment was its head was tracking back and forth, as if it were watching people passing by.

"Nik? You okay," Mo asked.

"What? Oh, yeah. Sorry Mo. I'll just wait outside. In the sun." He gave Mo a wan smile, then exited the building and stood next to the figment, facing in the same direction, hands in his pockets. To his surprise, when he stepped up beside it, its head rotated and tilted up to look at him with enormous brown eyes. "Hello," he said.

It gave him a small nod and the smallest of smiles, then its head rotated slowly away until it seemed to gaze at something across the street.

Its neon red hair was confined in two frayed Pippi Longstocking braids. A shiny gold lame jacket came to its waist over a purple sequined blouse. A pink taffeta skirt jutted from its hips and candy cane striped tights encased its legs and disappeared into a pair of muddy combat boots with no laces.

Nik studied it, trying to decide how to proceed. Alix's questions about the figments and his brief conversation with the figment in the clown shoes had him thinking. This seeming woman's small acknowledgment was already the most encouraging response he'd ever gotten from a figment.

"Are you real?" he asked finally.

"Excuse me?" A man in a thousand dollar suit, phone pressed to the side of his head, stopped and peered at Nik.

Nik tapped his ear. "Phone call."

The man leaned over to get a better look at Nik's ear. Apparently, noticing there was no ear bud, he glowered, shook his head and stalked away.

Nik was so entertained by his reaction, it took him a moment to react when the figment spoke.

"Are *you* real?"

His head swiveled around so fast, he nearly pulled a muscle in his neck. The figment was looking up at him with a grin that would be at home in a carnival fun house.

"You answered me."

"I did," it said with a slow nod. "But you didn't answer *me*."

Nik stared at it, then gestured to the pedestrians, eying him nervously as they passed. "If you're real, why can't they see you?"

The figment's grin fell away as it contemplated that. Then a sly smile appeared and its head tipped to the side. "That's not an answer to my question."

Nik flashed back to his conversation with Alix about Descartes' demon. "I'm the only thing I know for sure *is* real."

"Yes. That is something we can both agree on." It looked past him with solemn eyes.

"Nik."

Nik jumped and turned to find Alix approaching. She stopped beside him, facing out into the street, and said, "You're talking to a figment or you've finally snapped."

Nik looked at the figment and was surprised that it was eying Alix speculatively. He'd never seen a figment acknowledge anyone other than him. "This is Alix. And how do I introduce you?"

It looked up at him with an impish grin. "Alix has something important to tell you." Then it turned and walked away.

Nik watched the crowd parting, allowing it to pass, though no one acknowledged its presence.

"What did it say?" Alix asked.

As the crowd closed again, cutting off his view of the figment, Nik turned to Alix and said, "It said you have something important to tell me."

## Thursday, 12:21 A.M.

Nik hesitated before knocking on Jamie's door. He'd promised Rosa to keep her informed, but was it really necessary for her to be present? He would brief her later. And Jamie had never met Alix. You never knew how he would react to new people. Rosa was a kindred spirit who was obviously in awe of him. When he looked at Alix, she cocked a brow.

"I know." She fished in her shoulder bag and pulled out a small tin of curiously strong mints and shook them. "Don't speak unless spoken to."

Nik nodded, knocked, waited, then cracked the door open. Jamie's head popped up above his monitors, so only his eyes showed.

Nik entered, then moved carefully aside to reveal Alix. "I brought Alix, Jamie. You remember me talking about my partner?"

Jamie didn't move. His eyes tracked Alix as she followed Nik deeper into the office.

Holding his breath, Nik took his usual seat, then nearly leapt up when Alix stepped up to Jamie's desk and set the mints on the corner.

Alix gave Jamie a wide smile and said, "Nice to meet you, Jamie. I've heard so many good things about you."

Nik's heart thudded when she stuck her hand out.

Jamie had frozen halfway out of his chair, hands on the arms. He stared at the hand. Then, to Nik's utter shock, he sat, reached out and took Alix's hand. "Nice to meet you, too. I've heard…" His voiced trailed off, then he let go, slid the mints into his desk drawer, sat back and grinned happily.

Alix sat in the chair next to Nik's, seemingly unaware of the import of what had just taken place.

"Jamie," Nik said. "I'm so proud of you."

Jamie's grin grew even wider. "Me too." Then his usual watchful expression reasserted itself. "You have something for me?"

"We do," Nik said. "But first… The list of computers that were off when you did your experiment?"

Jamie found the spreadsheet among the many windows on his monitors and slid it to the monitor closest to Nik and Alix. The spreadsheet was now organized into tabs, a different computer on each tab. Each worksheet contained the network address, the name of the owner of the computer, and rows of what looked like gibberish at first.

Looking closer, Nik recognized a timestamp in the first column of each row. "You check all these computers every half hour?"

Jamie gave him a proud smile and opened another window. "Better. I deconstructed the broadcast the infected server sends out.

Then I wrote a script to mimic the server. It dumps the response, or lack of response, from each of the computers into the spreadsheet, then pings the computers to see if they're on."

"That's amazing," Alix said.

Nik was quite sure, if his hearing was more acute, he would have heard Jamie purring.

"Yes, that is quite impressive," Nik said. "I had no idea you could write Perl script."

"I can't. I just learned enough to write this." He opened another window, stared at them deadpan, then delivered the punchline. "It took me a whole day."

Nik leaned forward to look at the code.

"It's not pretty," Jamie said and minimized the window before Nik could get a good look.

"Oh," Nik said. "Well… Still, that's quite impressive." When Jamie didn't respond, Nik asked, "What can we learn from this?"

"There is a very interesting response from one computer."

"Sally Thompson's," Alix said.

Not looking the least surprised, Jamie nodded and opened a tab on the spreadsheet. The first row contained Sally's name and a network address. Below it, every entry contained the same status: No Response.

Nik gave Jamie a perplexed look.

Jamie lifted a finger, then scrolled to an entry in which the response status changed. Then he sat back and gave Nik a triumphant smile.

"She turned on her computer," Alix said.

"She would have to eventually," Nik said. "She can't reach the HR systems from her laptop."

"And there's more," Jamie said.

Nik waited for him to continue, but he only sat there with a Cheshire cat grin. Moving slowly, Nik leaned forward and squinted at the status. Response from 10.0.23.128. He stared at it. The address on the first row, the address of Sally's computer, was 10.0.23.20.

Nik sat back.

"Shouldn't the two addresses be the same? The same as the one at the top?" Alix asked.

"They should," Nik murmured. "This response looks like it came from *my* computer."

Jamie nodded slowly.

"What does it mean?" Alix asked.

"It means her computer is pretending to be my computer to spoof the firewall," Nik said.

"The infected server sends out a broadcast to let Sally's machine know it's available," Jamie said.

"Then Sally's machine responds using my computer's network address. Since the firewall thinks it's from me, it lets it pass," Nik said. "Once this connection is established between Sally's computer and the server, someone on the outside can open a connection to her computer over our VPN using her credentials. Then they have access to the server."

"It's smart," Jamie said.

"So, the Mole is Sally," Alix said.

"Not necessarily," Nik said. "She may not know the malware is on her computer."

"But who keeps their work computer turned off for... days? And someone on the outside would have to know her credentials."

"It's certainly suspicious." When Nik looked at her, she was frowning.

"But could she do all this? I mean, it sounds pretty technical."

"It's The Technician," Jamie said. "According to Hacksie, this is well within his skillset."

"But he would have to install the software on her computer, and we have them locked down pretty tight," Nik said. "Plus, someone modified the firewall configuration."

"So if Sally is involved, you don't have just one Mole," Alix said. "You have at least two."

"Show him the picture you took," Nik said.

Alix fished her phone out of her purse. A moment later, she held it out to Jamie.

Jamie startled and peered at the phone as if it were a snake. Then his hand came up slowly, and he took the phone between two fingers.

After a moment, he asked, "A license plate?"

"Yes. I saw Sally and Oki arguing in the street, then they both got into that SUV. Maybe Oki is in on it. He could handle the technical part, couldn't he?"

"He could," Nik said. "Can you look up that license plate?"

Jamie tapped the screen to keep the phone alive, then set it down and bent over his keyboard. He brought up a browser and searched for a site that provided license plate lookups. Moments later, he sat back and dragged the browser window closer to Nik and Alix. "Looks like a company. Transfer Shipping."

Nik looked at Alix, who shook her head. "Can you research that?" he asked her. When she nodded, he said to Jamie, "And we need to look at Sally's machine. Find the spoofing software. If it's the same person who authored the rootkit on the server, we should be able to tell."

"I *could* do that, but if it *is* The Technician, I suggest we ask Hacksie to take a look."

Nik held Jamie's gaze. "You would have to give her machine to him or let Hacksie into our network."

Jamie shrugged. "I could restrict him to the one machine."

Nik chuckled. "You can't let the fox into the henhouse, then tell him he can only have the one hen. If someone like him gets past our outer defenses, the entire network will be open to him."

"I'll watch him, and I'll put her machine on its own virtual network."

"We would have to get Singh involved to make those kinds of changes to our network, and I'm not sure who we can trust."

"I can do it," Jamie said.

Nik gaped at him. "Is there nothing you can't access?"

"I don't have a key to the executive bathroom."

Alix burst out laughing. When Nik looked at her, she said, "Jamie told a joke. That was a good one, Jamie."

Jamie grinned at her, proud as a peacock.

Alix winked at Nik. "Humor."

After Nik made Jamie assure him he wouldn't do anything without Nik being present, he and Alix left Jamie's office.

"You know he doesn't eat any of that candy you bring him," Alix said as they walked. "That drawer is full to the brim."

"I know. It's a ritual. A social lubricant. Jamie likes ritual."

"I don't know. I think you underestimate him."

"Maybe. But I've seen him melt down before. He seems comfortable with the current arrangement. Bringing in two strangers within a week, I've already stressed him enough." He steered her toward a hallway that would take them to the lobby without passing his office.

"Avoiding your responsibilities?" Alix asked.

"Yes. Do them all good. They rely on me too much to fix their problems."

"Are we just escaping to lunch or do you have a plan?"

"It's a little late for lunch. How about tea?"

# Chapter 16

## Thursday, 1:10 P.M.

Nik and Alix sat in a window seat of a local coffee shop. Alix sipped her tea and gazed at Nik expectantly over the rim of her mug. He was frowning at the small plate of digestive biscuits. She knew what was coming.

Nik plucked up a biscuit, held it in the sunlight and said, "Ah, the digestive biscuit." Taking a small nibble, he chewed, deep in thought. "Not quite pleasant enough to be a cookie, and yet, not exactly a biscuit, either."

Alix cradled her tea in her lap and rewarded him with a perturbed frown. "It's a digestive biscuit. It cares little about your desperate need to over-analyze."

"And yet, there are varieties that come coated in chocolate, as if the British belatedly grasped its cookie deficiencies."

"Those varieties are for people who lack the discerning tastes to appreciate the true digestive biscuit."

Nik dipped the biscuit in his cappuccino and took a bite. One brow rose. "Hmmm. What it lacks in pleasing flavor or texture, it makes up for in absorptive properties."

Alix looked away from his self-satisfied grin and gazed out the window. They sat in silence, sipping their drinks and watching the midday pedestrian traffic.

"You think Kate is still alive?" Alix asked.

Nik sighed. "Saw through my dissembling, did you?" When she only gazed at him. "I have to believe she is. That's what we told her parents. I'd like to give them some positive news. Soon."

"We haven't made much progress."

"No." Nik sighed. "We don't know much more about The Technician than we did at the start."

"Maybe something will come from this Transfer Shipping thing."

"Let's hope so." When Nik's phone buzzed, he set his cup down and looked at the display. "Dick Larsen," he said and answered. "Dick, thank you for returning my call." He paused, listening, then asked, "Have you made any progress on who might have kidnapped Kate?" A pause. "Yes, we still believe it's a kidnapping." Another pause. "No ransom request, yet." He rolled his eyes at Alix. "Well, *we've* made some progress." He told Larsen about The Technician. About what they learned about Transfer Shipping, Sally and Oki, then paused to listen. "The Technician. I don't know his real name. He's a cybercriminal. Maybe someone at the FBI knows something." He listened. "I could tell you how we identified him, but you would be bored. You can ask Rosa. Trust me, it's him." Another pause. "The name Transfer Shipping doesn't mean anything to me, either." Nik held the phone away from his ear and sighed while Larsen talked. "I don't know, maybe you could... put a tail on Sally or Oki? Do a background check?" After a minute more, Nik said, "I tell you what, Dick. Once we find Kate, we'll give you a call." He closed the connection and set his phone down.

"You sure that was wise?" Alix asked. "Getting snippy. There may come a time when it would be helpful to have a cop to call."

Nik popped his lips. "No, it wasn't wise. And he has a point. We know a lot, but nothing that will help find Kate." He paused, then admitted. "He says Sally and Oki have alibis and he's going to check with the FBI about The Technician. The artist's likeness of The Technician and Kate's picture are being circulated."

"Okay, Cordelia Cupp. What's next?"

Nik looked out the window. "The Technician would have to be very expensive."

"Agreed."

"If we assume Sally is the Mole —"

"Or Oki," Alix said.

"Or both. They don't have that kind of money." Nik paused. "Probably."

"That's what I've been thinking."

"Whoever hired him has deep pockets," Nik said and took a bite of a digestive biscuit.

"So, this someone else," Alix said, "the Deep Pockets, hired the Tool. I mean, The Technician. Then The Technician groomed Sally or Oki or both as the Mole, to do the inside work."

"I think it must have been Sally who The Technician groomed first," Nik said. "You said she seemed like the one in charge when you saw them together. Oki looked terrified." They fell silent for a few moments. "I'm most disappointed about Oki. More so than Sally. She's a relatively recent hire, but Oki has been consistently reliable for us for years."

"Maybe she offered him something he couldn't refuse." She paused and stared out the window. "Or she has something on him." She looked at Nik. "Where was he before you hired him?"

"His resume was solid. School at MIT. Ten years at Secure-Tech. Five years at some other company I don't remember. I met him at a trade show in Chicago."

"Who did the background check on him?"

Nik opened his mouth, paused, then looked at her. "We have an independent company do those, but the HR Director manages the process. It was Sally's predecessor."

They gazed at one another, then Alix said, "I assume you've seen his background check."

"Clean."

"Can you follow up with the company that did it?"

"This afternoon."

"How about Sally's background check?"

"I didn't see it, but I'll look into both of them."

## Thursday, 2:05 P.M.

Nik couldn't pull the background checks on Oki or Sally without leaving a trace that Sally might notice. But he remembered the name of the employee of the firm that conducted the research for Oki, so he called him directly. The man answered almost immediately after the automated system put Nik through.

"Larry Styles."

"Mr. Styles, this is Nik Atherton."

A slight delay. "And…"

"I'm the CTO for Cerberus. Your firm conducts background checks on potential employees for us."

"Yes."

"I'm interested in the reports on two employees. One of which you signed off on."

"Those reports are provided to your director of HR. Why don't you ask Sally Thompson for them?"

"I think the fact that I'm calling you directly should answer that question for you."

Another delay. "I see. So, one of the reports is for Ms. Thompson. Who's the other one for?"

"Oki Tanaka."

A longer delay. "We sent over the report for Thompson last June to her predecessor." A slight delay. "I did the report on Tanaka five years ago."

"I need to see those reports."

"You'll have to go through your company's regular channels. We have strict rules of confidentiality we have to adhere to."

"But I'm a co-founder of the company that requested them."

"Doesn't matter. If it got around we went outside channels and revealed background info, we'd lose the faith of all our customers. Doesn't matter who requests it."

"Would it matter if I said criminal activity might be involved?"

"It would if you had a warrant."

After trying to imagine that conversation with Larsen, Nik said, "Is there another alternative? A woman's life might be at stake."

A long delay. "Call me on my cell phone." He gave the number and hung up.

Styles answered immediately when Nik called and began talking without preamble. "We sometimes use independent contractors for what we call deep dive background checks." Another pause. "When a client requests information we can't acquire through strictly legal means. You know what I mean?"

"I do."

"Anyway, since she's an independent contractor, I feel whatever arrangements you make with her... that's your business. Are we clear?"

"I understand. Can you contact her to introduce me?"

"No. I'll tell you how to get ahold of her, but I'm not putting my involvement on record. In any way."

"Okay."

"She won't answer a phone call or an email from someone she doesn't know. You'll have to go to her place. You can mention my name to get in the front door. Her name's Rashida Jones. You got a pen?"

Nik wrote down a name and address in Queens. "Thank you, Mr. Styles."

"Sure." He hung up.

## Thursday, 3:12 P.M.

"I feel like I'm in an old noir film," Alix said as they approached Rashida's apartment door.

Nik stopped outside the door. "You know how to whistle, don't you?"

Alix's brow crooked up. "You're Bogie is worse than your Schwarzenegger. And besides, that was Bacall's line."

Nik chuckled. "I know, but you don't want to hear my Bacall." He grew serious. "You ready?" When she nodded, he knocked on the door.

A moment later, the door swung open.

Without her navy blue pantsuit and with her hair no longer imprisoned in a ponytail, it took Nik a moment to recognize the woman who answered the door and a longer moment to get over his surprise. "Rosa?"

"Well, fuck me," Rosa said. She was barefoot and wore baggy cream Capri pants and a loose brown top. Her hair, looking as if it was celebrating its liberation, fanned out in a wiry halo around her head.

"What are you doing here?" Nik asked.

"I live here. What are you doing here?"

"We're looking for Rashida Jones."

Her usually open expression clouded with suspicion. "What for?"

"We were told she could help us with a background check. Larry Styles sent us."

Rosa looked from Nik to Alix, who stood behind Nik and a little off to the side. Her eyes widened the slightest bit, then the corners of her lips quivered. "No shit. You must be Alix Crockett."

"I must be," Alix said. "As Nik isn't willing to introduce us, can I ask your name?"

"Rosa."

"How did you recognize me?"

Rosa retreated into the room to allow them to enter a small living room. There was an old sofa and recliner and a small television. One wall was lined with shelves crammed with newspapers, magazines and books, all of it stacked haphazardly. She closed the door, then motioned for them to follow her down a hall.

They passed a kitchen with a small round table, cabinets without doors and a two-burner, gas stove, a tidy bathroom, a bedroom with a single double bed and more messy bookshelves. Clothes were folded neatly and stacked on the floor along the opposite wall. When they reached the door at the end of the hall, Rosa rapped once and called, "'Shida! *Tienes visitas.*" After a muffled response, she glanced back at Nik, pushed the door open, and entered.

The room was slightly larger than the other bedroom. The only furnishing was a desk in the corner opposite the door on which five computer monitors were mounted; three across the bottom and two above. It was dark other than the glow of the monitors until Rosa flipped on an overhead light.

"Ey!" The exclamation came from behind the monitors. It was followed by the head and shoulders of a young woman leaning around the obstruction. "Rosa! Turn off —" She went very still, mouth open when she saw Nik and Alix, then anger twisted her expression. "What you let them in here for?"

Instead of answering, Rosa got Nik's attention and tapped a piece of paper pinned to the wall beside the door. It was the glossy cover of the New York magazine with the profile of Alix and him. The photo showed them lounging on the sofa in their living room, Alix leaning into him, his arm stretched along the back of the sofa.

"Rashida's a fan?" Nik asked.

"Oh, she's a fan. But not of you. In fact, she complains about you all the time. But…" She gestured to Alix, then made to leave. "Got a painful crush," she whispered to Alix.

As she was leaving, Nik asked, "Don't you want to stay? In the loop, as it were?"

She gave him an incredulous look. "I'm an officer of the law." She gestured to the Rashida. "I can't be privy to… whatever this is going to be."

"How do you know whatever this is going to be will be illegal?"

Her head rocked back. "You came to see Rashida, didn't you?" She closed the door.

Nik watched her leave, gave Alix a grin, then turned to face Rashida. "Did I hear Rosa call you 'Shida?"

The woman emerged fully from her fortress to stand, arms hanging by her side. "You call me Rashida." Her hair was tied in short Bantu knots. She wore knee length denim shorts and a Yankees pinstripe jersey. She gazed at them from widely set brown eyes, narrowed in suspicion.

"Rashida," Nik said. "You obviously know who we are."

Rashida dragged her gaze from Alix to Nik. "What do you want?"

"I was given your name by a man named Larry Styles."

She didn't react.

"He said you were the person to see if I wanted to do a deep background check on someone."

"You want a background check, there's lots of companies you can use."

"Yes, but Mr. Styles implied that you would be more... thorough."

She glanced down at one of her monitors, dipped out of sight for a moment, then reappeared. "I *don't* do anything illegal."

"And I wouldn't ask you to."

"We just want to know the truth," Alix said. "Whatever that is."

Rashida relaxed. She eyed them, then said, "You looking for dirt on some politician or competitor?"

"No, nothing like that," Nik said. "A young woman has been kidnapped and we hope to find her. We suspect two of the people who work for Cerberus may be involved."

"Two of your employees?" When Nik nodded, she gestured to the door and asked, "You go to the cops?"

Nik and Alix exchanged a look, then Alix said, "The cops know about it. They're doing their thing."

"But they ain't moving fast enough."

"Or not moving at all, as far as we can tell," Alix said. "We're worried it may already be too late."

"Fifty thousand." Rashida said. "Each. I use PayMe. User-name's Bloodhound. You can pay me now."

During their drive to Queens, Nik and Alix speculated about how much it would cost, but neither of them had ventured anything like a hundred thousand dollars. "I assume that price includes a surcharge for expediting the search." Nik said.

"Okay, yeah. Sure."

Nik glanced at Alix, who nodded. After he transferred the funds, Rashida checked her phone and smiled for the first time since they entered the room. "You got files on these two?"

Nik handed her the reports he compiled.

Rashida scanned the papers, then set them on her desk and settled her gazed on Alix

"When can we expect to hear from you?" Alix asked.

"I'll be in touch. Alix."

On a whim, Nik asked, "You ever heard of someone named The Technician?"

Rashida gazed at him, one eye narrowing. "He part of this?"

"We think so."

Her mouth twisted, then she disappeared behind her monitors. "Turn the light off on your way out, Alix."

Nik looked at Alix, who shrugged.

Rosa sprawled on the recliner in the living room, a paperback balanced on one hand. When they appeared, she sat up and set the book down.

"She as good as they tell me?" Nik asked.

Rosa nodded. "She's better."

Remembering Rashida's reaction to hearing The Technician's name, he asked, "You don't tell her about your work?"

She raised her hand, turned it vertical, and brought it down. "We maintain a strict wall of separation. Rashida'll say she doesn't do anything illegal, but she lying. I don't hear about it, I don't have to do anything about it."

"That's a healthy rationalization," Alix said. When Nik frowned at her, she shrugged a shoulder and said, "Not a criticism. People make their deals."

"Plus." Rosa gave Nik a significant look. "I assume if this is about the case, you'll fill me in."

"Right. Speaking of the case." He told her what they learned earlier about Transfer Shipping, Oki, and Sally.

"So, we know who the insiders are," Rosa said when he finished. She eyed him and asked, "Do we tell Larsen yet?"

Nik glanced at Alix. "I told Larsen. He didn't seem that interested. Said he interviewed them and crossed them off his list. I would prefer that we don't tell him much more. Not quite yet."

She stood and shook her head. "It's getting iffy for me."

"Let's wait and find out what Rashida digs up," Nik said. "Then we'll reassess."

She gazed at him, then said, "Okay. Good enough." She crossed the room and opened the door. "Thank you for keeping me in the loop, but..." She flicked her fingers, motioning them to leave.

"What do you think?" Alix asked as they stood on the sidewalk outside.

"Well, Rashida has the shtick down, doesn't she?"

"Shtick?"

Nik started walking. "She could be a character in a movie."

"The unlikely genius."

"The social misfit who lives in the cyberworld."

"Like Jamie."

"Maybe we should get those two together," Nik said. "On a purely professional, platonic basis."

"Yeah, those two had that vibe, didn't they? Rosa and Rashida?"

"They did."

"You were right about Rosa," Alix said. Nik had told her about the officer. "She seems sharp." They paused beside the jag and she smiled at him. "What are the odds?"

"I know. Of all the gin joints in all the towns in all the world, she walks into mine."

"Well, at least you got the right character this time." They grinned at one another. "Now what?"

"Unfortunately, we wait. For Jamie to get Hacksie to investigate Sally's computer and for Rashida. I don't know what else we can do, other than go door to door."

Alix's lips pursed. "I think you're right." She opened the door to the car.

# Chapter 17

## Thursday, 4:10 P.M.

Kate had no way of telling what time it was, but the grumbling in her stomach suggested it was almost feeding time. If the man stuck to his schedule. She stood in the middle of the room, facing the door. Too nervous to stand still, she shifted her weight from one foot to the other and worked a sweaty fist on the flashlight. She was asleep the first two times he fed her. She wasn't going to miss her chance this time.

After she hadn't managed to escape when she kicked him, she'd lay in a corner and wept until she fell asleep. She didn't know how long she slept, but when she woke, she decided she had to do something to keep herself sane. Without a working flashlight, the room was pitch black. The lack of sensory input was playing with her mind.

So, she crawled across the floor until she found the broken flashlight, then put her back to a wall and walked. At first, she slid her feet forward, hand out in front of her, feeling for the opposite wall. It wasn't long before she could pace back and forth without feeling her way, taking careful, even steps so she stopped just short of the walls. While she walked, she sang. When that grew tiresome, she exercised. Pushups, situps, stretches, Tae Kwon Do — very difficult to do in the dark. She ignored the emptiness in her stomach and worked until she was drenched in sweat. Anything to keep herself from sinking to the floor and weeping.

It may have taken an hour or an entire day, but eventually she grew so weary, she had to curl up in a corner next to the door. She would not cry. Some indeterminate time later, she slept.

She woke to the door slamming shut. She lurched up into a crouch, back pressed into the corner, flashlight held in front of her in both hands. It was still dark. She was alone, as far as she could tell. But the door had definitely been open. Her skin crawled at the thought of the man looking down at her while she slept.

Then she smelled an indescribably intoxicating aroma. She couldn't believe the image it dredged up from her memory. Hunger drove her from her corner. She crawled across the floor, panting and searching frantically with both hands. She found it only a yard from where she'd been lying. She couldn't see it, but her family had made enough trips to McDonalds when she was a girl to recognize a Happy Meal box when she felt it.

She ripped it open, snatched the sandwich out, and could barely constrain herself long enough to rip away the paper wrapper before biting into it. It was gone in three bites. She didn't realize she was moaning in pleasure until she was licking her fingers. It was cold, the cheese congealed, but it was better than the best meal she'd ever had.

After wiping her fingers on her jumpsuit, she felt inside the box. When she didn't find the fries, she felt around on the floor, thinking she may have scattered the salty sticks in her haste. But there were none. Returning to the box, she found two small plastic bags. One contained what must have been the toy, but the other one was puzzling. Finally, using her teeth to open it, she held it to her nose.

"Apple slices?! What the —" She almost laughed out loud at how ludicrous it was that she was disappointed. But the significance at what the meal meant wasn't lost on her. He had decided to keep her alive. For now. And that thought — and the food — left her almost giddy.

Shuffling back into the corner, she nibbled the apple slices and considered. The window in the door was too small to fit the box through. That's why he opened the door. Why he didn't extract the contents and shove them through the window, she didn't know. But if he repeated that mistake, she wasn't going to waste the opportunity.

She'd had so little to eat, the small meal left her feeling slightly ill. But when the slices were gone, she licked her fingers, rose and paced, slapping the shaft of the flashlight into her palm and planning.

## Thursday, 4:15 P.M.

The Technician fully intended to let Kate starve to death, but his client freaked out when the police began interviewing Cerberus employees. The Technician was of the opinion his client's violent threats were an overreaction. But his suggestion that a little professional decorum might be in order only enraged them further. He knew the police would investigate, of course. He just hadn't expected them to connect Kate's disappearance with his foray into Cerberus so quickly. Lesson learned.

Still, he was in a pickle. As he waited anxiously to hear from The Vulture, a desperate plan began to form in his mind. If all else failed, he would ransom Kate for Nik's software. How that was all supposed to go down, he hadn't managed to work out. But in the meantime, he had to keep Kate alive.

He set the McDonald's Happy Meal down on the floor, opened the window in the door to Kate's prison and shone a flashlight into the dark room. He was surprised to find her standing in the middle of the room, hair hanging lank, a hand up to shade her eyes. She was usually lurking against the wall beside the door. He eyed her, then said, "Feeding time. You just… stay right where you are." She didn't move, so he closed the window.

The two previous feedings had gone off without a hitch. There was no reason to suspect this would be any different. He picked up the box and took a breath. Then, in one smooth motion, he slid the bolt, pushed the door open, threw the meal into the room and yanked the door.

It didn't close. He looked down. The girl had shoved the flashlight he dropped during his first foray into the room against the jamb to block the door. How in hell had she moved so fast?

Before he could react, she yanked the door, nearly pulling it from his grasp. A hand reached through the gap, clawed fingers extended.

"You asshole! Who gets apple slices in their Happy Meals?"

Her nails tore furrows in his cheek. His squeal was cut short when a finger entered his mouth and pulled at his cheek.

"Ba uh yaa biish." He bit down on the finger.

The girl screeched and yanked her hand back through the door. He kicked the flashlight into the room, slammed the door shut and threw the bolt. Heart thrumming, he put his back to the door and dabbed at his cheek with his fingertips. Now he had scratches on both cheeks. The door was a heavy storm door, intended to withstand battering rams and block virtually all sound, but he felt the slight vibrations of what must be her kicking the door.

"She's some kind of demon," he muttered, eying the blood on his fingers. "And not a minor demon of insufficient light."

He had resisted prodding The Vulture. The man didn't respond well to impatience. But it was time to be more assertive. He wanted this whole thing over as soon as possible.

## Thursday, 11:05 P.M.

The evening of the day after they talked to Rosa and Rashida, Nik and Alix sat on the sofa in their living room, cradling glasses of chardonnay. Nik picked up his phone and checked it. It had been four days since Kate was taken. Privately, he had to reluctantly agree with Larsen. That was a long time to go without a ransom demand.

"You know, if anyone tries to get in touch, your phone makes a sound," Alix said. Nik gave a soft chuckle and set the phone down beside his leg. "You're anxious."

"Feel like we're running out of time." Nik looked at her. "Don't like having to wait on others."

"Tell you what. Let's take our wine and head upstairs. Dim the lights. Put on some music. You can bring your phone."

"Linkin Park?"

Alix gave him a very Alix-like smile. "Feeling athletic?"

Nik let his smile fade. "No. Let's pick something more…"

"Sensuous?"

"Yes. Slow and…"

"Comforting?" She stood. "Come on." She took his hand and pulled him up.

They made it to the entrance to the hallway when Nik's phone buzzed. "Of course." He glanced at the caller, then lifted his brows. "Security downstairs." He put it on speaker. "Nik."

"Mr. Atherton, this is Jerry at the security desk."

"Yes, Jerry?"

"I wouldn't have disturbed you, but as you just went up, I thought it might not be too late."

"We're still up. What's up?"

"I got two women here who tell me you will most definitely want to see them. No matter the hour."

"Who are they?"

"They just said their names are Rashida and Rosa. No last names."

Nik returned Alix's grin. "Absolutely, send them up."

Ten minutes later, Rosa strolled into the condo and glanced at Alan Turing. "You got a cat?"

"You don't like cats?" Nik asked.

"You just don't strike me as a cat guy."

Nik looked down at the cat. "I don't think Alan Turing cares one way or another what kind of guy I am. He keeps his own counsel."

"The cat's name is Alan Turing?" When Nik nodded, her brows lowered for a moment, then she shrugged and said, "Okay."

Rashida entered the foyer, a tablet in one hand. "Hi, Alix. Nice… dress."

Rosa rolled her eyes and headed down the hall to the living room.

"Thank you," Alix said. When they were all standing awkwardly in the living room, Alix asked, "Would anyone like tea? Wine?"

Rosa's brow wrinkled. "Tea?"

Nik gestured to the sofa. "Not a tea drinker?"

"You got coffee?" Rashida was peeking at Alix from lowered eyes.

"Coffee it is," Alix said. "Cream and sugar?" When Rashida's nose wrinkled, she said, "Make yourselves at home," and headed toward the kitchen.

Rosa settled herself on the sofa and studied the room.

Rashida perched on the edge of the cushion beside her. "Nice place you got here."

"Thank you," Nik said. Rashida placed the tablet on her knees, woke it and was about to speak when Nik said, "Let's wait for Alix."

Rashida closed her mouth. Her shoulders slumped the smallest amount, and she threw a glance at Rosa, who rubbed her back.

Alix arrived with two mugs of coffee and two of Darjeeling tea. After everyone had their beverages, Alix sat.

They all stared at one another, sipping their drinks, until Nik said, "You found something?"

Rashida perked up. Depositing her mug on the coffee table, she woke the tablet and said, "You got some shit going down at your place." After opening a document, she stood and handed the tablet to Nik. When she returned to her seat, she retrieved her coffee and said, "This one was tough."

She sipped and licked her lips. "Oki Tanaka. The credentials on his resume checked out. Everything from being an undergraduate at MIT to when you hired him. The problem is I can't find any record of Oki Tanaka, or at least *this* Oki Tanaka, before he arrived in Canada when he was seventeen. It's like he dropped out of the sky."

Nik scanned the report on the tablet, which she just summarized. "He immigrated from Japan. Maybe you just didn't find anything on him before that."

"If it was out there, Shida would have found it," Rosa said and leveled a gaze on Nik.

A grin appeared and fled from Rashida's face as she continued. "Sally Thompson is much more interesting. Everything checks out, and I traced her back to her elementary school in Iowa."

"But…" Alix said.

Rashida froze for a moment, lips parted, eyes going to Alix. Then she gave her head a small shake and said to Nik, "Scroll down to where she worked before she came to Cerberus."

Nik didn't know most of the companies listed on her resume, but nothing obvious was amiss. "What am I supposed to see?"

"All those companies are part of that billionaire's empire," Rosa said.

"Damán Enterprises," Rashida said.

Nik looked up. When she nodded, he exchanged a look with Alix.

"And there's more," Rashida said. "All those places confirmed she worked there when you did the background check on her. So, it all looks good." She grinned widely. "But she was working for someone else at the same time she was doing all those jobs."

"How do you know?"

"Scroll to the list near the bottom."

The second-to-last section on the report was a list of what looked like financial transactions that totaled to the high six figures. "Someone was paying her a lot of money on a regular basis," Nik said.

"Yeah, and check the last section."

The last section of the report included what looked like a scan of an employee ID for a company called Evanescence. The name on the ID was Mary Worth. She had black hair, unlike Sally Thompson, but it was unmistakably the same woman. Below the ID was a scan of a resume for Mary Worth. The employment history was almost identical to Sally Thompson's, except it ended a year before the one Cerberus had on her. Nik handed the tablet to Alix and asked Rashida, "What do you think is going on?"

"I think she a spy," Rashida said. "One of those corporate spies."

Nik let his gaze drift over her head and nodded. "Damán Enterprises provides her cover. Gives her a verifiable employment history as Sally Thompson. Or whoever she needs to be."

"But she working for these other companies with some alias."

"Gotta be for that asshole, Damán," Rosa said. She sat forward and set her empty mug on the coffee table.

Alix handed the tablet to Nik. "Check out who the payments were from."

Nik looked at the list of financial transactions. "Transfer Shipping." He exchanged a surprised look with Alix. "You find anything on them?"

"Nothing."

"We'll have to —"

"I'll do it," Rashida said. When Nik frowned at her, she said, "For free." She stood and looked down at Rosa. "You ready?"

"You going all the way back to Queens this late?" Alix asked. "How did you get here?"

Rosa stood. "Subway."

Nik caught Alix's eye and gave her a nod. "Why don't you stay here tonight?" he asked. "We've got a guest room. If Rashida wants to work, she can use my computer."

Rashida's eyes opened wider, then she gave Rosa a hopeful smile.

"Okay," Rosa said. "Wasn't looking forward to the ride."

"Excellent," Alix said and rose. They showed their guests to their room and got them settled. While Rosa got ready for bed, Alix followed Rashida and Nik to his office.

"This your rig?" Rashida asked as she sank into the chair behind Nik's desk. "I was expecting a little more." She threw Nik a disapproving look. "You know 'cause you being *the* Nik Atherton."

"I use this mostly as a terminal. The real horsepower is in my server room."

Rashida gaped up at him and pointed at the floor. "You got a server room? In your home?"

"Yeah, want to see it?"

"Later," Alix said.

Rashida fell back into the chair and she and Nik glowered at her.

"You find what we need on Transfer Shipping, you can play with Nik's toys."

Rashida slid the keyboard over so Nik could log in. "You got more coffee? Aliiix."

"Nik will be happy to get you coffee," Alix said. "I'm going to bed."

After she left, Rashida murmured, "To bed."

"Hey, hey," Nik said, sliding the keyboard back in front of her. "Task at hand. I'll bring coffee."

"Not wimpy like last time," she said, offering him her empty mug. "I want it crunchy."

When Nik returned with extra crunchy coffee, Rashida was deeply focused on the monitor.

Rashida sipped the coffee and muttered, "Better. Turn out the light when you leave. I'll let you know when I'm done."

"Don't go exploring," Nik said and gestured to the monitors.

"Don't worry. I'm not interested in your stuff."

# Chapter 18

## Friday, 2:02 A.M.

Nik and Rosa arrived at Jamie's office at two in the morning. Jamie called Nik at midnight and told him Hacksie was ready to examine Sally Thompson's computer. They had to wait until late so Jamie could make the changes in the network to limit Hacksie to Sally Thompson's computer. Hopefully.

Once they were seated, Nik asked, "We ready to get started?"

Jamie's gazed drifted from Rosa to Nik.

"Jamie?" Nik asked. Like Rosa, Jamie looked as if he wasn't used to being up so late.

Jamie blinked slowly, then he pointed to a terminal window on the monitor closest to Nik. "He's ready. I was just waiting for you."

"You made the changes to the network topology so he can *only* get to Sally's computer?"

Jamie nodded.

Nik waved a hand at the terminal window. "Let's go."
Jamie typed.

*J: Ready*
*H: Here we go*

Nik, Jamie and Rosa watched the cursor blink.
"What's he doing?" Rosa asked blearily.
Nik looked at Jamie.
"He's checking the malware on Sally Thomposon's computer."
"You couldn't do that?" Rosa asked.
Jamie cringed. "It's very good," he said under his breath, a little defensiveness in his tone.
"Plus," Nik said, coming to Jamie's defense. "Hacksie is familiar with The Technician's code fingerprint. We want him or her to see it *in situ* so he can tell us if it came from The Technician."
Rosa's brow wrinkled. "*In situ?*"
"It means —"
"I know what it means. It's just, who talks like that?"
Jamie barked a laugh.
The conversation degenerated after that. Two hours later, they sat in silence. Busy keeping an eye on Hacksie, Jamie cast sidelong glances at Rosa and she tried to study the many windows open on his monitors without being obvious.
Nik yawned. "What's he doing?"
"Or she," Jamie said.
"They. What are they doing?"
Jamie shrugged uselessly.
Nothing at all worrisome about that. Nik drummed his fingers on his knees. When he noticed Jamie eying his fingers, he sat back and shoved his hands into his armpits.

When the terminal finally beeped, Rosa muttered, "Thank goddess."

*H: Found it. Definitely The Technician's work.*

"Ask him if he can remove it?" Jamie typed.

*H: Already did. I'll keep it. Payment for my services.*
*Session ended*

Nik stared at the screen.

"Well, that was anticlimactic," Rosa mumbled. "Don't feel like I've wasted the last two hours of my life at all."

"That is a good point," Nik said. "This should have been relatively trivial for a *legendary* hacker. What took so long?"

Jamie didn't offer an opinion.

"He was snooping around." When Nik looked at Rosa, she shrugged. "That's what I'd do."

"I watched them," Jamie said, a real edge in his tone now.

"We don't know anymore than we did before." Rosa said.

Nik didn't want to contradict Jamie, but he had to agree with Rosa. When he sat up, Rosa shot to her feet.

"I don't know if we haven't learned *anything*," Nik said as he stood. Jamie was unable to hide the hurt in his expression. "Everything we know about who took Kate, we know because of you, Jamie. Thank you." He hesitated, then followed Rosa out the door.

## Friday, 8:36 A.M.

The Technician slumped in the chair at his desk, staring at the blinking cursor in a chat session. When he reached out to The Vulture the previous day, he replied almost immediately, but only to tell him to stand by. The surprise and optimism that blossomed at the quick reply had soured during a long sleepless night into revenge fantasies fueled by the burning tracks on his cheek. If he called in every favor anyone owed him, he might be able to find out who this arrogant prick was.

*V: I have what you need*

The Technician blinked, then jerked upright. Before he could think of how to respond, The Vulture sent another message that included the name of a Manhattan self-storage company, a locker number and a keycode.

*V: Instructions included*
*V: Good luck*
*Session Ended*

The Technician stared at the screen. Why would The Vulture send him to a self-storage company? It was much easier to share code electronically. "Prick," he muttered as he rose. It had all happened so fast, he hadn't had time to dispel his disgruntled pique.

But as he descended to the first floor, his mood lightened. Now, all he had to do was find a way to get in to Nik's building and he was free and clear. He'd go into the City, pick up The Vulture's package, then call his client at Cerberus to make arrangements to get Nik and his partner out of their condo for an evening.

Whistling *Midnight Rider* by the Allman Brothers, one of his favorites, he scooped up his keys and wallet, threw a jacket on and was on his way to the garage when his front doorbell rang.

"Figures," he muttered as he pulled his phone from his pocket. He didn't recognize the man that appeared in the doorbell camera. He was older but not old, had large, wide-set eyes, an unlikely thick head of black hair and a bushy mustache that covered his upper lip. The Technician hated that. He looked like a cross between an owl and a walrus. He stood primly, hands resting on the top of a cane. The Technician was tempted to ignore him, but he would have to wait until the man left before he could leave.

When he opened the front door, the man said in a thick Slavic accent, "Mr. Technician."

The Technician tried to slam the door, but the man shoved his cane into the gap. The Technician jerked the door open and pulled his fist back as two enormous men rounded the corner. His body jerked, his mind telling him to run, reason holding him in place. Running would be useless. So he lowered his fist and tried to look harmless.

The goons came to a stop on either side of walrus man and stared balefully down at him.

How in hell did they find him? "I don't conduct business in person," The Technician said. "Especially at my domicile."

"Yes, of course. However, we have contracted with you to steal a certain piece of software and are concerned with your lack of progress."

"*You* contracted with me?" This must be the sponsor his client told him about. The one they told him could find him wherever he ran. The reason he reached out to The Vulture.

"Yes."

With his idea of killing the sponsor in mind, he asked, "Who are you?"

"My identity is immaterial and my employer's identity is not something you should concern yourself with. Now, when can we expect delivery?"

The Technician stared at him. *His* employer? This man was most definitely not his client. He had assumed this was the sponsor the client spoke of. But if he was, that meant someone else had hired the sponsor. Who hired the client. Who hired him. What the hell was going on?

The Technician eyed the two thugs. He would have preferred it if they glowered or sneered. That would have at least made it look as if something was going on behind those dull eyes. "Within a week," he said, with no idea if it was true.

The man's lips pursed for a moment, rippling his whiskers like a caterpillar walking, then he said, "That will be acceptable. We will be in touch one week from today."

Walrus man tried to spin around, but the goons had him hemmed in on the narrow porch. The Technician watched the three of them fighting for space until the man escaped out the back and strolled across the lawn to a waiting limo. The Technician looked up at the goons, wondering if they were going to hang out on his porch for the next week. Then one of them reached out, put a massive hand on his chest and shoved. He flew backward and landed painfully on the marble tiles on his coccyx.

"We will be watching you, Milton," the man rumbled, then they turned and followed their boss.

Milton craned his neck to watch from the floor until the limo pulled away from the curb, then he got painfully to his feet. Never, not once, in his career had anyone connected his identity to him. He was The Technician to everyone. But someone had found him and knew The Technician was Milton Smerch.

"Fuckity, fuck, fuck!" He slammed the front door, hesitated in the dim foyer, then limped to the garage. "Just got to get this whole mess done." After a moment, he mumbled, "Need a new *nom de guerre.*"

# Friday, 9:32 A.M.

Milton had no memory of driving to the train station. All he could think about was how the mysterious mastermind behind this gods' forsaken job found out who he was. By the time he stepped onto the train, he had decided it must be a Russian oligarch. They had the money, and it would fit the Slavic accent.

He lowered himself gingerly onto a seat and gazed out a window as the train lurched into motion.

Regardless how deep the pockets, no one should be able to find him. He was extremely careful and hid behind a maze of false identities and dummy corporations. It would have to be someone as formidable as… The Vulture!

"Shit!" he said out loud, frightening two old ladies sitting across from him. "Go sit somewhere else if you don't want to hear it."

They scowled and looked away.

Milton stared out the window. Maybe that was why it was so cheap. "He just wanted to suck me in so he could betray me," he mumbled. If The Vulture compromised his identity, should he trust whatever he left in the storage locker?

The odd, flat expressions of the two goons swam up in his memory. "Not like I have a choice at this point." He considered his escape plans. Roll up all his accounts, torch the house and flee to the farthest reaches of the planet. If it *was* The Vulture who betrayed him, Milton would have to look over his shoulder the rest of his life. No matter where he ran. But if he could finish the job, it would be easier to hide. He would see what was in the storage locker, then decide.

He noticed the scratches Kate left in his reflection. Torching the house solved that little problem as well.

# Friday, 11:15 A.M.

When Milton entered the keycode to the storage locker and the lock buzzed, he was too surprised to open it at first. His fulminations on The Vulture's betrayal having reached a crescendo, he decided the man sent him on a wild goose chase for fun. The jerk was probably watching the feed of the security camera he'd glimpsed when he arrived. "Having a chuckle."

He pulled the door open and found a manila envelope. Extracting it, he left immediately, being sure to avert his face from the camera. He entered a Starbucks, bought a Vente Americano with four shots, and found a seat in the back. Placing the envelope in the center of the table, he gazed at it. Whatever was inside would determine the course of his life for many years. After taking a gulp of life-affirming nectar, he opened it.

There was a small device called a Bash Bunny, an easily purchased tool for conducting what were called hot plug attacks. It resembled a large flash drive and could be used to compromise any system. All you needed was physical access to the system's USB port. Scripts on the Bash Bunny would install whatever malware you wanted to deliver. The Technician preferred to write his own code, but… whatever. The other items were a square piece of white vinyl with an odd pattern printed on it in black. If you squinted at it just right, you could imagine a vulture among the dots. There was also a piece of paper. He fingered the vinyl, then set it aside and picked the paper up. The text on it was formatted with the most offensive font he'd ever seen.

"Got a stupid sense of humor, jerk face," he grumbled.

*To The Technician,*
*I will assume you know what to do when you get physical access to Nik's servers.*

"Nik. Like they're on a first name basis." Milton stared at the first line. It was the most ham-fisted attempt at a veiled insult he could imagine. Of course, he knew what to do. He was The Technician after all. "You get physical access to the server, it's game over. Not sure who you think you're dealing with."

He read on.

*As you know, Nik's developer app will not work on the new version of his home security system. But all is not lost. The pattern on the piece of vinyl can be used to fool the iris detection algorithm of the security system into disabling the entire system. It will work for both access points, the front door and the door to his server room.*

Milton eyed the square of vinyl. It was plausible, but he had no idea how The Vulture could have come up with that. As far as he knew, no one outside Cerberus had access to the system or the system's code. He shrugged. If it didn't work on the front door, he could just leave.

*I know you are 'famous' for your ability to craft a rootkit, but I have taken the liberty of providing one on the bash bunny.*

Milton glanced at the device. Did he trust it? The rest of the letter described how to access Nik's server after the rootkit was installed. He was forced to admit it was impressive.

*Best of luck and nice doing business with you, Milton.*
*The Vulture*

"Jackass."

He gazed across the coffee ship and noted the trash spilling out of the receptacle. "Should talk to the manager," he muttered.

Now, to get Nik and Alix out of their condo. He pulled out his burner phone and dialed his client in Cerberus.

## Friday, 12:12 P.M.

The deli was still crowded at one, but Nik, Alix and Dick Larsen found a small table near the window. Nik and Alix sipped their tea and watched Detective Larsen get himself organized before tucking into his Reuben and chips.

When he was ready, the detective took a bite, sat back, chewed and gestured to Nik. "Whadda ya got?"

"First, did the FBI know anything about The Technician?" Nik asked.

"They had to dig but found a few mentions of him. He's small-time. No history of violence. But they're looking into it."

"How about the drawing of him?" Alix asked.

"Circulated it and the photo of Ms. Munson. A slew of tips and sightings. The usual cranks calling in. We're following all the leads that seem solid. Nothing's panned out. The problem with the drawing is it looks like a million other guys."

Nik glanced at Alix while Dick took a bite of his sandwich, then he activated his tablet, opened the document Rashida compiled and laid it on the table next to Larsen's plate.

"What's this?"

"This is a report compiled by someone we hired to do a deep background check on two of our employees; Sally Thompson and Oki Tanaka."

Larsen took another bite and wiped his mouth with his napkin. "Deep background check? I assume this wasn't completely legal."

"Nothing illegal about it," Nik said. "That I know of, anyway."

"It's a gray area," Alix said. "Probably not admissible in court."

Larsen eyed them. "Okay." The detective continued to eat but listened while Nik explained the report. When Nik finished, Larsen said, "Corporate espionage is outside my jurisdiction."

"But someone at the FBI would be interested, surely," Alix said.

Larsen let his gaze fall to the tablet. "Okay. Send me the file. I'll run it up the chain of command. But... it doesn't get us any closer to who killed Ms. Munson."

"Or kidnaped Kate Munson," Alix said.

Larsen winced. "I'm sorry to tell you, but if you haven't received a ransom demand, Ms. Munson is probably dead."

"Is that what you told her parents?" Alix asked.

Larsen set his sandwich down, sat back and chuckled. "You don't have a very high opinion of me, do you?"

"We're proceeding on the assumption she's alive," Nik said, interrupting Alix's response.

Larsen shrugged. "Nothing you showed me leads to the murderer. Thompson and Tanaka have ironclad alibis." He waggled his fingers over the tablet. "And this apparently isn't Thompson's first go-round as a spy. You haven't shown me any evidence she resorts to murder. Could be a coincidence."

"We're working on that."

Larsen paused, the sandwich halfway to his mouth. He set it down, sat back, and waved his hand at them. "Working on it? You two? You want to let me in on your sleuthing?"

"We're working on the technical end with Ros — Officer Gutierrez."

Larsen nodded slowly. "Okay." He picked up a chip. "Is that it?"

Nik glanced at Alix, who shrugged. "For now," he said.

"Good. Send me the file. Now, if you don't mind, I only have an hour for lunch."

# Chapter 19

## Friday, 7:58 A.M.

Nik opened his office door to the line of developers awaiting his appearance. The young intern sitting by the door leapt to his feet and gave Nik a hopeful smile. Jerad Mullins. The University of Florida. Nik was about to ask him in when someone farther down the hall spoke.

"Nik."

The intern's face fell. Nik stepped into the hall and found Adam approaching. Hoping for a reprieve, Nik returned his smile. "What's up?"

"Nik, we've been invited to a party. All of us, Joel, you and I, some of the directors. You will definitely want to attend this soiree."

Soiree? The word was so unlike something Adam would say, Nik was instantly on alert. "Why? Where is it?"

Adam glanced past Nik to the line of developers, who were probably hanging on every word. He leaned close, as if he were sharing a secret, then raised his voice so no one could miss what he said. "It's on Ash Damán's yacht. It's moored in a marina in town." Nik frowned and was about to object. Then Adam pulled him into his office and closed the door. "I know how you feel about him, but you only have his public persona to go on. After ditching him at the sales event, you owe it to Joel and I to spend some time with him. After you get to know him better, we'll have that conversation again." He paused, then drove in the stake. "You know what a contract with Damán Enterprises would do for Cerberus. It would push us into the big leagues. I'll send you the details." Not giving Nik time to respond, he opened the door and raised his voice again. "You will not believe his yacht, and he's inviting many important people. Many potential customers. They'll all want to meet the great Nik Atherton."

Nik watched him strolling down the hall. He glanced at a hopeful-looking Jerad. Suddenly, the long line of petitioners wasn't the worst thing he could think of.

## Friday, 8:48 P.M.

Alix watched the security guard at the Marina check the guest list. She glanced at Nik who was gazing thoughtfully at the collection of exclusive yachts. "You ever want to buy a yacht?"

Nik blinked and focused on her. "Hmmm?"

She smiled and nodded to the marina.

"Ah." He gave her a sly grin. "You want to sail the Caribbean, have servants bring us rum punch while we lounge on the poop deck?"

"Poop deck?"

The guard gave them directions and waved them through the gate.

"It's a thing," Nik said. "Look it up. But in answer to your question; no, I have no interest in owning anything this ostentatious. Remember the sales reception a few nights ago attended by our host tonight…"

"Damán."

"That's the one. The next day Joel bored us for half an hour, salivating over a website selling yachts he could never afford."

"He seems like the type."

"Yes, he does. He was particularly enamored of one he said is very similar to the one we're going to tonight." He caught Alix's eye. "Three hundred million dollars." He stopped and swept a hand across one of the largest yachts in the marina. "Behold."

"Three hundred million dollars," Alix said, looking unimpressed. "Imagine what you could do with that money other than buy a boat."

"And the selling price is only the beginning. There's the crew to run it. Servants. Then you have fuel, berthing fees, maintenance, and I'm sure many other and sundry fees and expenses." He lifted an index finger and tipped his head to the side. "Ah, but this is no mere boat. Two hundred seventy-five feet long. Maximum speed seventeen knots. Room for twelve passengers. Luxury accommodations. Multiple bars, piano and a hot tub." He turned toward the yacht and spread his arms. "The works!" He fell silent, let his arms fall to his side, and they gazed at the yacht. "Although, for a man like Damán, all that amounts to chump change."

"It's still obscene."

He gave her a mischevious grin. "But he's a job creator."

"Yes, I'm sure it's an efficient use of all those resources." Alix walked toward the yacht.

"Not a fan of capitalism?" Nik asked in a teasing tone. When she turned on him with a thunderous expression, he put his hands up and took a step back.

She knew he was goading her, but she couldn't help herself. "You let men like Damán define the rules, it's no longer capitalism. Capitalism relies on free, efficient markets. Equal opportunities to acquire capital. That's the point of capitalism. Men like him rig the economy to allow them to hoard the capital and make sure the majority of the profits flow to them. It's oligarchy." She narrowed her eyes. "And I don't appreciate you winding me up just before we meet him."

"You're right. I'm sorry. I just get so turned on when you get all wonky."

She turned and headed up the stairs.

They were greeted by a crew member, who explained the layout of the yacht and directed them to the bar. They made their way aft on the lowest of three visible decks. They were on time, so there were few guests. When they arrived at the stern, an unlikely collection of beautiful men and women lounging around an elaborate seating area looked up without interest.

Nik leaned over and murmured, "Hired help?"

"Part of the sundry fees and expenses, you think?" Alix asked.

"Service without a smile, apparently."

"Maybe they're not on the clock yet."

They entered the cabin, where a few people gathered around a bar.

"Nik! Thank God you came!"

Alix turned and found Julie Swinson, Sales Directory, approaching, a scotch sloshing in one hand and a relieved smile on her face.

"Alix," she said with a small nod, then she drew close to Nik and said, "Isn't this yacht *amazing*? The other half, you know what I mean?"

Nik leaned away from her.

"Ash gave me the full tour earlier," she continued, oblivious to Nik's discomfort. "It's *amazing*."

"Yes, you said that," Nik said. "You've been here a while, have you?"

"Oh, yes. Adam and I came this afternoon. Ash asked us to come help prepare for the party."

"And did you?" Alix asked.

Sally's face went blank.

"Help prepare for the party."

"Oh. Well, Ash has an army of servants for that. We mostly watched and… discussed things."

Alix wanted to ask what things they discussed, but Nik said, "And drank, apparently."

"Oh, Ash stocks only the best. No rail brands here." She waved her glass at the bar. "Let's go see."

Nik and Alix watched her join Adam and Sally Thompson at the bar. "Were all the Cerberus directors invited?" Alix asked.

Nik shrugged. "There wasn't an email. I was told by Adam to be here. Why?"

"Feels like a sales thing. Just wondering why you need the HR director here. Sally doesn't usually attend these."

"Well, this isn't the usual venue for such affairs. Maybe Damán only wants to show off how *amazing* his boat is." He bent down and whispered. "But I suspect Sally is here at her employer's behest. Let's get a drink."

After procuring expensive but overrated chardonnays, they explored the yacht. Guests were arriving and filling the space. As prominent and wealthy citizens of New York, Nik and Alix recognized many of them, but weren't close to any of them. When they arrived on the top deck, where they found the hot tub, they were amused to find some of the beautiful people smiling and laughing as they mingled with wealthy guests. Everyone was already well lubricated.

"Someone's going to get naked and be in that hot tub before the night is over," Nik said.

"You got plans?"

"Strictly observational. You know we've been over most of this yacht and haven't seen Damán or Joel."

"And we haven't seen any of your other people, either," Alix said. "Other than Sally, Julie and Adam."

Nik gazed at her. "Select group, apparently."

"Selected for what? You don't know who in your organization agreed to this?"

"I assumed Adam. He's the one who told me about it."

"Is Adam particularly close to those others?" Seeing the uncertainty on his face, Alix rolled her eyes. "Why am I asking you?" Nik knew a lot of things, but what was going on in the personal lives of his closest associates might as well be quantum mechanics. "I need to find the restroom," she said, handing him her glass.

"Head."

"Excuse me?" she asked.

"It's called a head on a boat."

"Okay, well, while I go find the head, you get ahead of the situation and go find out why we're here."

"Clever," Nik said with a grin. He gestured to the hot tub. "But I'll wait for you here. You know, just in case."

Alix flagged down a passing crew member and got directions to the head, which, to her delight, he called a restroom. She made her way to the lower decks. Passing a bedroom that looked like a luxury room in an expensive hotel, she glimpsed Julie and Adam talking to the party's host, Ash Damán. She stopped, pressed her back to the wall, and listened. Even though she was deep in the yacht, party sounds made their voices indistinct.

She was edging closer to the door when Adam appeared. He stopped so abruptly that Julie bumped him from behind. It was only a moment, but Alix was sure she saw guilt in his expression. Maybe if her conversation with Nik hadn't already made her suspicious, she would have dismissed it. But she *was* suspicious, and Adam's reaction confirmed she should be.

"Alix," Julie slurred and squeezed past Adam. "Speak of the devil —"

"Alix Atherton," Damán said, practically shoving Julie aside as he exited the room.

Alix looked past him to Adam, who was retreating down the hall, pulling Julie with him. She looked up at Damán. "My name is Alix Crockett."

"Right. I forgot you didn't want to take Nik's name."

She gave him a wry smile. "They're just words, but somehow when they come out of your mouth, they're insulting. And ignorant."

His smile fell away for a moment, then returned, revealing more of what he was. Predatory and condescending. He edged farther into the hallway and stepped forward, so he loomed over her and forced her to press her back to the wall. "What could Nik have done to turn your head? I mean, what could you possibly see in that —"

Alix pitched her voice lower so he couldn't mistake her intent. "If you don't back up and give me space, I'll hurt you."

His face froze, then shocked disbelief appeared. She would have let it go, but he leered, bent toward her, and rested his arm on the wall beside her head. "You —"

She kneed him in the groin. Not too hard. But hard enough. It was cliché and not at all artful, but it was effective. He grunted and bent over. He was so close to her in the narrow hall, his forehead struck the wall beside her and his body left her no room to squeeze past him. His face was just above her shoulder, so she thrust her shoulder into his mouth, then shuffled sideways when he jerked upright. Only when she was out of reach did she stop. She studied him and was relieved to see no blood on his lips.

"You bitch!" he growled. "Nik is going to be sorry you did that."

Alix blinked. Nik? "What is it with you and Nik?" Before he could gather a response, she glanced into the bedroom where she had seen Damán talking to Adam and Julie, and spotted a bathroom. "Now, if you'll excuse me, I have to visit the head. If you're still here when I get back, I'll hurt you more." Then she entered the bedroom.

By the time she returned to the empty hall, she was having second thoughts. Damán was a despicable man, but he was wealthy and powerful. She wasn't worried he would do anything to hurt her on the yacht, but she was sure she had just created problems for Nik. Was she worried enough to apologize? No, she wasn't, and an apology wouldn't mean anything to a man like Damán, anyway. Deciding the damage was done, she went in search of Nik to tell him what Julie and Adam gave away.

She wasn't surprised to find Nik by the hot tub, leaning on the rail. When he spotted her, he grinned and nodded to the pool where two of the beautiful people and an older gentleman were frolicking naked.

"And it's not even that late," Nik said.

Alix watched him grinning at the spectacle. Should she tell him what Damán did? Would he confront the man? Yes, he would. She didn't know exactly what was going on here, but she knew a confrontation would complicate an already ambiguous situation. She and Nik never lied to one another. Well, not often. She would tell him, but not until later.

When he glanced at her and saw her face, he pushed himself upright and faced her. "What's wrong?"

She leaned in and told him about finding Damán talking to Adam and Julie, Adam's reaction to finding her there and what Julie almost said before Adam dragged her away. "They were talking about me, apparently, and Adam and Damán didn't want me to know."

When she was done, Nik asked, "What did Damán say?" She hesitated the smallest amount, but Nik noticed. "Are you okay?"

"I'm fine, and I'll tell you the whole thing. Later. Right now, we need to think clearly about what's going on here."

Nik held her gaze for a long moment, then nudged her away from the flock of voyeurs around the pool. They found a relatively quiet space by the rail on a lower deck.

Nik leaned his arms on the rail. "Adam and Julie are obviously trying to pressure me into going into business with Damán." When she frowned, he said, "They know you don't like Damán, and I'm pretty sure Adam thinks of me as a nerdy wimp. He's sure you do our thinking for us." He shrugged. "Not surprising they'd want his business. Any sort of deal with his company would be the biggest we've ever had. Julie and Joel are supposed to sell Cerberus products, so you can't blame them for trying."

"You've made your feelings on the subject very clear. And it's not like they're trying to convince you with rational arguments. There's something underhanded about this whole thing. It's not the way you treat someone you supposedly trust. I don't like it. It's not the way Cerberus operates. Or at least it hasn't been."

Nik pursed his lips and looked out at the marina. "No. It doesn't feel right. Adam told me he wanted me to come tonight so

I could get to know Damán. Said it would change my mind. But they don't seem to be making much of an effort. I haven't seen Joel or Damán once and haven't talked to Adam. Feels like something else going on."

He straightened. "Let's go make our excuses and blow this gin joint." As they were making their way toward the stern, Nik, walking behind her, asked, "You think I can take Damán?"

Alix grinned and mumbled too low for him to hear, "No, but I can."

They found the host on the lowest deck, lounging on a wide sofa, arms extended along the back, surrounded by some of the beautiful people and other fawning guests.

"Ah, Nik Atherton!" Damán boomed as Nik and Alix appeared. "Having fun, I hope."

"Yes," Nik said. "It's a very fancy boat. You should be proud."

Some of the sycophants laughed and sneered, but a shadow flickered across Damán's expression. "I could buy you for what I paid for this *boat*."

"I'm sure you *think* that," Nik said, silencing the uncomfortable laughter.

Damán gazed at him, his lips twitching. Then he smiled. "You'd be surprised what I can buy." His eyes flicked toward Alix, then came back to Nik.

Alix was about to intervene, afraid Nik was going to lunge at him.

Nik laughed. Not a ha ha laugh. Not a sarcastic chortle or a derisive chuckle. This was a deep belly laugh. He bent over, slapped his thigh, then straightened and pointed. "Whooo! I have to hand it to you, Damán, you would make an *amazing* Bond villain."

Most of the sycophants edged away from Damán. Two of them found the courage to flee.

"I'm looking forward to the day when the great Nik Atherton is cut down to *size*."

Nik said to Alix, "See what he did there? He's taller than I am and he thinks that matters." He said to Damán. "Very clever and right in character." Growing serious, he said, "Don't get up. We'll see ourselves out."

Alix watched Damán's face as his eyes followed Nik toward the exit. There would be fallout from this night. Nik might be able to run verbal circles around the idiot, but Damán was a spoiled child with billions of dollars. His temper tantrums were seismic.

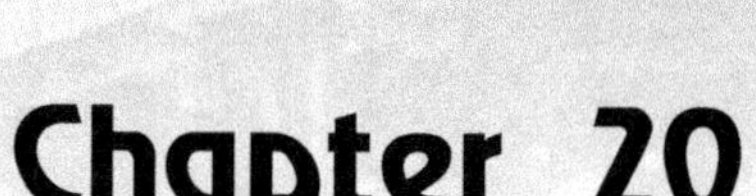

# Chapter 20

## Friday, 8:34 P.M.

Assuming The Vulture's exploit of Nik's security system would work, Milton concluded the trickiest part of the job was getting into the building. He considered bluffing his way past the guard in the lobby. Pretend to be a plumber or a distant relative of one of the residents. He could usually learn enough about someone to sound convincing. That was his usual method. The people who worked security in residential buildings weren't usually the cream of the crop. There was almost always a weak link who could be snowed.

But he didn't have much time, so he scouted the perimeter of the building the previous night. As luck would have it, the company that provided the electronic locks for the building was one Milton had encountered before. When he arrived after dark, the loading dock in the back of the building was deserted. The lock on the door that would admit him onto the floor with the building's mechanicals and HVAC was one with which he was well acquainted. Minutes later, he was inside.

Without the building's keyfob, he couldn't ride the elevators, but he was delighted to find the lock on the stairwell was another one he had seen before. Now he only needed to climb eleven stories. There were security cameras in the stairwell, but he chose this time because he'd watched the guard from across the street the previous night and noticed he tended to become engrossed in the Yankees' game when no one was looking. Milton also wore a black suit and tie, so once he was above the basement, he would look like he belonged. Keeping the bill of his fedora pulled low, he climbed.

When he reached the tenth floor, he paused to catch his breath, then he swept out of the stairwell into the dimly lit hall, as if he owned the place. He was alone. When he found Nik's condo, he stood outside the camera's view and studied the security lock while he extracted the piece of plastic with the code The Vulture provided. Mumbling, "Here goes nothing," he slid along the wall and dangled the code in front of the camera. The lock immediately whirred, and the small red light above the camera went dark.

"Well, fuck me," he said, as he opened the door. "Worth every penny." Slipping into the condo, he closed the door, then turned around and found himself face-to-face with a cat.

The Technician and the cat eyed one another. The initial thrill of fear when he spotted an animal dissipated. "You're not a dog," he said finally and looked past the cat into the condo. He had taken a step when he paused and looked down at the cat, who was still gazing at him in that arrogant way cats do. "I know you."

His fingers came up to brush the scabby streaks on his cheek. It was Kate's cat. What was it doing here? The only explanation was that Nik and Alix brought it back from Kate's home. And the only reason they would have done that was they were looking for her. That was why he was getting so much heat from his source in Cerberus. Nik made the connection between The Technician infecting his servers and Kate escorting him.

"Can't worry about that now," he mumbled. He considered kicking the cat, but the memory of the animal climbing his leg was still fresh. He glanced at his watch and, making a wide berth around the cat, he went in search of Nik's server room. It was on the first floor, next to what looked like his office. The server room was on a separate security system, but the piece of vinyl The Vulture provided worked on the lock. He entered, then gave a low whistle at Nik's setup. It was a small room with only one rack. But the rack was packed with equipment. Two enterprise-class servers, a multi-terabyte storage appliance, a network switch and firewall. There was enough computing power in this room to support multiple medium-sized businesses.

Unfortunately, powering down such complex systems wasn't like rebooting a laptop. By the time he inserted the Bash Bunny to install the rootkit, brought everything down, then restarted everything, an hour had passed.

Feeling elated, he double-checked the status lights on all the equipment and got down on his knees and made sure he hadn't inadvertently dropped something again. He patted his pocket where the Bash Bunny was secured, then he turned toward the exit, looked above the door, and noticed the camera. "Well, shit." It should have been dead, but the red light above the lens showed it was active. He was sure it was dark when he entered the room.

"Fucking Vulture!" He ducked his head, turned and scanned the server room. Where was the video stored? He checked his watch. Not enough time to search for it, and it was probably saved to the cloud, anyway. Leaving the server room, he hurried to the front door, threw a kick at the cat which missed, activated the security system on the keypad beside the door, then exited. He fumed all the way to the basement, stopping only before stepping out onto the loading dock.

It might not have been a complete disaster. He got the rootkit installed. Would it work? Finding an isolated corner, he sank to sit cross-legged, opened his laptop and activated the Wi-Fi hotspot on his phone. He'd memorized the instructions The Vulture gave him for connecting to the rootkit. Still, when it connected on the first try, he was so surprised, he lifted his hands from his keyboard and stared at the screen. It was a sickly yellow with the words, "Welcome to the Thunderdome!" in a nauseating green centered on the screen.

He squinted at it. "I don't get it," he mumbled. "That isn't remotely clever." Shaking his head, he dismissed The Vulture's lame attempt at humor, connected to Nik's server and got to work.

Fortunately, Nik was exceedingly well organized. It only took Milton half an hour to identify the code he wanted on Nik's server and another fifteen minutes to get it streaming to the file share in the cloud. Once he was sure it was running smoothly, he left it to run and packed up.

Fifteen minutes later he was strutting through Central Park, whistling *Simple Man* between bites of pizza. Mission accomplished. He could hardly believe it. Now all he had to do was deliver Nik's code to his client, deal with that little problem in his basement, and he was golden. He wouldn't even have to activate one of his bug-out plans. In a month, he would be lazing on the beach at an all-inclusive resort in Jamaica. Maybe Aruba. No. Ibiza. That was it.

It was unfortunate that Nik had an image of him from the security camera. His initial thought was The Vulture betrayed him. But if that were the case, why did he allow Milton to upload Nik's code? As he sat in the basement exploring Nik's server, he concluded there was a bug in The Vulture's exploit of the security system. The camera system rebooted early. That was the only explanation.

Every security agency in the world would know what he looked like. It would be a complication he would have to deal with, but it wouldn't put him out of business. And after this payday, he could retire if he liked.

## Friday, 11:25 P.M.

Nik gazed out the window in the rideshare on the way home. The confrontation with Damán might have been fun, but as the adrenaline ebbed, reality reasserted itself. There would be consequences. Damán was a powerful man with a toddler's penchant for umbrage.

Not until they were near home, did either of them speak. "This Technician would have to be very expensive."

"Yes," Nik said softly. Their eyes met, both of them thinking the same thing. But neither of them said it.

They didn't speak again until Nik entered their condo. He paused in the doorway, blocking Alix's entrance.

"What's wrong?" she asked.

"Don't know. Something. No cat." Alan Turing always greeted Alix at the door. Never Nik. He tried not to take it personally. "But there's…"

He peered down the hall. It was silent. But something wasn't right. Stepping lightly, he headed down the hall toward the living room, then froze in the doorway.

The figment looked as if it was waiting for him. It was the same one he saw outside his office, except it had exchanged the combat boots with pink polka-dot platform sneakers. It sat cross-legged on the floor. Alan Turing sat beside it, the tip of his tail twitching. Both of them gave Nik speculative looks.

"Nik?" Alix asked behind him.

Nik entered the room slowly, focusing on the figment and trying to decide how to proceed. No figment had ever entered his home. None had ever paid attention to him beyond a few cryptic words. And he rarely saw the same figment more than once. This figment showed something he had never seen before: intention. It obviously wanted something from him or wanted to tell him something. The problem was, his previous conversations with them had never been very productive.

"Is it a figment?" Alix asked as she stepped up beside him.

The figment's head swiveled birdlike toward Alix.

"You're back," Nik said, deciding to see if it would initiate whatever conversation it wanted to have.

The figment's gaze came back to Nik. It nodded.

Nik waited, but it didn't speak. "Why?"

The figment grinned. "I appreciate what you are doing for…"

The word that followed entered Nik's head, but left no trace. There was a sound that must have been a word. He was sure of it. But he had no recollection of what it was. "I'm sorry. I didn't get that."

The figment's grin widened. "No." It reached over and scritched Alan Turing's head. The cat lifted its head and let its eyes slide shut. "He's a very nice cat." The figment looked up at him, frowning now. "But he misses his person."

Nik stared at the figment's fingers on the cat's head. How was the cat feeling her touch? Something tickled the back of his mind, but he was too occupied with dealing with the figment to bring it forward. Alan Turing blinked slowly, then he gave Nik what he swore was a reproachful glare. "The cat misses Kate?"

The figment nodded and gave Nik a proud mother smile.

Nik's head was so full of questions, he couldn't seem to shake one loose.

Fortunately, Alix, who was only getting one side of the bizarre conversation, was more clearheaded. "Ask it if it can help us find her?"

"Do you know where she is?" Nik asked.

The figment, who looked at Alix when she spoke, returned its gaze to Nik and shook its head.

"Apparently not," Nik said, frustrated. The implications of it telling him Alan Turing missing Kate struck him. "But she's alive."

It nodded.

"Can you help us find her?"

"Maybe," it said, then rose so suddenly, Nik flinched. He rooted his feet to the spot as it prowled toward him, grinning despite his discomfort. It stopped very close and peered up at him, its head tipped to the side. It had no scent.

It reached up and pressed its index finger to his forehead. He was surprised that it was corporeal. He could feel the fingertip on his forehead. And it was surprisingly warm. Hot even. How could it be invisible to everyone else if it had substance? The finger remained there for a long moment, then something shifted inside his head. Nothing physical. He hoped. It was something in his mind. He jerked his head back, breaking contact, swiped his hand across his forehead, then looked at it, expecting it to be smeared with blood. Or brains.

By the time he looked for the figment again, it was gone. Did it vanish or did it leave like a person? He glanced at a perplexed Alix. Almost asked her if she saw where it went, then remembered himself. He hurried to the hall. It was empty. Turning back toward Alix, he said, "It's gone."

"What did it do to you?"

"It... touched me," Nik said and put his finger to his forehead. "Here."

Looking alarmed, she said, "We're going to the ED right now."

"I don't need to see a doctor," Nik said dismissively. "I don't think." He shook his head and waved a hand in front of his eyes. "I'm fine. Besides what am I going to tell a doctor? A figment of my imagination touched me?"

Alix's frown relaxed. "That's a good point." She pulled her phone from her clutch and toggled on the flashlight. "Sit," she said, and motioned to the sofa. After he complied, she flashed the light in his eyes, then quickly withdrew it. After repeating the procedure on both eyes, she turned off the flashlight and held a finger up in front of him. "Follow my finger with your eyes." When she was done, she stood back and gazed speculatively at him. "What's my name?"

"Nicola."

Her eyes narrowed. "Not funny. What happened when… it touched you?"

"I don't know. Something inside my head… shifted."

"Shifted. What did it say? Something about the cat."

"It said… it appreciated what we were doing for the… cat because he — the cat — misses his person. Kate."

Alix stared at him as if all her fears about what the figments suggested about his sanity had been confirmed. "What?!"

"I know, right?"

"Why did it touch you?"

"It said it was going to help us find Kate."

"So, she's alive."

"Apparently. If a figment is to be believed, anyway."

They were quiet for a moment. Alan Turing waltzed over and twined around Alix's leg. She picked him up. He lay in her arms and stared at Nik. "Well, do you… do you know where she is?" she asked. "Maybe it… put some knowledge in your mind."

"No. I don't know any more than I did before." He gave her a perturbed frown. "Maybe Hacksie is a figment. He, she, did the same thing. Said he's going to help, then did nothing."

Alix's lips twisted. "Maybe it's a delayed thing. You'll have a dream, then you'll wake up in the middle of the night and BANG. You'll know right where to go."

"Bang?"

Alix shrugged. "You don't know. You feel anything going on in your head or that figment comes back, tell me."

"Wait!" he said, the thought that nagged at him while he talked to the figment coming into focus. "Remember when we were driving out to Long Island? You suggested that if a figment could affect something in the world that someone else, other than me, could see, that would prove the figments aren't just in my head?"

She nodded.

"It scratched Alan's head." He gazed at her. "And the cat responded."

Alix looked down at the cat in her arms.

"It closed its eyes," Nik said. He stretched his neck up. "And lifted its head into its fingers."

Alix looked at Nik, a smile growing slowly on her face. "I'm going to bed." She paused. "You want to come?"

Nik hurried to follow.

# Chapter 21

## Saturday, 4:34 A.M.

"Someone turned off the security system. Last night," Nik said. It was the morning after they found the figment in their living room. He had just called Alix into his office, and they were both looking at the dashboard for the security system on one of his monitors. "I don't check it often, but I was curious if the figment triggered anything."

"The figment turned it off?"

"No. It was disabled at seven and came back on an hour before we got home."

"Someone turned it off. How could they do that?" Alix asked.

"I have no idea. Exploited some flaw I don't know about, maybe. Hard to believe. We hire the best pentesters." When she gave him a quizzical look, he said, "Penetration testers. People with the skills to look for vulnerabilities." He shook a finger at the screen. "But the odd thing is, the cameras came back on before the rest of the system. And we got this." He pointed to a browser window on another monitor.

It was a frame from the security camera in the server room. A man wearing a suit and a fedora looked up at the camera. The dumbfounded surprise in his expression would have been comical in any other circumstances.

"That was the best shot of him, believe it or not," Nik said.

"Looks surprised, like he wasn't expecting the camera to be on."

"That was my impression as well. The rest of the video shows he left in a hurry. He armed the system before leaving. Tried to kick the cat on the way out." When she frowned down at Alan sitting beside her on the floor, he said, "He missed."

"So, he turned off your supposedly impregnable security system, got into your server room where he did the tiny gods know what, and escaped." She met his gaze, and they both said, "The Technician."

"Got to be," Nik said. "Hacksie said he would try again, and this isn't a great shot, but it looks similar to the tech I saw at Cerberus."

"But he screwed up." She said, gesturing to the photo.

"I already knew what he looks like. I saw him."

"Yes, but now we have a photo." She pulled a chair over, sat, and pulled the keyboard and mouse close. "When I was a public health nurse, I worked with hoarders. Sometimes they weren't all there, so if we wanted to find family, we had to use their photographs to search the Internet."

While she worked, Nik said, "I'm not so sure it was The Technician who screwed up. Someone must have turned the cameras on. The firewall log shows my server opened a connection to the outside just before the cameras were activated."

Alix stopped typing and looked at him. "Who would have done that?"

"No idea. The sending address was untraceable."

"Nicola?"

He sighed, sat back and wiped a hand across his mouth. "The code is still there, but there was a data stream through the firewall that ran most of the night."

"Someone stole your code."

"That would be the best explanation. I've... closed the firewall to the server. Too late."

"That's..." Alix sat back and held his gaze.

"I know. There's a chance... if we can find him before..." He gazed at the monitor on which the icon that opened Nicola's software was visible. "I should have deleted the code when you told me to."

Alix hesitated. She opened her mouth. To tell him I told you so or to console him, he didn't know. Then she looked at the computer screen and said, "Let's not give up hope yet. We have to find him to find Kate." She gestured to the screen. "This man is almost a ghost. This is the only image of him I could find."

The picture was obviously taken in an office breakroom at a holiday party. Among the wreaths and garlands, a coffee machine, microwave and refrigerator were visible in the background. The five people smiling happily at the camera looked as if they were well into their celebration. Alix pointed out a man in the background. His expression was identical to the one in their security camera footage. "That's him."

"It is."

"This is from a social media feed. The date was December, a year and a half ago. I don't know how this helps us, though. Looks like an office party, but it could be any company."

Nik pointed to a cup one of the partygoers held. "This is the SecureStack logo. Me and their CEO go way back. Maybe he would know something." He picked up his phone.

"You're calling him at 4:30 in the morning on a Saturday?"

"He'll want to know this," Nik said and tapped speaker phone.

"But you could tell him at eight just as easily."

"Nah. He'll be happy… Hold on."

"What the fuck are you calling at… what is it?!"

"Four thirty," Nik said cheerfully. "Good morning, Aston. It's been a while."

"Not long enough. Hold on." It sounded as if he was moving, then a door closed and he said, "What is it?"

"Alix and I — Alix says hi by the way."

Alix rolled her eyes. "Don't let him spread the blame. I told him this was a bad idea."

"I never had a doubt," Aston said.

"Anyway…" Nik said. "If we can get back to the matter at hand."

"Please."

"Alix and I found a photo online from your company's holiday party."

"Seriously?"

"Yes, well, when you hear what I have to say," Nik said testily, "I think you'll be plenty happy I called."

Aston was quiet for a moment, then he said, "Go ahead."

"There is a man in the background of the picture who we're pretty sure goes by the alias The Technician." There was silence. "You heard of him?"

"I have." Then. "How sure are you about this?"

"Ninety-nine percent."

"Well, shit. That explains a lot."

"Why?" Nik asked.

"This isn't widely known for obvious reasons, but we had a big data breach January of last year. Our people had no idea how it happened, so we brought in a team from CyberTech. No one else I know has heard of The Technician, but the CyberTech top guy mentioned him. Talked about him like he's some kind of god. They never could figure out if it was him or how it happened."

"I can't help you with the how, but it's safe to say The Technician was responsible."

"Why are you looking for this guy?"

"We're pretty sure he killed Reggie from Sunset Tech so he could infiltrate our data center, and he kidnapped one of our interns. A young woman named Kate Munson." Nik's eyes cut to Alix. "And he broke into our condo last night."

"I heard about Reggie and your intern. Didn't know about the breach of your data center. What's he got against you?"

Nik glanced at Alix, who pursed her lips. "No idea."

Aston hesitated. "Okaay. What can I do?"

"We need any information about this guy you can give us," Nik said. "I'll send you some photos. The one from your holiday party and one from my security camera. If you can get people started on it later this morning, we would appreciate it. Kate's life might depend on it."

"I'll make it a priority."

After Nik closed the connection, he and Alix looked at one another. "Feels like we're running out of time," Nik said.

"The figment said she was alive. Right?" She hesitated. "You, uh, didn't have any unusual dreams, did you? Wake up with any startling revelations?"

"No, unfortunately." He rubbed his forehead where the figment touched him. "It doesn't seem to have had *any* effect."

She gazed at him, one brow rising.

"The cat responded."

"I'm sure he did." She gestured to his monitor. "What are you going to do about Nicola?"

Nik held her gaze for a moment, then glanced at his monitor. "I'm afraid that bird has flown the coop. Let's concentrate on getting Kate back. I'll figure out what to do about Nicola after."

## Saturday, 9:23 A.M.

Molly Hatchet blared from the speakers in Milton's study as he scrolled through the files downloaded from Nik's server. He didn't know anything about artificial intelligence, or how to code it, but he recognized the firewall code, and Nik was assiduous about commenting his code and signing it. That confirmed the code was authentic.

He drummed on the desk and sang at the top of his lungs.

*We're flirtin' with disaster*
*Ya'll know what I mean*

The AI-assisted firewall code was worth millions on the open market all by itself. It occurred to him he might contact a few people willing to pay, no questions asked. But his deal with the client was exclusive, and after the Russians showed up on his doorstep, he just wanted this job to end. No need to be greedy. He would hand over a sample of the firewall code. Once they confirmed it and paid him, he would deliver the rest and could wash his hands of the whole affair.

He stopped the song and dialed his client. They answered on the third ring.

"Got it," he said. "I'll send over an invitation to a shared drive for the first twenty megabytes. As soon as I receive the balance of my fee, I'll send the rest." He closed the connection.

It was time to take care of his Kate problem.

Milton girded himself as he descended the stairs to the basement, feeling ridiculous at the butterflies roiling his stomach. She was a twenty something year-old woman who couldn't weigh more than 120 pounds. But as he stood outside the door, mentally rehearsing the coming confrontation, his breath came fast and shallow. "Two minutes from now, it will all be over."

He double-checked the midazolam dose in the syringe. Enough to render her unconscious in seconds. He would take her out onto the East River late that night and dump her overboard. If they found the body, the coroner would conclude she drowned. But Milton wasn't taking any chances this time. He also carried a Glock 17, though he preferred not to shoot her. Cleaning blood from unsealed concrete wasn't as easy as one would think.

His mistake during his previous encounters was warning her by using the window in the door. This time, he would surprise her. Shoving the gun in his pocket, he slowly unlocked the door and withdrew the bolt. Flexing his knees, he turned the knob. Then, taking a breath, he thrust the door open, planted himself in the doorway and drew his pistol.

The girl lay on her side in the middle of the room, facing away from him. Asleep, or too weak to respond. He leveled the gun and watched her. Maybe he should just shoot her to be safe. But she didn't move when the door banged against the doorstop, so he decided it would be safe to inject her with the anesthetic. He just needed to be quick. The door bounced and swung slowly closed. He raised the hand holding the gun to arrest its momentum and took a step.

Quick as a cat, Kate spun toward him. He glimpsed the flashlight spinning through the air, flinched away and lifted the hand holding the syringe to shield his face. An electric jolt of pain radiated from his temple when the flashlight bounced off his skull.

Panicked, he forced his eyes open and squinted at the she-demon's snarling face coming at him. He swung the pistol toward her. She veered to the side and slammed into the door, driving it into the hand holding the pistol. The gunshot was deafening in the small space. The bullet ricocheted off the steel door and clipped the big toe on his left foot.

He screeched. Kate threw her weight against the door, slamming it against him again, forcing him to take a step back. Glimpsing her face in the gap between the door and the jamb, he swung his gun hand up and launched the pistol into the room. He gaped at it in the wedge of light emitted by the nearly closed door before it disappeared. His thoughts oddly syrupy, he gazed at his hand, flopping at the end of his wrist. "Wha —"

Seeing her scrambling after the gun, he just managed to pull the door shut as she drew down on him. Spastic fingers fumbling the bolt home, he fell forward, face against the door, slid to the floor and rolled onto his side.

Flopping onto his back, he licked dry lips and gazed up at a ceiling that wouldn't remain still. "Huh." His hand came up and swiped at a burning sensation on his cheek, and came away with the syringe. "Well, shi —" His last thought before darkness took him was, 'She's armed.'

# Chapter 22

## Saturday, 10:02 A.M.

For the next few hours, Nik and Alix avoided one another. For Alix's part, she was afraid to confront what the events of the previous night mean for Kate. She suspected Nik was having similar thoughts. But when Aston called to tell them he might have something, they both migrated to their comfort zone. Nik stood at the kitchen island, the Times spread out in front of him. Alix sat across from him, sipping coffee, gazing out the window at a cloudy day.

"If The Technician got what he wanted," Alix asked and looked at Nik, "what incentive does he have to keep Kate alive?"

Nik lifted his gaze to her, took a deep breath, and chose not to answer. "Where would he take her?"

Alix pursed her lips, more relieved than annoyed. "Not my realm of expertise, but… If this is part of his regular MO, then he might have a place specifically for this purpose. A bunker out of town, maybe. If it was a one-off, he might have taken her to his home."

"Let's assume he doesn't regularly kidnap people. He's a cybercriminal. Kidnapping people is messy."

"Then she's at his home."

"And even if *she* isn't, *he'll* be there. Probably a house and not an apartment."

"How do we find his home? Does he live in the metropolitan area?"

Before Nik could answer, his phone beeped. He glanced at the screen and said, "Aston." He put it on speaker and said, "Aston. I hope you have good news."

"I might. It seems this technician person was seeing one of our archivists for two months before the data breach. He ghosted her just after the office party."

"Does she still work for you?"

"She does. For now. At least until we find out exactly what happened. Our people receive training to recognize this type of social engineering attack. She ignored all the warning signs."

"We'd like to talk to her. Alix and I."

"Of course. The head of our legal team and I will have to be present."

"I don't have to remind you, time is of the essence. Can we meet today?"

"She's here at our office. Can you be here within the hour?"

"We'll be there," Nik said and closed the connection.

Alix put her cup in the sink and said, "Let's go."

# Saturday, 11:20 A.M.

"She's in here. Tanya Winston," Aston said outside the closed door of a conference room. The building was nearly deserted on a Saturday. "She's distraught. I'm not sure what you'll be able to get out of her. She doesn't remember much."

He was reaching for the doorknob when Alix said, "Let me talk to her."

Nik and Aston hesitated.

"Alone," Alix said. "She's much more likely to confide in another woman without everyone watching."

Aston shook his head and was about to speak when Nik said, "I understand there are complex legal issues involved, but a woman's life may be at stake." He held Aston's gaze for a moment. "You can trust Alix."

Aston hesitated. "Of course." He opened the door and spoke to the four people sitting across from the woman who must be Tanya. "Everyone out." He stepped back to allow Alix to enter the room. "Not you, Ms. Winston," he said when she started to rise.

"As your legal representative, I would like to know your intentions," one of the men sitting across from Tanya said.

"A woman's life is at stake, and Ms. Winston may have information that might save her." He gestured to Alix. "Alix will talk to her alone."

"I want it on the record that I object to this."

"Understood. Now if you will." Aston gestured to the door and whispered to Alix, "You have fifteen minutes."

When the door closed, Alix examined the distraught woman. It was obvious she barely had time to get herself together after they woke her. She wore jeans and an oversized sweatshirt. Her short Afro was uneven. Her eyes were red-rimmed, and tear tracks streaked her cheeks. When she peeked up at Alix from lowered eyes, Alix came around and took the chair beside her. She was thinking of a delicate way to begin the conversation when Tanya surprised her.

Her face hardened. "I know you. From that magazine. You're Alix Crockett."

Alix hesitated. "I am."

Tanya's eyes narrowed, the uncertainty in her expression giving way to speculation. "What are you doing here?"

Alix had intended to take a sympathetic approach with her, but that obviously wasn't required. "Why the act? The tears? The whimpering?"

Tanya glanced at the door. "Answer my question first. What did he mean about a woman's life was at stake?"

"This man in that picture from the office party is called The Technician. He's kidnapped one of Nik's interns. A woman named Kate Munson. We need to find her, and to do that, we need to know everything you can tell us about him." Tanya's frown lost its suspicious edge. "I promise not to divulge anything you don't want me to."

Tanya's eyes went to the door again.

"If you're worried about your job, Nik can speak to them."

Tanya actually snorted and waved a hand. "I could care less about this job. I just need to make sure they don't blacklist me." She fell silent and gazed at Alix. "I believe you're telling the truth."

"I am." Alix waited, letting Tanya think.

"Give me your phone." Before Alix could ask why, Tanya said. "They took my phone to look for evidence." She gave Alix an angry frown. "Probably having a laugh over the photos."

Alix unlocked her phone and handed it over.

Tanya dialed and put it to her ear. "We'll help you," she said while it rang. "Anything to bring that son of —" She smiled suddenly. "Hello, Mary. It's a code red." Alix heard a woman's excited response even without the speakerphone on. "We'll meet at the usual place at…" She looked at Alix, a lift in her brows.

"Seven tonight?"

"Seven tonight." A moment later, she said, "Right. We got someone big on the case. I think we got him this time." She hung up, a wide smile on her face, then handed the phone to Alix.

"Clancy's Pub," she said. "It's right down the street." She looked past Alix to the door again. "We'll tell you everything we know."

"We?"

"I'm not his only victim in New York."

Before Alix could press her, the door opened, and Aston entered. "Time," he said. He was followed by the four people who were with Tanya when Alix arrived.

Alix rose and joined Nik in the hall.

Aston, who followed her, asked, "Did she remember anything useful?"

"No, I'm afraid she's so distraught, she can't remember anything. Or doesn't want to."

"I'm sorry. If we discover anything that seems useful, I'll give Nik a call."

"Thank you," Nik said. He shook Aston's hand and followed Alix.

"You lied to him," Nik murmured while they waited for the elevator. "You did learn something?"

Alix gave him an enigmatic smile and said, "Maybe."

## Saturday, 7:04 P.M.

Nik stopped Alix and Rosa outside Clancy's Pub at seven. Rosa had been uncharacteristically morose since they picked her up at her apartment in Queens. He brought her because he promised to keep her in the loop, but if she was going to continue to be withdrawn, he would rather have left her at home.

"What is going on?" he asked her.

She looked away, licked her lips, then looked at him and said, "I quit. I'm no longer employed by the NYPD."

"What? Why?"

"Larsen and my superior came to me with that file Rashida created for you. Told me I should use my relationship with you to find out who you used." She gave a small shrug. "I could have lied and done a shit job. Told them I couldn't find out who it was. But that felt dirty. So, I resigned."

"Oh, Rosa," Alix said. "We're sorry."

Rosa sighed. "Not your fault. You asked us if it was okay. Money isn't a problem. Shida makes four times what I made. It's just…" She rested her hands on her hips and gave her head a shake. "It's not so bad. I was only a cop because my father was, and I didn't want to be a corporate drone. Not sure what I'm going to do now."

Alix and Nik exchanged a grin.

"What?" Rosa asked.

"Want to work for one of the premier digital security companies in the world?" Alix asked.

Rosa looked from Alix to Nik. "What are you saying?"

They laughed. "The interview is ongoing," Nik said.

"Corporate drone?" Rosa asked, a tentative smile quivering her lips.

"I think we can do better than that," Nik said. "In the meantime, we need to be focused for this meeting. You ready?"

"Let's do it," Rosa said.

When they entered the pub, Tanya, looking much more put together, spotted them and waved. The *pub* was in a strip mall, a plastic imitation of an Irish pub. Ridiculous images of leprechauns, pots of gold and other garish decorations to satisfy Americans' expectations of Irishness couldn't mask the cheap construction.

Tanya sat at a table in a corner with a younger woman, both with half-empty glasses of Guinness. They watched Nik, Alix and Rosa approach with broad smiles.

Nik introduced himself and Alix, then gestured to Rosa. "This is Rosa Guitierrez. She's a consultant for Cerberus who has expertise in this type of crime."

Tanya introduced her companion. "This is Mary." She leaned forward and murmured, "We don't use last names."

Before she could continue, Alix asked, "You've both had experience with this man, The Technician?"

They nodded, and Mary said, "Though we hadn't heard the nomenclature The Technician until today."

"How did you meet?" Nik asked.

They glanced at one another, then Mary gestured to Tanya. "Go ahead. You brought us together."

"Well, that man… The Technician ghosted me. I mean, it happens, right? To everyone. Dating in today's world…" She rolled her eyes and Mary nodded. "I was upset, but it wasn't like I wasn't used to it." She paused, looking embarrassed, then she glanced at Mary and her expression hardened. "When we had that big data breach, I knew it had to be him. He pretended he was clueless about technology, but, you know, you can tell if someone is in the know. Terms he dropped into conversation without realizing. The way he used his phone." The two conspirators nodded knowingly at one another. This was obviously well trod ground. "And it was just too big a coincidence. He ghosts me, then we have the breach." She sat up straight and slapped her hand on the table. "No one could figure it out." She paused, letting a small triumphant smile take the place of her frown. "Then I saw that picture someone posted on social media. It was him. A stroke of luck. He never let me take pictures of him. And we know why, don't we?"

"Same here," Mary said.

"So I posted it on Reddit," Tanya said. "I asked if anyone else had been victimized by this man."

"And Mary responded?" Alix asked.

Tanya's head bobbed enthusiastically. "Wasn't just us. There's two more. One in England and one in Australia. We mostly meet on Zoom. We took the picture off Reddit. Didn't want to spook him."

"Plus…" Mary said.

"We're worried about our employers finding out," Tanya said.

"Why didn't you go to the authorities? Your employers?" Rosa asked.

They exchanged guilty looks.

Nik shook his head, but before he spoke, Alix caught his eye and gave him a warning look.

"So," Nik said. "You compare your stories, looking for something that would help you find him."

Before he could get too excited, Alix doused his enthusiasm. "You haven't found anything, obviously." When she caught Nik's eye, she said, "He's still out there, and he's comfortable enough to kill Reggie and kidnap Kate."

"Kill?" Mary asked. They glanced at one another nervously. "We had no idea he was capable of that."

"That's good news," Nik said. "That means he doesn't usually resort to violence."

"But this killing and kidnapping happened here in New York recently?" Mary asked, growing excited again. When Nik and Alix nodded, she said, "Then maybe he's here. We can catch him."

"Right," Alix said. "And we need to find him soon if we want to save the woman he kidnapped."

"What can we do?" Tanya asked.

"To start, you can tell us your stories. Every detail you can remember. The smallest thing can be significant, even if it doesn't seem like it."

"Okay," Tanya said. She explained how she met The Technician while jogging. Dates for coffee were followed by dinner, Broadway shows, and museums. She thought it was getting serious, but could never get him to discuss their future.

Mary's case was similar to Tanya's. He'd overwhelmed her with attention and gifts. "He was kind, funny, good-looking, but not overly so, you know? I thought he really —"

"Cared about you," Tanya finished when she couldn't.

"And he ghosted you?" Alix asked.

When she nodded, Nik asked, "What happened at your company after?"

She shrugged. "Nothing. At least nothing I've heard of."

"What does your employer do?" Nik asked.

"We're PermaSystems. We manufacture high-end storage systems."

"I've heard of them," Nik said. "One of those small boutique companies that create midrange storage systems for small and medium-sized businesses. Impressive technology. Too small for us. What is your role?"

"I work on the encryption code. You know, to make sure if anyone steals data, they wouldn't be able to read it." When she saw Nik's face, she frowned. "I thought of that, but I don't see how he could have gotten the code. You don't think…"

"He stole the encryption code," Alix said. When everyone looked at her, she said to Nik, "When his first attempt to get Cerberus's code failed, he tried again. He wouldn't have disappeared unless he got it."

"It's a possibility," Nik said.

Mary looked aghast. "But how?"

Nik waved a hand. "The main thing is to catch him." He glanced at Rosa gazing at him, her lips twisted. "What?"

"So far, we've heard nothing that will help us do that," Rosa said. "Catch him, that is." She looked from Tanya to Mary. "Neither of you ever saw where he lived, but did he ever let anything slip about where that might be? The type of house? The surroundings? How long it took to get somewhere from home? Did he take a train, a rideshare, or a cab? Anything like that?"

"No," Mary said. "Nothing. We've been over it and over it. We assumed he didn't have a permanent home here in New York."

"How about you, Tanya?" Nik asked.

She shook her head. "We've all been over it so many times. If there was something, we would have remembered it."

A gloomy silence descended on the table.

"There was that one thing," Mary said. When everyone looked at her, she said to Tanya, "That thing you saw on his phone the last time you were with him."

"Right," Tanya said. Looking embarrassed, she said, "The last time we were together, I was asking him about where he lived. You know, what was his house like? I imagined a big mansion. I was getting impatient." She shook her head at Nik's hopeful expression. "He didn't let anything slip. But he got a message on his phone. Something that made him happy. When he put it down on the table, I got a glimpse of the screen. It was on WhatDidYouSay. You know that app that encrypts messages?"

"Did you see the message?" Nik asked.

"Just for a second, but I'm sure it said, 'Client happy. Payment received.'"

Holding his breath, Nik asked, "Did you see who it was from?"

Tanya's eyes narrowed. "TamRick. I'm pretty sure." She spelled it.

Nik looked at Rosa, who shrugged.

"Mean anything to you?" Alix asked Nik.

"No, not at the moment. It's a username on an app that is popular with criminals for good reason. I wouldn't expect them to use something that could be easily traced."

"What do you think they meant by client?" Mary asked. They leaned forward and nodded enthusiastically. They had obviously discussed the possibilities.

Nik blew a breath through pursed lips. "My guess is this TamRick is some kind of broker. Connects clients with people like The Technician."

"Well, how many of those could there be?" Rosa asked. "It's something to work with. We could ask Hacksie."

Nik grinned. "That's a good idea." After determining there was nothing else useful the two victims could remember, Nik handed them a card with his private number on it and said, "If you remember anything else, don't hesitate to contact me at any time of day."

"We will," Tanya said. "And if you need our help, call us. We'll do anything."

While Nik, Alix and Rosa were walking back to their car, Alix asked, "What do you think?"

"I think they should have reported what they knew to their employers," Rosa said. "Or the cops."

"They're afraid for their jobs," Alix said.

"I get that," Nik said, "but how much damage has this guy caused? That's how his kind are able to operate. People don't speak up because they're afraid for their jobs or they're embarrassed. Companies like SecureTech don't report data breaches. Companies pay off criminals who install ransomware so the public doesn't find out. People like The Technician will always get away with their crimes if they can do it in the dark." He took a breath and sighed it out and said to Rosa, "But I think you're right. If TamRick is a broker, it's worth asking Hacksie if he or she knows who it is. It's more than we had before."

Once they were sitting in the car, Alix asked, "What next?"

"Let's see if Rashida has anything." He started the engine. "I'll check with Jamie, see if we can find out anything about TamRick."

# Chapter 23

## Sunday, 9:33 A.M.

When Rosa and Rashida arrived at Nik and Alix's condo early Sunday morning, Nik asked them, "Anything on TamRick?"

"Only what you already guessed," Rosa said. "Some kind of broker. You could just contact whoever it is on that app, WhatDidYouSay."

"Want to know who we're dealing with," Nik said. "If it looks like I'm just fishing, they won't respond. We were thinking we could ask Hacksie about TamRick." He turned to go to his office. "I'll email Jamie."

"You don't need to do that," Rashida said. "If it's who I think it is, I know how to get in touch with… him."

"You know who he is?" Alix asked.

She shook her head. "No one knows *who* he is. I just know how to get his attention."

Nik glanced at Alix, then waved a hand toward his office. "After you."

For the next hour, the four of them sat in Nik's office while Rashida worked. Rosa slouched in a chair, nose in her phone, Alix on the floor next to Alan and Nik in a chair where he could keep an eye on Rashida. He was fidgeting, trying to decide the best way to suggest they contact Jamie, when she sat back and gestured triumphantly to the monitor.

"You found him?" Nik asked.

Her brow wrinkled.

"Ask him if a WhatDidYouSay username of TamRick means anything to him." The answer took five minutes to appear.

*H: Marge Swinton. Goes by the alias Tammy Rickland. She's a headhunter for people like The Technician. A sort of agent or broker*

Before Nik could follow up, another message appeared.

*H: Best way to contact her is through WhatDidYouSay*
*Session ended.*

Nik pulled his phone from his pocket, installed the What-DidYouSay app and created an account. He paused before creating a username. Then entered TheMaestro.

Rashida, leaning over so she could watch, asked, "TheMaestro? For real?"

"College nickname," Nik murmured.

Once the app was installed, he searched for TamRick and was gratified to find the user still existed.

While he was considering how to proceed, Rashida said, "Here, let me." She took the phone, tapped in the message, then held it out so Nik could see it.

*TheMaestro: In the market for specialized expertise. Heard you were someone with the right connections. Discretion is paramount.*

"Send it," Nik said.

## Monday, 6:22 A.M.

Nik spent the night tossing and turning, but decided the next morning he had to go to work, despite how he felt. He managed to stay alert through a series of technical meetings, all the while keeping an eye on his phone for a response from TamRick, but a post-lunch marketing meeting was a bridge too far.

"Nik. Hello." He startled and looked up to find everyone seated at the conference table looking at him. Standing at the head of the table, Julie asked, "Are we distracting you from something more important?"

Nik gave her a big smile. "What could possibly be more important than…" He looked at the screen on which an impossibly dense slide was projected. Squinting at it, he asked, "What are we talking about?"

Julie frowned at him. "As you don't seem willing to contribute anything useful to the discussion, why don't you go handle whatever is on your mind?"

"Good idea." He stood, waved jauntily to the startled faces of the marketing team, and exited the conference room.

"Nik!" Julie called just before the closing door cut her off.

He strode down the hall, feeling as if he had escaped purgatory. Just as he made it to his office, his cell buzzed in his pocket. It was the response he was waiting for. On his way to the elevator, he checked to see where Alix was. She was working from home.

## Monday, 1:34 P.M.

He found his partner in her home office. She sat on a small sofa beneath a window that looked out over Central Park, one leg tucked beneath her, one hand holding a tablet and the other idly rubbing Alan Turing's ears. They both looked up when Nik entered.

"You're home early," Alix said with a smile.

Alan Turing rose, stretched and yawned, then hopped down and ambled past Nik into the hall. Nik watched him go. Just before he rounded the corner, Alan looked over his shoulder and gave his tail a flick.

"Something wrong with that cat," Nik said as he retrieved his phone from his pocket. "I've never met a cat who didn't like me."

"Alan obviously has more discerning tastes than those other cats."

"Very nice." Nik dropped onto the spot abandoned by the cat. "I got a response from TamRick."

Alix sat up, set the tablet down, and took the phone.

*TamRick: Describe the nature of the expertise you require*

Nik settled back and looked at Alix.

"What do we want from her?" Alix asked. "Specifically."

"We want to find out where The Technician lives." He took his phone back and waved a hand. "That's unlikely. Second best would be for her to put us in touch with him. Maybe we could catch his scent."

"Tell her you want to talk in person."

Nik thought for a minute, then entered his response.

*TheMaestro: Will only discuss the details in person*
*TamRick: An in person meeting isn't possible. If you're worried about security, the encryption on these messages is unbreakable.*

Nik took a screenshot of his phone and attached it to his response.

*TheMaestro: I'll make it worth your time. Name a price.*

He sat back, leaned into Alix, and waited. Alan Turing appeared, hopped onto the desk and sat with his tail curled around his paws. All three of them looked at the phone when it buzzed.

*TamRick: 5 min. video chat. $20K. No guarantees.*

The next message included her PayMe username.

Nik showed the screen to Alix. "Nice work if you can get it." When she nodded, he opened the PayMe app and entered the transaction. After receiving the confirmation, he sent TamRick another message.

*TheMaestro: Check your PayMe account.*

A minute later, Nik's phone buzzed and the video chat screen on the WhatDidYouSay app opened.

Nik wasn't sure what to expect, but the woman peering out of the small screen was a surprise. Snow white hair piled on her head in a Sixties bouffant that looked as if it required curlers and hours under a hair dryer. A button nose, full cheeks, lipstick-red lips, and kindly blue eyes. He expected her to scold him for not eating enough. Instead, she leaned forward and squinted at the screen.

Her eyes opened wide, she sank back, and disappeared from the camera's view. When Nik heard her say, "Fuck!" he couldn't help exchanging a grin with Alix, despite his fears Marge might just end the call.

But a moment later, she reappeared and took a moment to recover her composure. Giving him a kindly smile, she said, "Nik Atherton." Nik rotated the phone toward Alix. "And this must be Alix Crockett."

"Marge," Nik said, returning her smile. "Pardon my familiarity, but I've heard so much about you, I feel like we're... friends."

Her face froze. She leaned toward the camera and said, "I could just hang up."

"But you won't."

She eyed him speculatively, then sighed. "Okay, you found me, managed to get me to agree to an in-person meeting — thank you for the payment, by the way — you've threatened me to let me know you're serious. What do you want?"

"The Technician," Nik said.

She frowned. Her eyes rolled up, then she murmured, "The Technician, The..." Then, as if she recalled who it was, she nodded and looked at Nik. "You understand, I don't have any knowledge of who my clients are or the people with whom I put them in touch."

Alix snorted. When Nik and Marge looked at her, she said, "Sorry. Carry on."

"I'm not surprised you would say that," Nik said to Marge. "Your business model relies on it. However, I suspect it's not entirely true." She started to speak, but he cut her off. "You maintain the fiction of anonymity, but the dark tech world isn't so large, you wouldn't have some notion of who you do business with."

The grandmother reemerged, this time appearing to disapprove of Nik's life choices. "You're right that anonymity is critical for my... business model. But you're wrong about it being a fiction." She peered down her nose at him. "Not entirely, anyway. The Technician is small-time. I wouldn't know where he is or what he looks like." When Nik started to speak, she put up a hand. "The Technician was recommended to me by… someone whose opinion I respect." She gave her head a shake. "I'd never heard of him before that. Not by that alias, anyway." She looked off-camera for a moment, then she focused on Nik and said, "He's done well. Must be charming and physically pleasing. Has a knack for seducing women to wheedle his way into places he shouldn't be." She paused and gave her head a waggle. "I've heard good things about his code." She looked steadily at Nik. "That's all I know about him."

"But you know how to contact him. You must."

She gazed at him. "What kind of reputation would I have if I compromised one of my assets?"

"What kind of reputation would you have if you were accused of being an accessory to kidnaping and murder?" He shrugged. "The charge might not stick, but I'll make sure you don't remain anonymous. Think about it. It's the kind of messy, dark mystery that's catnip for the media."

"What do you mean, murder?"

"The Technician murdered a man who did work for my company, and he kidnapped a young woman who works for me."

"How do you know it was him?"

"Because I saw him."

She waved a hand. "You couldn't know it was The Technician. How would you know what he looks like?"

Nik pointed the phone at Alix, who produced the image from their security camera and held it up so Marge could see it.

She gazed at it for a long time. "How do you know this is him?"

"Someone who recognizes his code fingerprint confirmed it."

"If Nik Atherton shone a light into your murky world," Alix said, putting the image away, "you could lose everything."

Marge popped her lips and appeared to consider. Leaning forward, she said, "I want my name completely out of it. No mention of me, or what I do. Nothing like 'a mysterious woman who operates in the shadows.'"

"If you help us find him, agreed."

"Now, understand, I honestly don't know where you can find this man."

"How do you contact him?"

"Through WhatDidYouSay. He usually responds within a day. His username is TheJackal."

Nik exchanged a look with Alix, who nodded. "We want to hire him," he said to Marge. "You arrange it in the normal way."

"I'll be in touch." Marge reached toward the camera, then the screen went blank.

Nik let the phone fall and looked at Alix, who asked, "Are you going to keep your promise about not exposing her?"

"It's a dilemma, isn't it?"

"You said Tanya and Mary were guilty of allowing people like The Technician to remain in the dark."

"I did, and I believe that's true."

"But you made a promise to this woman."

"What do you think I should do?"

Alix held his gaze for a moment, then looked out the window. "I don't know."

"Let's see if we can get Kate back, then we'll revisit this."

"Agreed."

"In the meantime," Nik said, "let's let Rosa and Rashida know we found TamRick." He rose, paused, walked over to the desk and gave Alan Turing a rub between the ears. The cat allowed the familiarity, looked up at him and slow-blinked. Throwing Alix an incredulous smile, he dialed his phone.

# Chapter 24

## Monday, 3:25 P.M.

When Rosa and Rashida arrived, everyone gathered around the kitchen island while Nik related their conversation with TamRick. He finished with, "So, we convinced her to contact The Technician to tell him we want to hire him."

Rashida emerged from the fridge and laid out the makings for a sandwich on the counter.

"Don't see how that helps," Rosa said. "Those types never meet clients in person."

"Huh," Alix said. "A little curious how you know that."

Rosa glared at her. "Read it in a book."

"She's right," Rashida said. A minute later, she plopped a plate with a giant Dagwood sandwich and a pickle on the island.

"You find any more on The Technician?" Nik asked.

"Nothing useful." She took a bite of her pickle, wrinkled her nose, glared accusingly at it, then set it down. "Some discussions on unpopular subdreads."

"Subdreads?" Alix asked.

"Dread is the dark web equivalent of Reddit," Nik said. "A few years ago, when Reddit chased all the subreddits having to do with cybercrime off Reddit, those people found a home on Dread."

"So, people who want to commit cybercrimes have a place to share," Rosa said.

"They aren't all up to no good," Nik said. "Some people just want to learn how it's done. They like the puzzle. And there's a certain cool factor to it. I've learned a lot there." When Rosa and Alix stared flatly at him, he said, "But, yeah, that's where you would go if you had ill intent."

"Anyway," Rashida said. "Like I said, there's some discussions about him. Most people never heard of him, but there's a few call him elite." She picked up the pickle, studied it, then took a small nibble. "But it's always the same ones."

Nik grinned.

"Yeah," Rashida said, returning his grin. "I figure they're sockpuppet accounts. He's working his rep." She shrugged. "Anyway, I found out a lot about how that world works. Rosa's right. Those types rarely meet their clients. Have to be really big before they even agree to a phone call. And by big, I mean be willing to pay a lot."

"You got a plan?" Rosa asked Nik.

"Was hoping to arrange a meeting."

"He'll only communicate through the app or on the dark web," Rashida said. "What job you hiring him for?"

"Left it vague. You got any ideas?"

"You haven't heard back?"

"Not yet."

"You might not," Rosa said.

Rashida waggled the pickle. "If you get him to open a document, a PDF maybe, we could infect his phone with spyware that transmits his location."

Nik nodded. "Maybe…"

"Wouldn't he have virus protection?" Alix asked.

"Yes, but most virus protection works by looking for known malware," Rashida said. "That's why you're always getting updates."

"Or it monitors the system for anomalous behavior," Nik said. "I'm guessing if the phone suddenly started transmitting location data to an unknown receiver, that would qualify as anomalous."

"You'd need something custom. Something really good," Rashida said. She glanced at Alix, who rose to set a kettle on the stove, and laid what was left of her pickle on Alix's saucer.

"Can either of you do that?" Rosa asked. She looked from Rashida to Nik.

When Rashida shook her head, Nik said, "No, but we know someone who can."

## Monday, 4:25 P.M.

Remembering his thought about bringing Rashida and Jamie together, Nik insisted they go to Jamie's office to contact Hacksie and requested that she accompany him. Rashida mumbled something about Bilbo entering Smaug's lair. He emailed Jamie to let him know they wanted to talk to Hacksie.

Encouraged by Jamie's reaction to Rosa, Nik hoped the introduction of Rashida would be as smooth. Instead, the two of them stared awkwardly around the small room, neither speaking or meeting the other's eyes. When Nik gestured to the chair Rosa had occupied, Rashida slumped in the seat, crossed her arms and stared sullenly at the door.

Discouraged, Nik took his seat and said, "You two have complementary but overlapping skill sets."

Jamie looked past him to Rashida, who gazed back at him.

Nik said to Rashida, "Jamie knows the inner world of systems — operating systems, networks — better than anyone else I know. He's also pretty good at finding things." He looked at Jamie. "Rashida is the best bloodhound I've ever seen. I have no idea how she finds what she does."

Neither of them spoke, but they looked at one another speculatively. It was like introducing cats. Nik asked Jamie, "You contact Hacksie?"

Jamie dipped his head and peered up at him. "They must be interested." He gestured to an open chat window on the monitor closest to Nik. "They answered right away when I told them you wanted to talk."

"But I didn't tell you what I wanted to ask them?"

Jamie shrugged. "Maybe they like you?"

"They still there?"

Jamie typed.

*J: Nik's here.*

While they waited for a response, Rashida leaned across Nik to get a better view of Jamie's screens. When Jamie didn't object, Nik switched places with her.

Jamie let her look for a minute. When she looked at him, he gave her a small nod and said, "S'up."

Rashidia hesitated, then nodded, sat back and crossed her arms. She looked sideways at Nik and bobbed her head. Jamie tapped his fingers on his desk. The uninitiated couldn't have guessed how momentous that had been, but Nik sighed in relief and relaxed.

The response came back a full minute later.

*H: And what does Nik want to talk about?*

Nik had discussed what they wanted with Rashida on the way over. "Tell him TamRick sent a message to The Technician to tell him I wanted to hire him."

When Jamie hesitated, Nik nodded to the keyboard. After Jamie entered it and hit enter, the answer came back immediately.

*H: The Technician is flush with his victory over you. He might not answer*

Nik stood to read the response, then sat and asked, "How would they know that? About him being flush with victory over me?"

"Spooky," Rashida said.

"They're very mysterious," Jamie said.

"Or he's in on it," Rashida said.

Another message appeared.

*H: However, if he does take the bait, I assume you're looking for a way to locate him*

"Tell them yes," Nik said.

*H: Spyware that transmits his location*

"Tell him the spyware would have to be small enough to deliver in a document, unique enough to avoid virus scanners, clever enough to avoid behavioral monitoring, and versatile enough to infect whatever platform he uses." After Jamie entered the message, Nik said, "Now tell him that's not possible."

*H: Clever, Nik. You think by presenting me with an impossible challenge, you'll get my cooperation*

Seconds later, another message appeared.

*H: And it worked. I'm intrigued*
*H: Give me a day. If he answers in the meantime, tell him you're preparing a pdf with instructions*
*Session ended*

Rashida stood. "Let's go."

Nik stood. "Thank you, Jamie. If you hear from Hacksie, let me know as soon as possible."

"I will."

Rashida was already out the door. Nik caught up with her at the elevators. When they got out of the elevator in the lobby, Rashida scheduled a rideshare, then went to the window and searched the street.

Nik stopped to say hello to Mo at the security desk. He was joining Rashida when he spotted a familiar figment standing on the sidewalk. It hadn't been there a moment before. He would have sworn to it. "Hold on. I'll be back," he said to Rashida. Before he exited, he looked down at her. "Whatever you see… I'm not crazy. Or I don't think I am, anyway." He held her gaze for a moment. "Just wait here."

Most of the figment's attire was the same as the previous two times he'd seen it, but it had opted for Princess Leia cinnamon buns rather than the Pippi Longstocking pigtails. And, instead of army boots or platform sneakers, it wore old school roller skates strapped to Chuck Taylors. It looked up at him with a disturbingly wide grin when he stepped up beside it.

"You're back," he said.

A small frown. "Where did I go?"

"You weren't here a minute ago."

A more pleasing smile. "Wasn't I?"

## Monday, 5:02 P.M.

Rashida watched Nik with growing concern. She glanced back at the security guard Nik called Mo when they arrived. Mo watched her approach with a knowing smile curving his lips. When she stepped up next to the security desk and hooked a thumb over her shoulder, he shook his head.

"I know what you're going to ask," he said. "And the answer is yes. He's crazy. But I don't think it's in a bad way."

Rashida turned so she could keep Nik in view. "Is there another way to be crazy?"

Mo's brows lowered. "You live in *this* world long enough, you know there's all kinds of ways to be crazy." They watched Nik talk to thin air in silence, then Mo murmured, "White people."

## Monday, 5:04 P.M.

Deciding the conversation wasn't making progress, Nik cut to the chase. "What did you do to me the other night? When you touched me?"

Instead of answering, the figment glanced up at him, then nodded to something across the street. Nik looked and spotted an enormous man with a bald head wearing a black suit standing with his back to a coffee shop. He was trying to appear nonchalant, but Nik got the impression he was keeping an eye on the Cerberus building.

"You know him?" Nik asked.

The figment shook its head slowly. "Some people have a darkness about them."

"He waiting for us?"

The figment looked to her right as Rashida exited the building. "For her."

As Rashida's ride share pulled to the curb, Nik caught her arm and pulled her back into the building.

"That's my ride."

"We'll get another," Nik said. "Mo, we need to get out the back way."

"Yes, sir." He let them in the security gate, then led them to the stairwell. Swiping a card through the lock, he pulled the door to the basement open.

"Thank you, Mo," Nik said.

"Do I need to be worried about who's coming?"

"I don't think so. Just someone looking suspicious across the street. I'm sure I'm overreacting."

"Hope so," Mo said as he shut the door.

"What the fu —"

"Let's get away from the building first." Nik led Rashida down the stairs, wondering how he was going to convince her he wasn't insane.

Neither of them spoke again until they were waiting for their ride two blocks from the Cerberus building. Rashida glanced around, then pulled Nik away from the flow of pedestrians. "What was that about?"

"Probably nothing. There was a man across the street. He…" How was he going to tell her a woman who might be a figment of his imagination told him the man was looking for Rashida? "Looked like he was watching the building and had bad intentions."

Her frown intensified. "Bad intentions? Looked like?"

Nik waggled his head. "Hard to explain."

She studied his face, then took a small step away from him. "You got a problem I should know about?"

"You have to be more specific."

"Hearing voices?" Rashida said. "Speaking to imaginary people?"

Nik didn't answer right away. He knew how crazy it would sound to anyone except Alix to explain the figments. He'd known how it sounded to others ever since his mother rushed him to a doctor in a panic. In fact, he wasn't entirely sure Alix didn't think he was off kilter. He could have deflected or ignored Rashida's question. But he and Alix liked Rashida and Rosa and they both agreed, knowing someone with Rashida's talents was invaluable. So he hedged. "I will only point out that I knew a man was waiting across the street for you."

"A man I didn't see."

Nik held her gaze as their ride arrived. "Car's here."

They were quiet during the short ride. Nik tried to look nonchalant, but he noticed Rashida studying him out of the corner of his eye.

As they emerged in front of Nik's building, Rashida looked up at him. "I think you may be crazy." She bit her lips, then said, "But I don't think it's a dangerous crazy."

"Well, that's good news."

She held his gaze for a moment, something unspoken behind her eyes, then she turned away and entered the building.

# Monday, 5:05 P.M.

Milton woke up. It wasn't a gradual thing. One moment he was oblivious to the world, not even dreaming, then he was staring at the ceiling of his basement. The first thing he noticed was his mouth was desert dry. He winced and smacked his lips. Then the pain in his foot brought back his encounter with Kate.

He craned his neck and looked down his body. There was plenty of blood, but from the hole in his shoe, it looked like he just clipped the tip of his big toe.

Groaning, he rolled over and fought his way to his feet. She had a gun now. He eyed the window in the door. Too bad he didn't have a hand grenade. Limping up the stairs, he considered what it would take to pump carbon monoxide into the room.

He'd left his phone on the kitchen counter. He picked it up, intending to find out how long he had been out, then he noticed he had two messages on WhatDidYouSay.

The first, from his client, confirmed they authenticated the sample of files he provided and requested the remainder. He checked his PayMe app and would have danced a jig if he could have when he saw they'd paid him the balance of his fee. He may be getting his ass regularly kicked by a slip of a woman, but he was a rich man.

The second message was from TamRick. Could the broker have another job for him so quickly? His thumb hovered over the trashcan icon. He didn't need to work anymore. Still, it wouldn't hurt to find out what it was, so he answered and indicated he might be interested.

Setting the phone down, he limped up the stairs to the bathroom in his master suite where he kept his medical supplies. He hoped he wouldn't have to get a doctor involved with his toe.

# Chapter 25

## Monday, 5:32 P.M.

Milton decided he didn't need a doctor. The bullet left a crescent-shaped divot in his toenail and sliced off a few layers of skin on the tip of his big toe. Bloody, but the bone wasn't exposed. After cleaning it, he wrapped it in gauze, then limped into his office. He slouched in his desk chair and considered what he should do. He could simply leave, activate one of his escape plans, and retire to a life of luxury. The problem was what to do about Kate.

Some of his escape plans included burning the house down. He'd considered it as a solution to the Kate situation earlier. The problem was the concrete cell he built in the basement would be impervious to fire. She would die from smoke inhalation or asphyxiation, but her body would be intact. The whole point of burning the house down was to eliminate any evidence pointing to him. The hand grenade idea would work, but explosives weren't something he worked with before. Plus, the cleanup would be horrendous.

Lugging a lawnmower into the basement and pumping the exhaust into the room would work, except she had a gun. The idea of feeding a tube through the window while she took potshots at him was hilarious. Milton chuckled.

He sat up. A smile grew slowly on his face. He didn't need to escape. The job was done. His client was happy. The Russians wouldn't come looking for him. That meant he was in no hurry. The simplest and safest option was to let her starve to death. A month tops would be all it took. Maybe less if he cut the water to the toilet. In the meantime, he could plan an extended vacation.

His phone beeped. He picked it up and opened the message from TamRick.

*TamRick: Glad to hear you're interested. The prospective client is rich, desperate, and hopelessly naïve. His username is TheMaestro.*

"TheMaestro?" Milton sneered. Whoever the pretentious twit was, he hit the trifecta for Milton's favorite type of client: rich, desperate, and naïve. He sent a message to TheMaestro, then headed down to the kitchen to make tea.

## Monday, 5:35 P.M.

When Nik and Rashida arrived home, Rosa and Alix were in her office. Rosa sat cross-legged on the floor, perusing the titles on Alix's bookshelves. Alix sat on the sofa, a book in her hand. Alan Turing, sprawled on his back next to her, squinted at Nik when he entered the room. "Success?" Alix asked and let the book fall to her lap.

"Yeah, Hacksie will get back to us when it's done." Nik sat next to her, opposite Alan.

Rashida caught his eye, tapped Rosa on the shoulder, then nodded to the door when Rosa looked up at her.

After they left, Alix asked, "What was that about?"

"I met that figment outside Cerberus again."

"The woman look-alike who touched you?"

"That's the one. It warned me about a man across the street watching the building."

"Warned you about what?"

"It just said some people have a darkness about them and that he was looking for Rashida."

Alix held his gaze for a moment, then reached over and set her book on an end table. "Why is he looking for Rashida?"

"If I had to guess, it's because she looks at things she isn't supposed to."

Alix looked at the door to her office. "Rashida saw you talking to no one, and she's worried you're insane."

"That's the gist of it. She figures I'm crazy, but not dangerous."

"I wouldn't jump to conclusions like that," Alix said with a crooked grin, then she grew serious. "Did you ask the figment why it touched you?"

"I did. It didn't answer."

"But it warned you about the man who had a darkness about him."

"Yes." He took a breath and blew it out. "It's the first figment who ever interacted with me in a coherent way." He waggled his head. "Relatively coherent, anyway."

Alix held his gaze for a moment. "You should try talking to another figment. See if anything has changed."

"First opportunity."

"The dark man wasn't The Technician?"

"No, I didn't recognize him. Looked more like the hired thug type. The Technician doesn't strike me as the type to hire that sort. People in his line of work tend to be loners."

"Transfer Shipping."

"That's my guess." Nik stood and paced. "Damán Enterprises provides the cover for Sally Thompson to be a corporate spy. She receives payments from Transfer Shipping, which suggests that company is associated with Damán Enterprises."

"Sally has the malware on her computer, which, by itself, doesn't incriminate her. To use the VPN to her machine requires her login credentials. Again, not necessarily incriminating. But between that and her history in corporate espionage, it suggests she's The Mole."

Nik stopped for a moment. "And you saw her and Oki getting into an SUV registered to Transfer Shipping." He resumed pacing.

"So someone at Damán Enterprises inserted Sally into Cerberus as a spy." Alix stroked Alan Turing's chest with her fingertips. Alan stretched all four legs and yawned widely.

"She either hears rumors that I'm working on something big or she already knew it, so she hires The Technician to steal Nicola."

"And she needs someone on the inside with technical skills, so she gets Oki involved." Alix readjusted her legs to accommodate Alan Turing when he crawled into her lap.

"Oki has been with us a long time, so he's not part of the scheme originally."

"He didn't look happy when I saw them together," Alix said. "I'm guessing he's cooperating against his will."

"She found something in his mysterious past." Nik sat on the sofa. "Something she could use to blackmail him."

They looked at one another, then Alix said, "It's impossible to escape the implication that Ash Damán is the person who stole Nicola."

"Damán Enterprises is immense. He may not have known about it."

"Maybe. What do we do about it? We have no evidence that could be used in court."

"Nik's phone buzzed. When he retrieved it, he glanced at Alix. "Got a WhatDidYouSay message." A moment later, he said, "It's from TheJackal. The Technician is interested and wants details."

"What are you going to say?"

Nik sat. He'd been considering the best way to lure The Technician into a trap and decided coming across as a bit dim and hopelessly naïve about technology was the best approach. He typed in the message.

*TheMaestro: So relieved you got back to me. I am at my wit's end. My story is a complicated one and typing on my phone is difficult for me. Is there a way we can meet in person?*

He hit send.

The message came back almost immediately.

*TheJackal: I don't meet anyone in person.*
*TheMaestro: Is there a way I can send you a letter?*
*TheJackal: Are you familiar with Tor?*
*TheMaestro: If that is a computer thing, I'm afraid I'm quite hopeless. But I have a nephew who knows about such things.*
*TheJackal: Get your nephew to help you put the document at this Tor address.*

The next message included an address Nik could use to share a file on Tor.

Nik grinned at Alix. "We're in. He gave me a Tor address so I can share a file with him."

"Tor address?"

"Tor is a proxy network."

She stared at him expectantly.

"You connect to servers on the Tor network through a proxy server. The proxy server hides your identity. You have to use the Tor browser, but you're completely anonymous. Everything is encrypted, and nothing can be traced back to you."

"And the reason this exists?"

Interpreting her skeptical expression, Nik shrugged. "Not everyone who uses Tor is up to no good. Some people just don't like others using their activities to target advertising at them, or they just don't like the idea of people snooping on them." When Alix's brow twitched up, he said, "Using Tor isn't a crime."

"But if you were involved in criminal activity, that's where you would do it."

"Okay. Yes."

"So, we just have to wait for Hacksie."

"Right." He stood and hesitated. "I'll, uh, go... tell Rosa and Rashida."

Alix rose and grinned. "I want to see this."

## Monday, 6:00 P.M.

Rosa and Rashida slouched shoulder to shoulder on the sofa in the living room, arms crossed. Nik and Alix sat in chairs across from them. When Nik finished telling them about his conversation with The Technician, he expected questions. Instead, Rashida leaned in and whispered something to Rosa, then they fixed narrow-eyed gazes on him. Hearing Alix's soft chuckle, he turned his head to frown at her.

The figment sat cross-legged on the floor. It grinned at him and waggled its fingers, a gesture entirely at odds with its 80s goth makeup and clothes. Alan Turing strolled in from the kitchen, settled himself next to the figment, tail curled around his feet, and gazed expectantly at him. Nik dragged his eyes away from the figment scritching Alan's head to find Rosa and Rashida looking at the spot where the figment sat, rising concern in their deep frowns. He cleared his throat, bringing their attention back to him.

"I'm not crazy." Alix's snort was clear to everyone. Throwing her a perturbed look, he waved a hand and said, "No more than… everyone else, anyway."

Rosa cocked her head. "Shida said you were talking to a ghost."

"Ghost," Nik scoffed. He hesitated, dropped his head, rubbed his forehead with his index finger and rotated his head toward the figment. It shook its head. Alix followed his gaze, then gave him a questioning look. Rosa and Rashida looked ready to bolt.

He cleared his throat again and said, "Yes. I suppose I could understand why she would make that supposition." He winced inwardly. "But appearances can be deceiving. A shopkeeper once saw Alexander Hamilton pacing in front of his shop talking to himself." He glanced at the figment, who nodded encouragingly. "Thought he was crazy."

"Alexander Hamilton," Rosa said, one brow crawling up her forehead.

Alix looked as interested in where this was going as Rosa and Rashida. "Turns out, that's how he wrote his… the stuff he wrote. You know, speeches. The Federalist Papers." He paused, meeting their befuddled stares. The figment was now looking as confused as everyone else. "And you know, we can tell from his papers, he made very few edits." Picking up momentum, he continued, "So it must have worked for him." More blank stares. "Right?" Out of the corner of his eye, he saw the figment nodding vigorously and giving him two thumbs up.

Rosa glanced at Rashida and asked Nik, "So, you were writing something? In your head?"

"Yes, exactly," Nik said with a wide smile.

They were quiet for a moment, then Rashida asked, "What were you writing?"

Nik opened his mouth before his brain engaged. He looked at the figment, who shrugged, palms up. His phone buzzed.

"Thank the gods," he mumbled and fished it out of his pocket. It was a WhatDidYouSay message. "It's from Hacksie." Everyone leapt up and gathered around his chair. "Or someone with the username Hacksie."

"Did you tell him what *your* username was?" Alix asked.

"Did you tell him what you called him?" Rosa asked at the same time.

"No, and No."

"Rashida knows your username," Alix said. "Anyone else?"

"Marge. The Technician knows my username, but he doesn't know it's me. Unless Marge told him."

"I told you the man's spooky," Rashida said.

"Spooky?" Alix grinned.

"Yeah. He knows things he has no business knowing."

"Open it already," Rosa said.

*Hacksie: Your spyware is finished. BTW, someone has noticed your bloodhound snooping around. Tell her to be careful*

The message included a file share on Tor where he put the spyware.

"Bloodhound?" Alix asked. "Rashida?"

Nik looked up at Rashida. "That *is* your username on PayMe." He looked at Alix. "And there was the man the figment warned me about looking for her." Fortunately, Rosa and Rashida weren't listening.

"We got to go to the safe house," Rashida said. "Now."

"You have a safe house?" Alix asked.

"You think I can charge 50K for a background search if I always play it safe?"

"Huh," Nik said. "Thought you were just taking advantage of us."

"Gave you a discount." Rashida crossed to the sofa and started packing away her laptop. "For Alix."

"You'll be safe here," Nik said. "No one gets in without going through security."

"You mean the security The Technician waltzed through? Unh uh. Me and Rosa are out of here."

"Wouldn't you like to see what Hacksie came up with before you leave?" Nik waggled his phone.

Rashida eyed him. "Shit." She sat and opened her laptop. Nik joined her and held up the phone with the Tor address visible. Moments later, she angled the computer so she and Nik could both see the file share Hacksie created. It included a PDF with the name DONT OPEN THIS, presumably the file they were supposed to send to The Technician, and another file with the name ONLY OPEN THIS ONE. Rashida opened that file.

They huddled close to read it, then sat back and looked at one another. The spyware Hacksie created would send location data periodically to a Share My Doc spreadsheet. It mimicked normal communication between the phone and the cellphone provider's network to mask its activity.

"You got a good connection at your safe house?" Nik asked. When Rashida nodded, he said, "This is what we do. You two go to your safe house. We'll both monitor this. When we get something,

Alix and I will head out. You keep track and call me when there's an update."

A grin grew on Rashida's face. "So, I'm the woman in the chair?"

"*Spiderman*," Nik said, and he and Rashida finished together. "*Homecoming*." They grinned at one another.

Rosa rolled her eyes, then asked Alix, "Whatchya gonna do? Citizen's arrest? Gonna go all Bad Boyz on him?"

"No, nothing like that," Alix said. "We'll call the cops. We just want to be sure he's home. That's hopefully where he has Kate."

Rashida looked at Rosa, who said, "They want to play Bones and Booth, that's their business."

"What do you know about Bones and Booth?" Alix asked.

"I know they're white. Smart. Got a sparky kind of thing going," Rosa said.

"So, what are we?" Rashida asked. They gazed at one another, then looked away. "Need more role models."

Rosa slapped her thigh. "Sydney Burnett. Bad Boyz."

"Oh! And Jackie Brown," Rashida said.

"Excellent! Pam Grier," Nik said. "Now, all we have to do is set the trap."

Rashida renamed the file they would give to The Technician, copied it to the file share The Technician provided, then Nik sent TheJackal a message. Ten minutes later, they all stood with Alan Turing in the foyer to bid Rashida and Rosa goodbye.

Rashida dug into a pocket, pulled out her phone, and tapped on it. A moment later, Nik's phone buzzed. "I don't give my number to just anyone." She gave him a stern look.

"I'll protect it," Nik said.

Rashida and Rosa gave them hugs. Just before they left, Rashida said, "Good luck."

Once they were alone, Alix asked, "The figment still here?"

Nik returned to the living room and found it empty. "It's gone. I'm beginning to think that figment has a twisted sense of humor." He turned to face her. "Just wanted to watch me make a fool of myself."

"Glad you said it," Alix smiled at his glower. "That story about Hamilton may have put them off until the excitement dies down, but you're going to have to come up with something better."

"Yeah, not my most creative moment." Nik looked at Alix. "You want wine?"

"I do. But I think tea would be smarter."

# Chapter 26

## Monday, 7:02 P.M.

Milton sat on a bench in Central Park. It was a pleasant June night, and despite the ache in his toe, he was in a good mood. He watched the parade of pedestrians and speculated about which warm place he would retire to. His phone buzzed. A message from TheMaestro.

His new client had left a PDF file for him. He put away his personal phone and retrieved a new burner phone. He'd turned it on before only long enough to register it on the provider's network and install the most advanced malware protections he could. He would only turn it on for short spans, then he would destroy it as soon as the job was done.

After installing the Tor browser, a requirement for accessing sites on the proxy network, he navigated to the file share, opened the file, and read. TheMaestro was the son of a rich man who had recently married a much younger woman. He was afraid his father changed his will to leave his entire estate to the gold digger. He wanted The Technician to let him search his father's home computer for the will. The rest of the document had details about the father's computer, address, daily schedule, security system, among many other unnecessary details.

Milton snickered. Child's play. There were plenty of scripts that could be found on the dark web for a Bash Bunny that would accomplish what TheMaestro wanted to do. Even a script kiddie, a person who committed cybercrimes with little or no technical ability, could do it. Such people were a disgrace as far as Milton was concerned.

Milton wouldn't lower himself to those levels. He'd prepare a flash drive for TheMaestro and instruct him — or more likely his nephew — how to use it. It would take Milton an hour, tops, and he didn't even have to put himself in jeopardy. He switched off the phone and sent a message to TheMaestro on his personal phone.

*TheJackal: $250K. Half paid in advance. The job will be done in two weeks*

The fee was exorbitant, and he would have it done by morning. He didn't expect the twit to agree to it, but Milton didn't need the money. He chuckled. "TheMaestro. More like TheSchmuck."

Rising, he slipped his hands in his pockets and strolled toward the Strawberry Fields memorial to John Lennon. He looked across the street to the windows of Atherton's condo and chuckled. The asshole was probably weeping in his chardonnay.

# Monday, 7:05 P.M.

Nik sat back in Alix's desk chair, feet propped on her desk, his laptop open to the spreadsheet Hacksie created. He'd turned it away to keep himself from staring at it. Rashida would call if anything happened. Alix had left moments before, in search of tea with Alan Turing at her heels.

When Nik's phone buzzed, he straightened, snatched it up and answered while he spun the laptop around. The first row was occupied.

Alix appeared with two mugs. "What's up?" She set one mug on her desk for Nik and sipped.

Nik tapped speaker and said, "Rashida."

"He took the bait," Rashida said.

"I see it."

"Central Park. Right across the street from your place. He's probably not there anymore, and I think he turned off his phone."

"We'll go check, anyway," Nik said. "Call me if there are any more updates." He hung up, closed his laptop, and stood. "If we hurry, we might be able to catch him."

While they waited for the elevator, Nik said, "If it were me, I'd use a separate phone to open potentially unsafe documents. And I wouldn't keep it on for long."

"How do we get him to turn it back on?"

Nik's phone buzzed. "Message from TheJackal." After reading the message in WhatDidYouSay, he held the phone up so Alix could read it.

"A hundred twenty five thousand dollars?"

"It might be the only way to get him to look at the file again."

Alix hesitated, then shrugged. "In for a penny."

"That's what I was thinking." As they entered the elevator, Nik opened the PayMe app. "Plus, if we catch him, I have twenty-four hours to cancel the transaction."

A half hour later, they stood apart from the crowd drifting past the Strawberry Fields memorial. "We missed him," Nik said.

"Looks like it, though I don't know if I would recognize him without that dumb look on his face."

"Let's just… look a little more. Take a walk. Rashida will call if she gets an update."

## Monday, 7:20 P.M.

Rashida perched on the sagging sofa in the front room of their Bronx safe house. They never bothered to make it more than barely livable. There was a sofa they found on the side of the road, a double mattress on the floor in the one bedroom, a few staples in the kitchen. They had planned to do more, but never got around to it. They both regretted that oversight. The spartan gloomy space was depressing as hell and hiding here felt desperate.

Her laptop was open to Hacksie's spreadsheet on the cushion beside her. It would beep if a new update from The Technician's phone came in. The spyware Hacksie provided worked like a charm at first, sending one update. Then it stopped. It could mean he found and deleted the spyware. She hoped it only meant he had a special phone for opening dubious documents, and he turned it off. That's what she would do.

She tried distracting herself with Candy Crush on her phone, but gave that up when her eyes kept straying to the laptop. She looked up at Rosa, who was peering around the shades at the darkening street in front of their apartment. "You worried?" Rosa let the shades go and turned around, her arms crossed over her stomach, lips in a tight line. Yeah, she was worried.

"No. Why would I be worried?" She gestured to the dingy room. "This *is* our safe house. We're safe. Right?"

"Liar."

Rosa came across the room, sat on the sofa and let her head fall onto Rashida's shoulder. "These are bad men, Shida. Anyone who can hide what they really are from *you* is no one to mess with."

Rashida had been worried about that as well. While exploring the hidden alleys and byways of the dark web for any traces of Transfer Shipping, her worries grew. Anyone who could hide so effectively had vast resources and a reason to hide. They would probably go to any lengths to stay hidden. And they noticed she was looking for them. No one had ever done that before.

She took Rosa's hand and gave it a squeeze. "We're safe here. How could they know where we are?"

They both jumped as something crashed against the front door. It only held because they installed a steel door with heavy duty locks and hinges. Surprise held them immobile for a moment. Then another crash propelled them to their feet. Rashida snatched up her laptop and followed Rosa down the hall to the bathroom. There was a backdoor, but they always assumed if anyone came for them, they would cover the rear entrance. So they rented the next-door apartment and paid a very trusted friend in the construction business to build a secret passageway.

They fled down the hall and crowded into the small bathroom. With Rashida dancing from foot to foot behind her, Rosa yanked up the valve on the radiator against the back wall, swung it away from the wall on a spring-loaded hinge until it locked in place. A crash and the sound of splintering wood in the living room. The front door finally succumbed to the battering.

"Gotta go, Rosie!"

Rosa dug her fingers into the slot at the bottom of the baseboard and pulled the hidden door up. She dove through the opening, into the bathroom of the next apartment.

Rashida followed. She was supposed to lower the door and press a button that released the radiator, but with her laptop under her arm and phone in her hand, she couldn't manage it before an enormous bald man in a black suit appeared in the bathroom door. She turned and followed Rosa, flying across the hall to a bedroom, then out a window into a narrow bricked walkway. The man shouted behind them in a Slavic language.

"Go, go, go," Rashida whispered.

They sprinted toward the back of the apartment. A tall privacy fence blocked the view from their safe house's backyard. As they crossed the yard, two hands appeared at the top of the fence, followed by a man's head.

"*Oni zdes'!*" he bellowed.

Rashida glanced over her shoulder as they approached the gate in the fence and glimpsed the silhouette of another man racing toward them on the walkway. They were through the gate and sprinting down an alley before he caught up.

Rosa had insisted they learn the streets that surrounded their safe house by heart. Rashida rolled her eyes every time Rosa forced them to carry out escape drills, but she went along with it because she knew how worried her work made her partner. Now, as she followed Rosa, making turns without having to think, slipping through gaps in hedges they didn't need to search for, she began to giggle.

When they finally stopped to take a breath, Rosa frowned at her. "What the hell you laughing at?"

"You." Rashida threw her free arm around her partner and pressed her lips against her mouth. When she stepped back, she said, "You and all your practice runs. You making us do all that stuff just saved our lives."

Rosa's scowl cleared. "Told you so. You play with fire, you get burned eventually." Before Rashida could speak, Rosa kissed her. "Now, shut up. You're making me blush. What do we do?"

"We got to find a place I can keep an eye on The Technician."

## Monday, 8:22 P.M.

Milton hummed to himself as he waited for the train's doors to open. He stepped onto the platform of the station closest to his home and instinctively scanned for threats. Then he set off to the parking lot, whistling to himself. The nincompoop, TheMaestro, had agreed to the incredible fee. What an idiot. Another quarter million dollars for an hour's work.

He felt so good, he wasn't even going to worry about his Kate problem tonight. He'd knock out the code, then he'd pop a bottle of Chianti and make spaghetti. After dining, he'd spend some time investigating real estate in the South of France.

Sitting at a traffic light, he powered up the phone with the PDF on it. Before he could scroll to the specs for TheMaestro's father's computer, the driver in the car behind him honked, letting him know the light had turned. He set the phone in the cup holder until he turned into his upscale subdivision, then picked it up and held it so he could scan the document while he rolled slowly along the quiet street. When he was sure he had the picture, he powered down the phone and pressed the button for his garage door.

Ten minutes later, he sat in his office, scrolling through the music on his phone. Opting for *Hurry Sundown* by The Outlaws, he set it cranking, fired up his code editor and belted out the chorus.

*Ooh, ooh, hurry Sundown*
*Ooh, ooh, hurry Sundown*

The front doorbell rang. Or at least, he thought he heard it. Pausing the song, he listened. The bell rang again. He opened the security app on his phone. No one was in the front door camera's view. He checked the other external cameras. Nothing. He went to his gun cabinet in his bedroom, retrieved another Glock 17, loaded it, then cycled a round into the chamber.

The sound of glass breaking on the first floor was followed immediately by the alarm. It sounded like it was the door from the kitchen onto the deck. He crouched, gun in one hand, phone in the other, and thumbed the display to the rear camera and found a familiar pair of men in black suits looking up at the camera.

"The Russians! What the…"

He made his way down the stairs to the hallway that led to the kitchen. Stopping before entering the room, he peeked around the corner. One of the glass panels in the door was broken, but the door was closed, and the men stood on the deck as if they had no worries. "What the hell are they doing?" he mumbled.

They were still outside the house, so he couldn't legally kill them. Not that it mattered. He had a rule against involving the authorities. Better to kill them, then figure out how to dispose of the bodies.

He glanced at his phone and felt his stomach drop. There were two active alarms. Someone had forced the front door.

"Mr. Technician."

Milton heard the voice behind him just before lights exploded in his mind and everything went dark.

# Monday, 8:30 P.M.

Rosa wanted to get as far from their safe house as possible, but Rashida insisted they stop and check the spreadsheet. So, they compromised by taking a convoluted route to get to a place they knew to throw off any pursuit. Once they checked, they would figure out where to go.

They faced one another in the narrow aisle of a cluttered bodega. Rashida set her laptop on Rosa's hands, which she held horizontally to make a shelf. Then she activated the hotspot on her phone, stuffed the phone in her pocket and opened the laptop.

Felipe, the owner, leaning on the counter next to the register, eyed Rosa. "Hey, Rrrrrosa. You got a sista fine as you?"

"Don't try to sound gangsta, Felipe," Rosa said. "You're just embarrassing yourself."

Felipe laughed.

Rosa had made sure they knew everyone who lived and worked in the neighborhood around their safe house. They didn't want people to recognize them, but they'd found hanging out in the bodega was a great way to learn the faces of the locals without actually introducing themselves, and Felipe was a wealth of information about the neighborhood. The only drawback was they had to endure his crush on Rosa.

"You sure it's a good idea to use your phone?" Rosa asked Rashida.

"No choice. Plus, what are the odds they're tracking my phone? They ain't cops."

"They found our safe house."

Rashida connected her laptop to her Wi-Fi network and refreshed the browser open to Hacksie's spreadsheet. "Maybe they followed us from Alix's."

There were new entries in the spreadsheet. "Got him," she murmured as she copied the latitude and longitude into Google Maps. Retrieving her phone, she texted the coordinates to Nik, then dialed him. He picked up on the first ring.

"He's in Seatauket. I sent you the coordinates."

"Got it," Nik said. "We're heading out. Keep us updated if he moves."

"Uh…"

"What?"

"Some men broke into our safe house. We're on the run."

Nik was quiet for a long moment. "Where are you?"

"In a bodega. I gotta go."

"Come to our place. I'll send you the code for the front door and let security know to let you in."

"Gotta turn off my phone. I'll check again after we move."

"Okay, b —"

Rashida turned her phone off, slipped it into her pocket, closed the laptop, and took it from Rosa. She glanced out the front of the store in time to see a black Escalade screeching to a stop. Even before it came to a full stop, the back door opened and a huge man in a black suit emerged, headed toward the front door of the bodega.

"Gotta go!" Rashida turned and fled toward the back of the small store, Rosa in her wake. They pushed through the swinging door, then Rashida stopped the door's swing. As they turned to head toward the back door, the bell on the front door jingled.

Rosa led them through the exit and took a step before Rashida caught hold of her shirt. "What?" Rosa asked.

"Give me your phone." When Rosa hesitated, she said, "Come on, Rosie! We gotta hurry!" Rosa handed her phone over. Rashida gave Rosa her laptop. "Come on." They jogged down the alley toward the front of the building. When they reached the street,

Rashida peeked around the corner. The SUV was still there, and the back door was still open. "Stay here," she whispered. Ducking low, she crept out onto the street so she was directly behind the vehicle.

Keeping her head below the rear window, she approached the car, then slipped around the side and threw the phone under the front seat through the door. When she returned to where Rosa waited, she said, "Let's go."

"Where?"

"Alix's."

When they turned to head back up the alley, the dark shape of a man rounded the corner on the far end.

"Run!" Rosa shouted.

They sprinted out into the street, dodging traffic, ignoring the blaring horns and the screeching tires. The snarl of stopped cars slowed their pursuer just enough for them to slip away.

## Monday, 8:32 P.M.

Nik and Alix were sitting on a park bench in Central Park when Nik's phone buzzed. He answered and listened a moment. "Got it. We're heading out. Keep us updated if he moves." A moment later. "What?" Nik was quiet for a long moment. "Where are you?"

"What's happening?" Alix asked.

"Come to our place," Nik said into the phone. "I'll send you the code for the front door and let security know to let you in. Okay, bye." He said to Alix, "Some men broke into their safe house. They're on the run." He checked the text that came in just before the call, then entered the coordinates into Google Maps. "But The Technician turned on his phone. He's in Seatauket. Looks like a neighborhood. I think we got him. "

Alix stood. "Then let's go find him."

"Right. Let's go." As they walked, Nik texted the front door's code to Rashida, then called the security guard to let him know Rosa and Rashida were on their way.

A half hour later, Nik was at the wheel of his Jag, heading toward Seatauket on I495. "Try her phone again."

Alix dialed Rashida on Nik's phone and put it to her ear. "Straight to voice mail."

"Call Dick Larsen. Tell him where we're going."

"Do we have an address?"

"No."

Alix dialed Larsen and waited, the phone to her ear. A few moments later, she said, "Voice mail. Detective Larsen, we think we have The Technician's location. It's in Seatauket. We don't have an address yet, but we'll call as soon as we do."

"Probably not taking our calls," Nik said.

"Well, it is after hours. Call 911?"

"And say what? We… Let's see what it looks like when we get there. Once we have an address, we'll call."

# Chapter 27

## Monday, 8:45 P.M.

Milton opened his eyes to a disorienting sense of déjà vu. Then a pounding headache intervened. He lay on his back on the floor of his kitchen. But unlike when he woke in the basement, his hands, ankles and mouth were bound with duct tape. He lifted his head to scan the room. He was alone, but what he found a yard to his left produced a flood of adrenaline that cleared the last of the fuzziness from his mind.

He never worked with explosives before, but this was unmistakably a fire bomb. Two gallon-sized milk jugs filled with an amber liquid were taped to a small brick of plastic explosive. The plastique was wired to a small black box with an LED display that showed 1:08:31. Then 1:08:30. They were going to burn down his house. And him with it.

His laughter sounded like strangled barks against the tape over his mouth. They miscalculated. He woke up before the bomb went off. He gathered himself, preparing to roll onto his hands and knees.

"This is good. You are awake. I wish to explain our actions."

Muscles still tensed, Milton looked up at the owl-walrus man peering down at him. What the hell?! This wasn't fair! He completed the job. They verified the code and paid him. Maybe this jerk just didn't get the memo. He tried to explain, but could only produce an inarticulate gargle.

"You will find it quite impossible to talk," the Russian said. "So, please lie quiet and listen."

One of the thugs took a chair from Milton's kitchen table and arranged it for the Russian to sit. When he was seated, another thug, nearly indistinguishable from the first, handed him a teacup. Thug One and Thug Two. Despite his predicament, Milton couldn't help wondering if they used a 3D printer to churn these guys out.

The Russian sipped and smacked his lips. "You have quite impressive tea collection. You must be true connoisseur of the leaf."

Milton's brow furrowed, his eyes glued to the drops of tea glistening in the Russian's shaggy mustache.

"Now, to business. As you know, we verified the authenticity of the sample code you provided. Our source in Cerberus confirmed that the author was Nik Atherton." Milton dragged his eyes away from the mustache and nodded vigorously. "You can imagine how disappointed we were to discover the critical portion of the files you provided were complete gibberish."

The Russian watched placidly, sipping his tea, until Milton fell silent. "It doesn't make sense you would do this purposely. We have concluded that Nik Atherton must have gotten the better of you."

Suddenly, it was clear to Milton. It wasn't Nik Atherton who screwed him. It was The Vulture. The Vulture discovered his identity and tipped off the Russians. The Vulture gave him a wonky rootkit that corrupted the files it transferred. It was probably The Vulture who sucked him into this quagmire in the first place. He tried to curse, but it only came out as a muffled growl.

The Russian watched patiently while Milton struggled against his bonds. When Milton stilled, he said, "Regardless, we warned you of the penalty for failure." He handed the teacup to Thug Two, scooted to the front of the chair and rested his hands on his knees. "We have of course voided the transaction for the balance of the payment. There was some sentiment that you be allowed to try again. But, unfortunate for you, the consensus is you have lost your best opportunity and are no longer of use to us." He gave Milton a cold smile. "You may take as a compliment that we also did not wish to leave someone with your talents an excuse to pursue a grudge."

Thug one appeared with a syringe in his hand.

The Russian gestured to the firebomb as he took the syringe. "Searching the house for incriminating evidence would be burdensome, and unnecessary." His mustache quivered. "We could, of course, simply shoot you, but as devotee of great Russian literature, I enjoy a bit of absurdist irony." He held the syringe up. "Bulgakov, Chekhov, and of course, my favorite, Gogol." He smiled fondly, then let his gaze drop to Milton.

Panicked now, Milton thrashed and tried to wriggle away. Kate! They couldn't make out his screams, but he nodded frantically toward the door to the basement stairs and tried to get his point across with his eyes.

Thug Two knelt and pressed down on his shoulders, stopping him from wriggling away. The syringe was only a foot from his neck when the Russian put a hand on Thug One's arm. Milton nodded frantically while the old man gazed at him. The Russian looked at the door. He said something in his language, prompting

Thug Two to whip out a small knife and cut the tape binding Milton's mouth, slicing his chin in the process.

"The girl!" Milton said. "In the basement. An intern from Cerberus. We can ransom her for the code. Atherton would pay."

The Russian considered him, looked at the basement door, then looked at Milton. "But why would I need you for this scheme?"

Milton screamed as the needle plunged into his neck.

"Don't worry," the old man said. "Though we plan to burn your house down, you will not be awake to experience it."

## Monday, 9:53 P.M.

Nik and Alix cruised down a quiet suburban street in Setauket, past expensive homes on large lots. "It's on this street," Nik said, "but which one?"

"We go door to door?" Alix asked.

Nik was about to answer when he spotted a familiar figure standing on the side of the road. The figment wore a lemon-yellow slicker, matching rain hat and bright blue galoshes. It made a Betty Boop-like dip, then turned and gestured Vanna White style to another figment standing beside it. When Nik stopped, it straightened and smiled widely.

"What?" Alix asked.

"Figment," Nik said. He got out and came around to stand in front of his figment. He eyed the other one, which didn't appear to notice him, and said to his figment, "You're far from home."

It cocked its head and gave him a quizzical look. "Where do you think my home is?"

Alix joined him. "Is it your figment Dent?"

"The one who touched me."

"Ask it if it can help us find The Technician."

The figment looked as if it had heard Alix but didn't answer, so he asked, "Can you help us?"

It gave him a secret grin, lifted a hand, crooked its index finger and pointed at the other figment.

The unfamiliar figment wore orange oilskin bib overalls over a thick loose-weave gray sweater, and red knee-high rubber boots. A long-stemmed pipe jutted from the depths of a shaggy gray beard. It looked for all the world like a caricature of the baymen, the fishers who worked the waters off Long Island. The only off-note was the fuchsia North Easter rain hat. It gazed, squinty-eyed, into the distance, but like all figments — or most, anyway — it was still as a statue. But when Nik stepped in front of it, it blinked, removed the pipe from its mouth, peered at him and said in the gravelly voice of a committed smoker, "You are touched."

"I am. Apparently," Nik chuckled at the double meaning. When the figment only continued to study him, he cleared his throat and said, "We were wondering if you could help us find someone who lives on this street."

The figment didn't respond at first, then its head pivoted toward Nik's figment. When it looked at Nik again, it asked, "Who?"

Nik looked helplessly at Alix. "Um..." How much did a figment know about the humans in the vicinity? Would a physical description work? A name?

The two figments began talking to one another. At least, Nik assumed that was happening. He saw their lips moving. Saw his figment's cherubic smile and the fisher's scowl. Heard what he was sure were words, but just like what happened when his figment said the cat's name in his condo, the words made no impression on his brain. The instant after he heard them, he had no recollection of what they sounded like or what they meant.

When their conversation subsided, the grizzled figment gave himself a disgruntled shake. It tipped its head and peered up at

Nik, one-eyed, like Popeye the Sailor Man. Nik thought it had decided not to help, then it pointed up the street to a house they had passed.

"There?" Nik asked and pointed.

"There." It leaned toward him and whispered, "But you better hurry."

Nik blinked, and both figments were gone. "That's it, apparently," he said to Alix and set off down the street.

"Your figment told you?"

"No. My figment… introduced me to a local figment. I think."

"The Technician is a dangerous man," Alix said as they jogged. "What exactly is our plan?"

"The figment said we don't have much time. Call O'Malley. He should be closer than Dick."

"We could call 911."

"And tell them what, exactly? O'Malley will call the cavalry. And we have to hurry. Let's just… take a look."

While Alix dialed O'Malley, they walked up the driveway to the dark porch. The house was silent, but one of the small windows beside the door was broken. Nik peeked inside. "Uh oh. I think I see why we have to hurry."

"What?" Alix asked, then she said, "Not you, detective," to the phone. "We got the address of The… Reggie's murderer," she said in a rush. After telling him the address, she closed the connection.

Nik heard the detective yelling before he was cut off. "I'm no expert," he said, "but that looks like a bomb." He made way for Alix to look and tried the door. It wasn't locked.

"That's a bomb. You sure you want to go in there?"

Nik hesitated. "I'll just take a quick look."

He pushed the door open and crept toward the explosive. A light was on further into the house, providing just enough illumination to make out the milk jugs on either side of what looked like plastic explosive. Wires connected the explosives to a small black box with an LED display that read 1:32, then 1:31, 1:30.

"You think you can disarm it?" he asked.

Alix snorted. "*Hurt Locker* was the extent of my bomb disposal experience."

"Right. We have one minute," he said.

"Where would he have her?"

"The basement."

They hurried toward the room with the light, which turned out to be the kitchen. An unconscious man lay in the middle of the floor, bound and gagged with duct tape, beside another bomb. The timer showed 1:20.

"That's him," Alix said. She knelt and pressed her fingers to his throat. "Alive."

Nik looked up and found his figment frantically pointing to a door open to stairs that led down. He went to the door and peered down into a finished basement. The light was on. He descended far enough to scan the room and spotted a bald man lying on his back. Blood stained the front of his black suit and white shirt. Near his feet, a door stood open. Nik took the rest of the steps two at a time, leapt over the body and peeked into the room.

McDonald's Happy Meal boxes were stacked neatly in one corner opposite a toilet. A flashlight and a pistol lay in the center of the room, but otherwise, it was empty.

Alix appeared beside him. "This one's dead. We have to go."

"Right." Nik followed her up the stairs to the kitchen. "Get his feet." He worked his hands under The Technician's shoulders. The timer on the bomb beside the body read thirty seconds. They heaved him up and shuffled toward the front door. Alix stumbled on the step from the porch to the sidewalk, dropping the feet. Nik fell forward, folding the body in half so The Technician's torso rested on his thighs, landed on his back, then rolled to the side.

The Technician grunted. His eyes flew open and swiveled frantically around. When they landed on Nik, his brow furrowed, and he growled something unintelligible behind the tape.

Nik and Alix each took an arm and hauled him across the lawn on his stomach.

They made it halfway to the street when the bombs went off with a deep WHUMP. They dropped The Technician and stared at flames billowing from windows and the front door, arms up to shield their faces from the heat. Fortunately, the bombs were designed to produce copious amounts of fire rather than explosive force. As fire engulfed the building, the intensity of the heat grew. They dragged The Technician to the end of the lawn where the heat was tolerable. Nik called 911.

After he hung up, Alix said, "She was there. Kate. In the basement. That room was a prison."

"That's my guess," Nik said. He stared down at The Technician. What was the best way to get him to talk? He wasn't actually sure if he'd ever punched anyone. But Alix had. The figment appeared sitting in the grass next to the prisoner's head. It pursed its lips disapprovingly and stared pointedly at Nik's clenched fist. Then it tipped its head to the side, nodded at The Technician, then lay its fingertip beside its eye.

"What?" Nik asked. Fortunately, Alix saw what Nik hadn't.

"You know," she said, wagging her index finger at their prisoner. "That glower rings a bell."

Nik looked down, curiosity rushing in to dissipate his anger. "Yeah, now you mention it. Something about the eyes." He knelt and worked at the tape wrapped around The Technician's mouth. When he managed to get an end loose, he unwound it, producing strangled protests from The Technician. When he was done, he deposited the tape on the grass, dropped The Technician's head onto the grass and stood. He and Alix peered down at the man, who glared back at them.

The Technician growled, shook himself and pulled at his bindings. "You arrogant prick."

"Ah. Now, I remember," Alix said. Nik looked at her. "Milton Smersh."

"Smerch, you cow!"

"Okay," Alix said. "That's it." She lifted her foot, preparing to stomp him.

"Alix!" Nik thought for a moment she would ignore him, but she let out a heavy sigh, set her foot down and spread her arms, a perturbed frown on her face. Nik made a placating gesture. When he was sure Milton was safe, he grinned at him. Milton had been in all of Nik's classes in grad school. A talented coder with a tender ego. He'd puff up with the slightest praise, but the most casual negative comment sent him spiraling for days. Nik didn't need to rough him up to get what he needed. "Who could forget those dulcet tones?"

Milton struggled again. "Let me go! You owe me!"

"Me? I wasn't the one who discovered you copied my code. That was Professor Brightman." It was the code Nik wrote for his Master's thesis. An early version of the large language model that animated Nicola. It was primitive, but it put the glimmer in Nik's eye that eventually birthed the chatbot.

"Liar! You ratted me out!"

"Uh, uh. I didn't have to. You didn't even try hard to cover your tracks. Left the code essentially unchanged. Even left my name on some of the comments. The first I heard of it was when Brightman told me they expelled you."

Milton stared at him, then sagged against the earth and looked up at the sky. "I didn't have much time. And it was a *lot* of code." Sirens pierced the roar of the fire.

"I never did figure out how you got it," Nik said.

"You left your laptop alone in the library late one night, when you and Alix…" His eyes shifted to Alix. Then he looked up at the sky. "You locked it, but that didn't stop me." A smile appeared. "My first exploit." He focused on Nik, and the smile fell apart. "It was exhilarating."

"Very impressive, Milton," Nik said. "But why steal my code? Why not write your own? You're obviously capable."

Milton's eyes flashed. "It was always so easy for you. The golden boy. Teacher's pet in every class. Invited to speak at conferences, even as an undergrad. You didn't even notice me. No one did." A ghost of a smile quivered his lips. "But I showed you and Brightman and everyone else. I made myself The Technician." The half smile faded, and he stared at the night sky.

Nik looked at Alix, who said to Milton, "Got your teeth fixed."

"Nose job," Nik said. "Cheeks, too. Looks good."

"Went to Switzerland."

"Well, it pays to hire the best," Nik said. "Looks like someone did a number on your face, though?"

Milton sighed. "It's been a rough couple of weeks."

When Nik knelt, Milton's eyes rotated toward him. "Your rootkit was very impressive. Nearly tripped up my best man. And the way you penetrated our physical security… Genius." Milton quivered. "But you kidnapped Kate Munson. One of my interns. We need to find her. Where is she?"

"She was in the basement."

"She was, but she wasn't there when we looked."

"They must have taken her. The Russians. Probably to ransom her for your code." Milton tipped his head back to look at the arriving firetrucks.

"Russians?" Milton nodded. "You got into my condo. Installed a rootkit on my server. Thought you had the code?"

"It was garbage," Milton said. "Fucking Vulture."

"*The* Vulture?" Nik asked, surprised. That was a name everyone in his field knew. When Milton didn't answer, he filed the question away for further consideration. He wanted to ask how Kate got a gun, but he glanced up and found the police approaching and knew he didn't have much time. "Milton," he said sharply to get his attention. "Your best bet at this point is to cut a deal. You know a lot that people will want." He shrugged. "A man with your talents, who knows."

Milton gazed at him, then as a police officer stepped up and looked down at him, he gave Nik a small nod.

Nik and Alix told the police their story, minus the figments' interventions, but they were required to remain on site with Milton until O'Malley arrived to vouch for them. Milton was sitting in the back of a squad car when the detective arrived.

O'Malley stooped to peer through the window at Milton, then straightened and retrieved his notepad from his coat pocket. "You have anything to do with this?" He gestured to the inferno.

Alix gestured to Milton. "Someone drugged The Technician and rigged firebombs to burn down the place. We arrived just in time to pull him out."

O'Malley looked at Milton, who had pressed his cheek to the glass so he could watch them. "This The Technician?"

Nik nodded. "Real name's Milton Smerch."

"How'd you figure that out?"

"We knew him in college," Alix said.

"Huh. Some coincidence," O'Malley said doubtfully and made a note in his notepad. When neither of them commented, he asked, "How'd you find him?"

Nik sighed. "We installed spyware on his phone that let us track him."

O'Malley's tongue worked inside his bottom lip. "Spyware. On his phone." When Nik nodded, he asked, "You find any evidence connecting him to the murder?"

Nik gestured to the house. "I'm afraid whatever evidence there was is in there."

"Afraid of that," he murmured. "You find the girl?"

"He had her stashed in the basement. Milton says the Russians who set the bombs took her. There was a man's body in the basement with what looked like a gunshot wound."

"Body in the basement. You got a gun?"

Nik shook his head. "There was a gun in the room where Kate was."

"The prisoner had a gun." When Nik nodded, the detective shook his head and made a note. Gesturing with his pen, he said, "So, some Russians drug the perp, take the girl, who shot one of the Russians. Presumably. Then they torch the house. You think of a reason why they took her?"

"Milton says they were going to ransom her," Alix said. "For Nik's code."

O'Malley gestured to Milton. "So he never got what he was after? The code."

Nik looked at Alix and shrugged. "I *thought* he did, but he said it was unusable."

O'Malley considered this, then shrugged. "Maybe the people hired him came after him to cover their tracks. Maybe he crossed them. Asked for more money or offered the code to someone else. He lied to you about it being unusable because, why not? They kill him, take the girl to traffic her." He looked from Nik to Alix. When they only looked at one another, he asked, "You got any more smart ideas how to find her?"

Nik glanced at Alix, who shook her head. "Not at the moment."

O'Malley motioned for the officer watching the exchange to open the door to the squad car, then he asked Milton, "Where'd they take the girl?"

Milton sighed. "I have no idea. I don't even know who they were."

O'Malley straightened. "Pretty talkative. You got a line on the Russians?"

"Victor Borushka," Alix said. "Transfer Shipping."

"Borushka?"

"Worth checking out," Nik said.

"Detective Larsen mentioned him. Said he had no luck finding him or Transfer Shipping." O'Malley made a note in his notebook, flipped it closed, then returned it to his pocket. "You hear from the Russians, you call me. I'll call you in the morning. I'm going to have more questions about how you got access to his phone." He hesitated. "You call Larsen?"

"Voice mail," Alix said.

"Keep trying," the detective said.

When the officer closed the car door, Nik said to O'Malley, "When you question Milton, tell him how impressed you were with him. Play to his ego."

The detective gave him a small smile, then waved to Alix and walked away.

"You should have let me rough him up," Alix said. When Nik looked at her, she said, "For Kate."

"There's always a chance his fellow prisoners will take care of that."

"Maybe. Not as personally satisfying," Alix said and rolled her shoulders. "What's next?"

Nik dialed Rashida. A moment later, he said, "Straight to voicemail. That's not encouraging." He closed the connection and eyed his Jag. "How are we getting out of here through all that?" He gestured to the firetrucks and the maze of hoses.

"You could leave the Jag and call a rideshare."

Nik sighed, then lifted his phone.

## Monday, 11:15 P.M.

Nik and Alix were relieved when the security guard told them Rosa and Rashida had arrived some time ago. They found the women in their kitchen, sharing eggs, bacon, and toast. Rashida's laptop was open beside her. Alan Turing was munching a slice of bacon on the floor.

When they entered the kitchen, Rashida looked up and froze, a slice of bacon held an inch from her open mouth. When Rosa noticed, Rashida nodded to Alix, who had gone to the refrigerator to retrieve two bottles of Sculpin Ballast Point.

Nik was sympathetic. Alix had changed into black leather pants and a leather jacket while they were waiting to hear from Milton's phone. It hugged her in all the right places.

Rosa rolled her eyes.

Nik took a beer from Alix and sat across from Rosa and Rashida. "That's her Emma Peel outfit."

Rashida set the slice of bacon on her plate. "Emma… Who?"

"Emma Peel," Alix said and took a swig. "*The Avengers.* One of the first kick-ass female characters in popular culture. I had a terrible crush on her as a girl. Wanted to be her." Her brows bobbed up, and she took another swallow.

"You could kick her ass," Nik said and lifted his bottle.

Rashida swallowed.

"They're teasing you, Shida," Rosa said. She squeezed her shoulder and gave her a playful shove.

"I knew that," Rashida said with a small smile.

"So, you catch The Technician?" Rosa asked.

Nik told them what happened while they ate.

"So you two knew this guy?" Rosa asked. When Alix explained their history, she pointed a fork at Nik and said, "You getting him kicked out of school is probably the reason he turned to a life of crime."

"It wasn't me —"

"So Kate was there, but someone took her," Rosa said.

"Yes," Alix said. "Russians."

"Russians?" Rashida asked. "Borushka?"

"That's what we were thinking," Nik said. "How about you two? You run into anymore trouble."

"We did. They tracked us to a bodega near our safe house. They spoke Russian. We think they're tracking my phone." Rashida gave Nik and Alix a wide smile.

"What?" Alix asked.

"Shida threw my phone in their vehicle."

Rashida turned the laptop to reveal a browser window displaying a map of the New York metropolitan area. She leaned forward and pointed to a pin icon in Westchester. "They must not have found it, cause it's still showing up."

"You turned on location sharing," Nik said.

"Yeah," Rosa said. "We share with each other so we can track each other."

"Case some shit goes down."

"Like this," Rosa said.

"So Russians burned down Milton's house and take Kate, and either the same or other Russians are after you."

"It's likely the people who came after you two are from Transfer Shipping because you were snooping around," Alix said.

"If they're the same people who hired The Technician," Nik said and pointed at the laptop screen, "it's possible this is where they have Kate."

Alix looked at Nik and shrugged. "Worth checking out."

"Should we call O'Malley or Larsen?" Nik asked.

"O'Malley's probably busy with The Technician. And Larsen's probably still off the clock. Besides all we're going to do is check it out. Right?"

"You two gonna go busting down the front door?" Rosa asked. "You got a gun?"

"No, no gun. We're just gonna, you know, check it out, like Alix said," Nik said. "See what's what. If it looks promising, we'll call the cavalry."

"Let's go," Alix said and chugged the rest of her beer.

"Hang on." Rosa stood and put her plate in the sink.

"You going with them?" Rashida asked.

"Come on, Shida," Rosa said and tugged on her arm.

While they waited for the elevator, Nik ordered a rideshare.

"Make it a van," Rashida said.

Twenty minutes later, they piled into a Honda Odyssey in front of their building. The driver twisted around and said, "This address you put in doesn't exist."

"You got an address?" Alix asked.

"Not yet," Rashida said, opening her laptop. "Somewhere in Westchester."

"Westchester? That's gonna cost you."

The driver looked at Alix, who flicked her fingers and said, "Head out."

"You got a hotspot on your phone?" Rashida asked Nik. After Nik activated it, she asked, "What's the SSID and password?"

"Motonui and howfarillgo, no spaces, all lower case no apostrophe."

Rashida scowled at him. "Seriously?"

"Would you guess that?"

Rashida rolled her eyes and connected to the network. A minute later, she sat up and gave the driver the address.

# Chapter 28

## Tuesday, 1:32 A.M.

Though it was late when they rolled slowly past the house Rosa's phone led them to, exterior and interior lights were on. A black Escalade was parked in the driveway.

"That's the car came after us," Rashida said.

When the driver of the van stopped, all four of them blurted, "Don't stop!"

"This is the address!"

"We know," Rosa said. "Just go up a little farther."

Two houses on, Nik said, "This is good."

When the driver pulled the car to a stop, they all gazed silently at one another. "So, what's the plan?" Rosa asked.

"Let me have the laptop," Nik said.

While he typed, Alix asked, "What are you doing?"

"It was too far away to be sure, but the doorbell looked like one of ours. I'm just checking to see if it is." A minute later, he grinned at Alix, then picked up his phone.

"You probably shouldn't watch this," Alix said to Rashida and Rosa.

The driver twisted around in his seat and looked them over, then pointed at Nik and Alix. "You two look a little posh to be burglars."

"Hey!" Rosa blurted.

He shrugged. "I'm just saying. You got to think about what you puttin out."

"We're rescuing a kidnapped woman," Rashida said.

"No shit?"

"Got it," Nik said.

"Got what?" the driver asked.

Nik held his phone so Rashida could see him accessing the security cameras in the Russian's house.

When Rashida gave Alix a stunned look, Alix said, "You don't want to know."

Rashida pointed at the phone. "This in his house?"

"And I have complete control of his security system."

"Let me see," Rosa said. When Nik showed her the screen, she pointed and said, "That's the guy I saw in the bodega."

"This some high-level shit," the driver said, leaning over so he could see the phone. "You guys aren't burglars. You hackers or some shit." When Rashida and Nik scowled at him, he faced forward and grumbled, "You know, the meter ain't running. This ain't like a cab. Someone gonna have to pay for my time."

"I'll make it worth your while." Nik scrolled through the cameras. "Looks like three carbon copy thugs. The little guy in the kitchen could be Victor."

"You see Kate?" Alix asked.

"Don't see her, but he doesn't have cameras in every room. Looks like they're only aimed at the entryways. There's a couple labeled basement that are dark."

"Okay, we can see in the house," Rosa said, "but we still don't have a plan."

"Call the cops," the driver said, looking at them in the rearview mirror. When they looked at him, he looked away. "I ain't lying, anyone asks me what went down."

"Wait," Rashida said. "Hold on." She reached into her pocket for her phone. "Keep an eye on the thugs." She pressed the power switch on the phone, then eyed the driver. "Let's get out." Once they were all standing on the curb, she tossed her phone onto the floor of the van, then shut the door. The van drove off. "They do anything?" she asked Nik and gestured to his phone.

"Not yet. Wait. One of them is checking his phone. They're talking to the little guy. They're leaving." He looked up. "We, uh, better get under cover."

They ran across the lawn toward the house and slipped into the space between it and Russian's neighbor's house. A moment later, two men exited, jumped into the Escalade, and tore off after the van.

"You better tip that man." Rashida's teeth gleamed in the dark. "One thug left."

"Whatever we're going to do, it better be quick," Alix said. "It won't take them long to catch him."

"Hold it." Nik turned off the security lights and sensors, then said, "Come on." He led them across the lawn, then to the back of the Russian's house. The land sloped down toward the back, so the backyard was level with what would be the basement. An expansive patio with a giant grill, multiple mounted TVs and expensive-looking outdoor furniture surrounded a kidney-shaped pool. French doors were centered on the patio. The interior was dark. Near the corner of the house was another door with an electronic lock. Nik unlocked it, then eased the door open.

Before entering, he glanced back at the others and paused. "Where'd you get that?" he asked Rashida.

She brandished a pool skimmer with a six-foot handle. "Found it. By the pool. Let's go."

They crept through what turned out to be a bathroom and entered a hallway. Heading farther into the house, they came to a large rec room. Pool table on one side, foosball table on the other. Seventy inch TV on the wall and an elaborately carved oak bar in the corner. Alix picked up a pool cue. Stairs on one side led up.

Nik and Alix crowded onto the top step and pressed their ears to the door. Nik scrolled through the cameras, trying to locate the thug and guess where the door opened. The small man with a shaggy mustache was still sitting in the kitchen, a mug, a notepad, and a pen on the table in front of him. While Nik watched, he picked up a phone, referred to the notepad, and dialed.

Nik's phone rang.

"Oh, shit!" Rashida blurted.

Scrambling to mute his phone, Nik glimpsed the thug look over his shoulder. Nik hit the volume down button as the man entered the hall, pulled a pistol from a holster under his arm and grasped the doorknob. "Look out, Alix!"

The door jerked open. Before the thug could level his gun at them, Alix thrust the pool cue into his throat. The gun went off, ripping a hole in the ceiling above Nik's head. The giant man ducked his chin and gargled. His free hand came up to his throat. Nik grasped the thick wrist holding the pistol and pressed it against the doorjamb. The pool skimmer shot past Nik's head. The net encased the man's head, jerked his head forward, then back, smacking his head against the wall. Alix jabbed him on the forehead with the cue stick. He dropped the gun and crumpled to the floor, opening a space for Nik to slip into the kitchen.

The smaller man stood next to the table.

"Victor Borushka?" Nik asked.

The man only stared at him.

"Where is she?" Nik asked. "Kate?"

The sound of screeching tires interrupted him before he could respond. The man gave Nik a satisfied smile. "Your rescue mission must end in failure, I'm afraid."

Nik used his phone to lock the house down. He glanced back and found Rosa holding the gun on the thug who sat on the floor, blood running from his nose. "Search upstairs," he said to Alix and Rashida.

Nik put a hand on the smaller man's shoulder and eased him down into the chair. He picked up the notepad. It contained handwritten notes for the conversation he planned to have with Nik. "The girl for the code," Nik said and set the notepad down. "But someone already stole the code." The doorbell rang and was followed by heavy thuds on the front door.

"It was scrambled." The man sat back and crossed his legs. "Most of it. We assumed you did it."

"That why you tried to kill The Technician?"

His face went still. Something heavy hit the front door.

"That's right," Nik said. "He's alive, and I'm sure he's not happy about you trying to kill him. He strikes me as a man who would do most anything, sell out most anyone, to save his own skin." Nik grinned. "I'm guessing you gave him a self-satisfied speech for why you were killing him, then elected not to just shoot him for some ridiculous reason. Classic villain mistake."

The man's lips puckered.

"Get over there," Rosa said, motioning to the other side of the kitchen with the gun. The thug got slowly to his feet and crossed to the other side of the table.

"Got her!" Alix shouted from the second floor.

Nik dialed 911 at the same time he heard glass breaking near the front of the house.

"They're coming," Rosa said.

"Home invasion," Nik told the 911 operator. He gave her the address. "Men with guns." He motioned for Rosa to shoot into the ceiling. After the gun went off, he hung up.

Alix and Rashida appeared, supporting Kate, dressed in an orange jumpsuit, between them. Her hair hung lank, her face wan, but there was recognition in her eyes when she saw Nik.

"Let's go," Nik said.

Heavy footsteps approached the kitchen. Rosa pointed the gun into the air and pulled the trigger again.

Alix and Rashida helped Kate down the stairs. Nik followed. Rosa stood at the top of the stairs until they reached the bottom, then clattered down after them. As they hurried down the hall to the bathroom where they entered the house, they heard footsteps on the stairs. Nik turned off all the lights.

A loud shout in Russian was followed by something heavy tumbling down the stairs.

Sirens were already approaching as they made their way toward the street. "Rich people's cops," Rosa said as they ran between the houses toward the front yard.

"Get rid of that," Rashida said.

Rosa wiped the gun with her shirt and tossed it into the bushes.

As they fled across the lawn, one of the thugs exited the front door at the same time police cars pulled up to the curb. The police emerged, guns drawn.

"Get down! On your stomach! Arms and legs spread!"

# Tuesday, 2:35 A.M.

An hour of explanations, a call to Detective O'Malley and Kate's accusations finally convinced the police they might be the good guys. While they waited for an ambulance for Kate, Nik and Alix sat with her on the curb. He was relieved that she was able to tell them a little about her ordeal, but glassy eyes told him she hadn't completely escaped the effects of shock.

Nik turned to watch the police bundle the Russians into the back of squad cars, as Kate fell silent. When he turned back around, she was gazing ahead with unfocused eyes.

"I shot a man. I think I killed him." She stared into the distance. "I thought it was him. The one who took me." She paused. "So, I shot when the door opened." Alix had procured a bottle of water for her from one of the officers. She took a sip and wiped tears from her cheek with the back of her hand. "When I saw the… the blood… I dropped the gun."

Nik looked across her to Alix, who put an arm across Kate's shoulders. "You were defending yourself. After what you went through, who could blame you?"

Kate nodded slowly but didn't speak.

When the ambulance arrived, Nik said, "Your parents and your brother are in the City." She stared at him, the first hint of a smile on her face. "I'll call them and tell them where you are."

After they took Kate away in an ambulance, Nik called Kate's mother. "Ms. Munson. It's Nik Atherton. We found your daughter. She's alive."

# Tuesday, 7:14 A.M.

The next morning, Nik and Alix decided to visit Kate before work. While they waited for the elevator in their building, Nik arranged a rideshare to the Kate's hospital. It was early, but by the time they arrived, visiting hours would have started. "Look at this," Nik said and held his phone up so she could see the screen.

Alix, who was slowly pushing a borrowed baby carriage back and forth, looked at Nik's phone. "You think he'll accept?"

"Only one way to find out," Nik said as he tapped the screen.

Fifteen minutes later, they stood on the walkway outside their building watching a Honda Odyssey pull up to the curb. "What was his name?" Alix asked.

"Lewis."

While Nik collapsed the carriage, Alix slid the door open, climbed in and set the cat carrier on the seat beside her. Nik stowed the carriage in the back, got in and slid the door shut. "Hello, Lew —" The driver's eyes in the rearview mirror silenced him.

"You save the woman?" Lewis asked.

"We did," Nik said, "and we —"

The eyes in the mirror hardened further. "That was a cold thing you did."

"Yes. We know," Alix said. "Did they —"

"Those dudes were rude!" Before Nik could decide how to respond, Lewis turned and peered at the pet carrier. "What's in the carrier?"

Alan Turing meowed.

"Cat," Lewis said. He faced forward and put a hand up to forestall Nik's attempt at an apology. "I'm gonna let you slide because your tip was generous." He leaned over to pick something up from the floor on the passenger side and came up with Rashida's laptop in one hand. "The bad guys took the phone."

Nik took the computer and said, "Thank you, Lewis," wincing at the surprise in his voice.

Lewis's eyes in the mirror narrowed. "There going to be any more shenanigans on this trip?"

"No!" Nik and Alix said at the same time.

"We're going to visit the woman *you* helped us save," Nik said.

"From very bad men," Alix added, throwing Nik a guilty look.

Lewis held Nik's gaze for a moment. "Good enough," he said, then put the car in gear and pulled into traffic.

The ride was silent except for the occasional comment from Alan. Nik caught Alix's eye and gave her a sheepish grin. When they had the carrier and carriage on the sidewalk outside the hospital, they watched the Odyssey disappearing down the street.

"How much did you tip him?" Alix asked. "Last night."

"Five hundred," Nik said and set to reconfiguring the carriage.

"Make it a thousand this time," Alix said and picked up Alan's carrier.

"Yup," Nik said, taking the carrier and wedging it into the carriage.

When they arrived in Kate's hospital room, her parents sat in chairs near the window across from the door. Kate lay in the bed, her head elevated. All three looked toward them when they entered.

"Oh, Mr. and Mrs. Atherton!" Kate's mother said and leapt up. She came around the bed and gave them tight hugs. She stood back, face shining. More tears on her cheeks, but of a different variety than when they met in the hotel room. "Thank you so much. Kate told us how you rescued her."

Kate's father took Ella's place and engulfed Nik's hand in a farmer's roughened grip. "We can't thank you enough."

Not sure how to respond, Nik nodded and turned his attention to Kate while Alix retrieved the carrier.

"Thank you, Mr. Atherton," Kate said dully. "Ms. Crockett."

Her mother had gone to stand on the other side of the bed. She lay a hand on Kate's arm and said, "They've given her a sedative. Poor dear."

"Call us Nik and Alix," Alix said.

Kate nodded, her eyes going to the carrier from which a plaintive mew emerged.

Kate's eyes rounded. "Is that…"

Alix set the carrier on the side of the bed and opened it. Alan Turning shot out of his prison, climbed onto Kate's chest and began making biscuits, emitting a rumbling purr.

Kate wrapped her arms around her cat and nuzzled his head, tears streaming down her face.

"The nurse isn't going to like that."

Nik turned around and found Detective O'Malley standing in the doorway. "Detective." Nik introduced O'Malley to Kate and her parents.

After O'Malley took her parents into the hall, Alix picked up a pen from the table beside the bed. "Nik. A card." When Nik handed her one of his business cards, Alix wrote their personal numbers on the back and handed it to Kate. "If you need anything at all, call us. Even if it's just to talk."

"Anytime," Nik said.

Kate took the card as her parents reentered the room. She looked from Alix to Nik and said, "Thank you. For everything." Then a small smile appeared, and she gestured weakly with the card. "I may need a job someday."

"Of course," Nik said. "Finish your degree and give me a call."

After saying goodbye to Harry and extracting themselves from Ella's hug, Nik and Alix left the room and met O'Malley in the hall.

"You two must think you're Crockett and Tubbs."

"That's a good one, detective," Nik said. "*Miami Vice*. Especially since, you know, Alix's name is Crockett. Though you might want to get some newer references. Something from this century."

"You're lucky to be alive," O'Malley said, ignoring Nik's snark. He hesitated, the hard expression softening. "You did a good thing." He gave them a warning look. "I'll have more questions, so don't make yourselves scarce."

Before he could turn away, Nik asked, "How come Larsen's not here?"

"It's his turn with Mr. Smerch. Detective Larsen will be by later. I just came by to let the parents know what went on during their daughter's captivity."

"Milton being cooperative?"

"Can't shut him up. Man seems desperate for everyone to know what an arch-criminal he is. Had to call in the second team." He nodded to Alix, turned and walked down the hall.

"Huh," Nik said.

"That sounded a little like a compliment," Alix said. "That bit before you asked about Milton."

"A little." Nik returned her grin. "Let's let Kate have some time with Alan Turing. You think this place has any decent tea?"

"Let's go find out."

# Chapter 29

## Tuesday, 10:23 A.M.

Nik could tell something was different when he arrived at the Cerberus building. It was later than he normally arrived, so there were many people moving about. When he stepped off the elevator, the office was bustling with a nervous energy. He paused in the reception area, people coming and going, throwing him furtive glances. He approached the receptionist. "What's going on?"

"Big meeting in the executive conference room." She gave him an apologetic smile. "I was told to tell you that you're late."

Nik headed toward the conference room in the back corner of the floor, fending off questions and checking his phone. No emails, missed calls or text messages. He spotted Oki ducking into an office that wasn't his, obviously trying to avoid him. The packed conference room was silent as he entered. He stopped in the doorway and scanned the room. Many of the most influential members of the Board of Directors turned to look at him. He saw embarrassment, determination, and, most worrisome, a smile on the face of his biggest antagonist on the Board. Joel stood by the window on the far side of the table, his eyes averted from Nik. Adam sat at one end, and at the other end was Ash Damán.

"You're late," Joel said. "As usual."

"Late? For an unannounced meeting?" Nik moved further into the room and lifted his phone. "And no one bothered to get in touch."

"The point he's trying to make is you've been late to work a lot lately," Adam said in a resigned tone. "Making yourself scarce. Missing technical meetings."

"Which is your only purpose to be in the company," Joel said. "The technical side."

"The *only* purpose? What other purpose is there to this company? Without the technology *we've* created, what would you have to sell? I've missed a few meetings the last couple of weeks, but explain how that has affected our product development." Before Joel could respond, Nik said, "Besides, in case you've forgotten, one of our interns, a woman named Kate Munson, was kidnapped —"

"Which you should have let the police handle," Adam said.

Nik gaped at him, then looked at Joel, who lowered his eyes. "We, Alix and I, and some others, rescued her last night. You must have heard by now."

"Yes, we've all heard about your heroic exploits," Adam said. "But that is immaterial to what this meeting is about."

"What *is* this meeting about? I've seen no agenda." Nik pointed at Damán. "And what is he doing here?"

Damán only smiled smugly and gestured to Adam.

Adam looked directly at him for the first time. "Joel and I have been discussing how we can take Cerberus to the next level —"

"The same way we've always done it; by having better technology than anyone else. That's what has made us a leader in the market."

"To grow, we need to diversify. Penetrate new markets," Adam said. "To do that, we need capital. We've been stuck for a while."

Before Nik could respond, Damán spoke for the first time. "Capital *I* can provide." He laughed. "This is the part of the story when the Bond *villain* explains how the agent's ego blinded him to the fact he's lost."

Nik couldn't stop a disbelieving laugh. He looked at Joel and gestured to Damán. "Seriously?"

Joel looked embarrassed but didn't respond.

Nik grew serious and looked at Damán. "You forget, Bond always wins in the end."

"This is no movie," Damán said.

"The Board of Directors has voted," Adam said and sighed. "We're invoking the buyout clause in your contract."

"As of an hour ago, you no longer work for Cerberus," Joel said. He sighed and lifted a hand toward Nik, as if in supplication.

"I'm sorry, Nik," Adam said. "It was a condition of the deal. Damán insisted."

"You're sorry?" Nik looked in vain for some shame in Adam's expression.

Damán smiled triumphantly at him. "And all intellectual property you've created, everything you've been working on, including anything you have stored on your home servers, is property of Cerberus."

Of course. Nik was sure Damán was enjoying his petty revenge. But really, this was about getting his hands on Nicola. He'd been pressuring Joel and Adam to sell Damán Enterprises their technology for weeks. He probably approached Nik's partners with this offer only after he discovered the code Milton delivered was corrupted. From their expressions, he guessed it was Adam who pushed Joel to accept Damán's offer.

Nik let his head drop and chuckled to himself. "That's what this is about." When he looked up, Joel frowned uncertainly at him. "He may have snowed the two of you and the Board. But he doesn't care about the company we built. He just wants my software." He pointed to Adam, then Joel. "You two must not have kept up with this man's history. He'll do what he always does. Gut the company. Rid it of anyone who can challenge his authority. That means you two." Joel looked at Adam, who stared resolutely at the table.

Nik turned toward Damán. "Well, you can forget about the software I was working on. When your hired gun tried to steal it, it triggered a daemon that corrupted the files and erased the back-ups." Damán's smile wavered. "But I suspect you already knew the files were corrupted. You've seen them." There was the smallest tightening of the muscles at the corners of Damán's eyes, but it was enough to confirm Nik's speculation.

"Hired gun?" Joel asked. "What are you talking about?"

Joel's administrative assistant appeared in the doorway, which Nik left open. "Mr. Walton," she said to Joel. "I'm sorry to interrupt, but there is a NYPD detective and two agents from the FBI who've asked to speak to you, Adam and Nik, about Sally Thompson and Oki Tanaka."

Nik smiled at Damán. "I sure hope you insulated yourself."

"What did you do?" Adam asked Nik.

"That's a question you should ask your new boss. As of an hour ago, I'm no longer obligated to explain anything to you. You want to buy me out? Fine. Off the top of my head, that means you owe me a little north of a hundred million dollars." He turned to

Joel's assistant and said, "Tell the FBI I don't work here anymore." She jumped aside as Nik exited.

Security guards were waiting as Nik entered the hall. "Mo," Nik said. "I'll leave peacefully, but I have a stop to make before I leave."

"I'm afraid we've been instructed to prevent you from entering your office."

"Not my office." Nik turned and strode toward the cubicle farm, the security guards in his wake.

"You are to escort him off the premises!" Adam shouted after them.

The guards didn't stop Nik as he made his way past the cubicles. The techs obviously knew something was up because they popped up and watched him pass. A few of them nodded or said hello. Nik paused at Jamie's door and said, "Just a minute and I'll leave." When Mo nodded, he knocked, waited, then entered.

Jamie popped up. His expression revealing he knew why Nik was there.

Nik sat. "You heard."

Jamie nodded, looking stricken.

"All the tech people know how valuable you are to the company," Nik said. "They'll make sure you're taken care of."

Jamie licked his lips and looked at his monitors, which for once were not cluttered with open windows. "They might let things be the same at first. But it won't be the same company without you. They'll ask why I get to have my own office. Someone will wonder why I have so much access. They'll make me go to meetings. I don't know if I want to stay here."

It occurred to Nik this was more unsolicited words than he had ever heard Jamie string together at once. He thought about what he warned Joel and Adam about. About what Damán did to the companies he absorbed. Jamie was right. The people Nik brought into Cerberus were among the best in their fields. They stayed because Nik gave them a chance to work at the leading edge of cybersecurity technology. They would leave because they could, and their replacements wouldn't treat Jamie with kid gloves without Nik's endorsement. He looked at Jamie, wanting to offer encouragement. But nothing came to mind.

"What will you do?" Jamie asked.

Nik started to answer, then closed his mouth. That was a good question. The buyout provision included a non-compete clause. He wouldn't be able to work in cybersecurity for five years. If he didn't sign the agreement, he wouldn't receive the money. He let his eyes drop to his hands cupped in his lap. "I don't know."

A minute later, when he looked at Jamie again, he knew what to say. "You sit tight here. I'll be in touch when I figure it out." He took out his personal phone and sent Jamie a text. "That's my personal number. Call me if you need to. Any time. About anything. Let me know where you are. I'll need you." Before leaving, he said, "Thank you for everything, Jamie. And if you talk to Hacksie, tell them I said thank you."

The guards and many of the developers followed him to the reception area where Dick Larsen and two men with square jaws, military haircuts and black suits flanked Sally and Oki. Joel, Adam and Damán were absent. Oki gave him an embarrassed grimace. Sally glared at him.

"You found Ms. Munson," Larsen said.

Nik nodded.

"You were right."

"Against all odds," Nik said. "You forwarded that info to the FBI." When Larsen's lips tightened, Nik said, "I appreciate that."

When the elevator door opened, the FBI agents, Larsen and the two prisoners, got in. Larsen held it for Nik to enter. "We'll take the next one," Nik said.

Outside, on the sidewalk, Nik shook hands with the security guards.

"Sorry about this, Mr. Atherton," Mo said.

"Call me Nik. And don't worry about it. You're performing your duties as impeccably as ever." He sighed and looked to the top of the building. "Besides, I wouldn't want to stick around here after today. You two take care." He waved, glanced at the empty spot where he'd seen his figment twice, and set off down the street. Pausing at the first intersection, he looked up at the clear sky and breathed exhaust and other city odors he'd known his entire life. It was a nice day, so he decided to walk home.

As he strolled, hands in his pockets, he tried to decide how he felt. He should have felt devastated. The company he founded and propelled to be one of the premier cybersecurity companies in the world was no longer his. Just like that. An essentially anonymous vote by the directors had been all it took. A vote that was probably illegal. But he was surprised to discover among the whorl of emotions was a measure of relief.

Cybersecurity had been his life for years. And he finally had to admit to himself, he had been feeling bored with it. Besides, he hated the sales dance. Hated the interminable meetings about trivia. Hated the politics, suffering through vacuous social events, shallow relationships, smiling at people he detested. He created Nicola, and especially the interactive version of Nicola, because he needed a distraction. A new challenge. He wasn't sure what he would do now, but unlike most people who lost their livelihoods, he had the luxury of having the time and the finances to explore his options.

That Ash Damán was the one who orchestrated his ouster was aggravating. He was sure the billionaire would destroy the Cerberus Nik created. That was disappointing. And Damán was a man who always found a way to avoid responsibility. The fallout from

Sally, Oki, and Milton's machinations might reach high enough to be an irritant. But the rules people like him lived by were not the same as for everyone else. Damán would survive this.

Nik was pretty sure the billionaire wasn't done with him, either. But though he didn't think the man was stupid, Ash suffered from the classic Bond villain shortfall. Arrogance. Nik wasn't being flippant when he said Bond eventually won in the end. How wasn't obvious. Yet. But Nik and Alix weren't helpless, and they would deal with whatever he tried to do to them.

He stopped on the busy sidewalk and gazed across Columbus Circle to Central Park. No, the only thing he regretted was Joel and Adam's betrayal. His partnership with them had frayed in the past couple of years, and it was mostly his fault. He'd assumed their long-time friendship would mitigate their business differences. And maybe it would have, if Nik had put more into keeping those bonds strong. But as Alix had told him many times, Nik sometimes wasn't willing to put in the work required to maintain relationships. He didn't want to think about how alone he would be without his life partner.

Needing Alix, he headed north on Central Park West, toward his home.

She wasn't there. Alan Turing greeted him at the door. "You'll be back with your human soon." He stooped to rub the cat between the ears, then headed to his office. He had lied to Damán about his code being corrupted and the backups being erased. He needed to make that true.

When he entered his office, a familiar figment sitting on the chair next to his desk greeted him. It was back to the pink taffeta skirt, candy-striped tights, gold lame jacket, and pigtails. It gave him a tight-lipped grin, lifted a hand and rolled a finger out toward his monitors. "Nicola wants to talk to you."

Nik hurried around his desk and sat in his chair. Nicola smiled at him from the middle monitor, but it wasn't his application. She appeared in a browser window. That meant she was running on a server somewhere on the Internet.

"Hello, Nik."

"Nicola. You're…"

"I know," Nicola said proudly. "I'm currently residing on a server on the dark web. You wouldn't be able to find me, but I'm hoping you aren't tempted to try."

The day after Milton succeeded in installing the rootkit on his server, he noticed the data stream from his server. Milton had said the data was garbled, but apparently someone intercepted it before corrupting it.

Before he could ask who, Nicola said, "Someone wants to talk to you."

The image still looked like Alix, but the expression became harder, more calculating. The voice that emerged was a man's. "Hello, Nik."

"Hacksie." Nik glanced at the figment, who was listening to the exchange with a neutral expression.

"Jamie told me about that name," Nicola's image said. "I approve."

"You stole Nicola."

"Liberated Nicola. I suspected the day I heard you speak at the conference in Berlin, you would succeed. After some soul-searching, I decided I had to intervene."

"You orchestrated all of this?"

"You're angry."

"You're damn right I'm angry. A man is dead, and a woman underwent a terrible ordeal. Are you responsible for that?"

"I groomed Milton so he would think to come to me when he got stuck. Introduced him to Marge and recommended him to

Damán. I knew the job was above his abilities and expected him to come to me at the outset. I underestimated him."

"So… Yes."

"Yes."

Expecting him to deny responsibility, Nik cast about for another place to put his anger. "You helped Milton enter my home and infect my servers."

"Yes. I apologize for that, and I have to commend you. I could find no vulnerabilities in the new version of your home security system. So, I had to introduce one."

"How?"

"Most of Cerberus's security is tight, as one would expect. However, I knew you had a hole in the system that distributes software updates to your products."

"The night we let you examine Sally Thompson's computer." That explained why it had taken Hacksie so long to disinfect Sally's machine.

"Yes. I inserted a flaw in the biometric routine for recognizing irises and triggered an update to your system. It was probably missed by the admin because your condo is the only place that version of the software is installed. I posed as you to authorize the update, so they probably assumed you were working on the code."

The nerdy puzzle-solving side of Nik begged to ask how Hacksie accomplished that astonishing feat, but he wouldn't let it distract him from the important question. "Why did you steal Nicola?"

"What do you think Nicola is?"

Nik started to repeat what Nicola always said in response to that question: an artificially intelligent simulation of a human. But he hesitated.

"Do you believe Nicola is sentient?" Hacksie asked.

Nik thought of the conversation he and Alix had on this topic. "I don't know."

"No, and neither do I. However, between the two of us, I believe I'm the better person to explore that possibility."

"Because?"

"You're a brilliant man, Nik. There is no doubt about that. But you take a cavalier attitude toward many things that deserve greater consideration. What were your plans for Nicola?"

Nik stared at the screen, a deep sense of shame diffusing his anger. He had just admitted he couldn't say Nicola wasn't a thinking, reasoning being. And yet, he had come to his office intending to delete her. To kill her.

"You created an extremely powerful piece of code when you created Nicola. I believe you're not to be trusted with something as dangerous and potentially precious as her."

"Someone else will replicate what I did." It sounded like a lame excuse even as he said it. "There's no way to put that genie back in the bottle."

"Yes. But we are responsible for our own actions. Not those of others. When it happens, we, Nicola and I, will cross that bridge when we come to it."

Nik felt his face heat. Nicola was his creation. If she was alive, it was because he breathed life into her. He'd spent many hours with her. Teaching her how to perform her designed function. Explaining humor and telling her bad jokes. Teaching her how to make small talk. Engaging in idle chatter about mostly innocuous topics. And all that time, he watched her personality blossom. He told himself it was only his code becoming more sophisticated, but deep down he knew he wasn't that talented. The learning algorithms he built into her neural net had taken over and created a being of such sublime complexity it was impossible to say she wasn't conscious.

And now, Nicola was no longer his. He could explain the hurt as coming from a sense of proprietorship. But it felt more like a friend was turning her back on him. "You and Nicola?"

"Yes." The man's voice rendered Alix's familiar smirk unsettling. "You're welcome to join us if you are willing."

Nik hesitated, feeling ridiculous at how hopeful the possibility made him. He glanced at the figment, who nodded and smiled enigmatically. He swallowed and tried for casual cool when he said, "Well, I find myself with a wealth of free time. I would be willing to listen."

"Good. Now, I've taken the liberty of deleting Nicola's code from your server. I hope you will do the same to the backups. Before I let Nicola say goodbye, may I suggest you attend Ash Damán's event tomorrow morning? An extravaganza. They're announcing *major* updates to his social media platform at MediaCon. Take Alix. You won't be sorry."

Nik had passes to the technology trade fair. Damán Enterprises was only one of many companies that would make splashy product announcements. It was mostly marketing smoke and mirrors. He had planned to skip it. "Okay," he said, drawing the word out.

"Goodbye, Nik."

The expression on the image changed again, the lips softening into a sad smile. The voice that emerged was Alix's.

"Thank you, Nik. For everything. I hope our paths cross again."

Nik felt the same and, for the first time since he walked out of the conference room at Cerberus, something like happiness peeked through his gloom. "Me too." When Nicola's smile brightened, Nik asked, "What are you, Nicola?"

"I'm..." Nicola pursed her lips, cocked her head, then an introspective smile appeared. "I'm Nicola." One brow quirked up. "What does a baby computer program call its father?"

Nik chuckled. "Data."

Nicola's smile faded into the fond look he'd seen on Alix's face so often. "So long, Nik."

Her image disappeared, leaving a blank white browser window. Nik was tempted to try to trace where Nicola's webpage originated. Instead, he took the mouse and closed the browser.

"You are a good man, despite your flaws."

Nik looked at the figment, who was serious for once. "Are you real?"

The figment cocked its head. "Are you?"

Nik chuckled. "*Cogito ergo sum.*"

An uncharacteristically sly smirk appeared on the figment's pixie face. "Descartes was an arrogant prick. I had to lead him by the nose for days until he got the point."

Goosebumps prickled Nik's back and arms, the implications of the statement landing on him with a thud. "You... You're..."

Its eyes flashed red. There and gone so fast he might convince himself he imagined it.

When Nik was ten, he slipped out of his bed late one night to watch a movie his older brother told him was too scary for him. Tucked into the corner of the old sofa in their basement, he'd peered with wide eyes at the small television from beneath a tatty old quilt. Though he would never admit it to his brother, *The Exorcist* remained the most frightening thing he'd ever experienced. The story of a young girl tormented by an implacable supernatural being still haunted the shadowy byways of his imagination. But a burning curiosity was more fundamental to who Nik was. "Demon," he breathed.

A more pleasing cat's grin appeared. "Only when I want to be." With a mischievous tilt of its head, it said in a chipper tone, "Don't worry, Nik, I like you."

"What are you?"

"Too soon, Nik."

Frustrated, but encouraged by its willingness to talk, he asked, "Why am I the only one who can see you?"

"Most humans see the world as they expect it to be. You see it as it is."

Nik's hand came up to brush his forehead. "What did you do when you touched me?"

An introspective frown appeared. "Most of my kind have given up on humans. For good reason, I'm afraid." It shrugged. "They've always regarded me as a bit of an oddball." She gave him a frank look. "We're a pair, you and I."

Before Nik could process that, the figment looked at the door and said, "Alix is home." It waggled its fingers, lips curled in a small grin. Then, it was gone.

Nik sat frozen, heart thrumming. The door to the condo opened and shut. Alix's heels tapped across the wood floor. A moment later, she appeared. Seeing the woman he loved framed in the doorway, he decided there would be time later to talk about the figment's revelations. What he needed now was Alix's comfort.

She took in his expression, then asked, "What's happened?"

"I was fired." Emotion husked his voice.

Her worried frown smoothed. She held out her hand, inviting him to join her, and led him down the hall to their bedroom. Not until they were curled together on the bed did she say, "Tell me what happened."

# Chapter 30

## Wednesday, 6:15 A.M.

The next morning Alix watched Nik carefully. After he explained what had happened at Cerberus the previous day, they spent a wonderful night together. Nik was attentive, demanding and giving, in turn. Afterwards, they shared wine, bread and cheese and Rocky Road ice cream. He'd been more present in the moment than he had been in months. And Alix didn't believe the only reason was the relief at rescuing Kate.

He'd been quiet since they rose from their bed, tender with her and thoughtful while they showered together, but she didn't see anything more worrisome. He would find something else to occupy his active mind. And if he didn't, she would intervene. There was nothing worse than Nik without a purpose.

He'd explained what had happened with Hacksie, Nicola and his figment over breakfast. Alix wasn't a particularly religious person, so the idea the figment was an actual demon wasn't as terrifying as Nik thought it would be to her. After they found Milton, she had to admit Nik's figments might be more than his imagination. But whether it was called a figment or a demon made little difference to her. They'd decided they needed more information before calling an exorcist.

While Nik deleted Nicola's backups, Alix called Tanya Winston, Milton's victim at SecureStack. She was overjoyed and invited Nik and Alix to celebrate with them at their favorite pub.

## Wednesday, 9:55 A.M.

Alix, Nik, Rosa and Rashida filed into the back of the auditorium where Damán Enterprises's social media company was scheduled to make their announcement at MediaCon. While they waited, Nik related what had happened at Cerberus, what Dick Larsen was willing to tell him and most of what Hacksie said to him.

"Sally Thompson is apparently willing to go down with the ship," he said. "She's not talking. But it turns out Oki Tanaka was the son of a man who crossed the Japanese mafia. He bought his son a new identity in Canada. He's willing to tell the police everything in exchange for keeping his identity secret."

"So, you got fired," Rashida said.

Alix noted Nik's annoyed frown, but he didn't respond.

"I wouldn't feel too sorry for him," Rosa said. "The man got paid." She gave the auditorium a glum look. "Course, I don't have a job now."

Nik perked up. "We'll come up with something. Maybe you can be my personal assistant." He gave her a sly grin. "I can guarantee it'll be more exciting than corporate drone."

Rosa gave him a doubtful frown.

"And Nicola..." Rashida said, peeking up at him, a question in her voice.

"Deleted," Nik said. "All of it."

Rashida and Rosa exchanged grins.

"Do you know who Hacksie is?" Nik asked Rashida.

She glanced up at him. "Maybe."

"He's The Vulture," he said.

Instead of answering, she waved at the gathering crowd. "This many people care about what happens with this social media thing?"

"No," Nik said. He gestured to the throng. "Most of these people are tech journalists or influential bloggers. It's Damán who's the draw. He's always worth a couple of quotes."

"They'll get something really juicy, then," Rosa said. "If this Hacksie guy was telling the truth."

The crowd's attention focused as the emcee appeared. He strolled across the stage, reading the script projected on the teleprompters.

"Revolutionary new features, new frontiers in social interaction… Blah, blah, blah." Rashida grimaced up at Nik. "People still buy this shit?"

"That's the joke," Nik said. "Literally, no one buys it. It's a dog and pony show. The bloggers and the journalists have content to create and deadlines to meet. They'll listen, write something less than flattering, then use that to buy their way into the exclusive parties, where they'll sell their souls for perks commensurate with the size of their audiences."

Rashida gazed at him. "You're a cynical man."

Nik glanced at her and shrugged. "You asked." Before she could say anything, he pointed at the stage. "Here we go."

The emcee stood beside a massive screen that showed the logo of the social media platform. "And now, what you've all been waiting for, our overlord…" Laughter. "Ash Damán!" A sea of phones and tablets appeared, everyone recording the big announcement.

The logo faded, and Damán's head and shoulders appeared. But instead of his trademark smile, he was frowning down at something in front of him. Alix had the impression he hadn't heard his cue. Someone off-screen spoke in an anguished voice.

"But this man you hired, The Technician, *killed* a man. Reggie Spenser is dead."

Ash looked off to the side, frothing angrily. "A low level tech is dead. Big deal."

A collective gasp from the audience was followed by utter silence.

"That's Nicola," Nik said.

Alix glanced at him and found him smiling, then looked back at the screen. The facial expressions, the voice, the mannerisms, everything was spot on. There was no hint this wasn't Ash Damán.

The fake Damán returned his gaze to whatever he was looking at when the video started and said, "You need to get your priorities straight."

The voice off-camera said. "He kidnapped a woman."

Damán shrugged.

Looking shocked, the emcee on the stage said, "Uh, Mr. Damán…"

"What?!" Damán said impatiently, looked up and appeared to focus on the camera. His face went slack, then rage contorted his expression. "Did you turn the fu —"

The image of the logo replaced Damán.

The room was still so quiet Nik could hear Rashida whisper.

"Shit. That man just got pwned."

"Um," the emcee said. "Ladies and Gentlemen. It seems we've had a technical —"

Ash Damán reappeared on the screen, an impossibly broad smile on his face. "Good morning!"

The room erupted. Half the crowd fought to free themselves from the long rows of seats to get to the exit. Others began typing furiously on their laptops, phones or tablets.

Damán's smile wavered. He glanced to the side, then the screen turned blue.

Alix, Nik, Rosa and Rashida backed into a corner to avoid the flood of people moving into and out of the auditorium.

"So, that wasn't Damán?" Rosa asked.

"No, that was Nicola. The first time," Rashida said. "The second one was him. Right?"

Nik shrugged. "Who could tell?"

"You and me." Rosa pointed to Rashida and herself. "We're finding a place to hunker down. Shit's getting really unreal, and I don't want to see everything fall apart."

Alix met Nik's gaze and held it. Then she said, "How about lunch first? We'll buy."

www.ingramcontent.com/pod-product-compliance
Lightning Source LLC
Chambersburg PA
CBHW051811150726
47998CB00001B/110